The Whispers of the Streets

The Whispers of the Streets

*J. Earl
Loving, Jr.*

Edited by Carolyn Gaither Ellis
Published by the Author

Printed in Victoria, Canada

National Library of Canada Cataloguing in Publication

Loving, J. Earl, 1946-
    The whispers of the streets / J. Earl Loving, Jr.

ISBN 1-55395-852-7

    I. Title.

PS3612.O88W49 2003   813'.6   C2003-901034-1

TRAFFORD

This book was published *on-demand* in cooperation with Trafford Publishing. On-demand publishing is a unique process and service of making a book available for retail sale to the public taking advantage of on-demand manufacturing and Internet marketing. **On-demand publishing** includes promotions, retail sales, manufacturing, order fulfilment, accounting and collecting royalties on behalf of the author.

Suite 6E, 2333 Government St., Victoria, B.C. V8T 4P4, CANADA
Phone   250-383-6864   Toll-free   1-888-232-4444 (Canada & US)
Fax   250-383-6804   E-mail   sales@trafford.com
Web site   www.trafford.com   TRAFFORD PUBLISHING IS A DIVISION OF TRAFFORD HOLDINGS LTD.
Trafford Catalogue #03-0215   www.trafford.com/robots/03-0215.html

10   9   8   7   6   5   4   3   2

Although totally a work of fiction, it is believed that this work reflects what can and often does go wrong in our urban communities. The characters reflect the good, bad, and ugly in all of us. As you read, please be reminded that we can do much in order to correct what seems to be uncorrectable. We can change what seems to be unchangeable. Above all, we must maintain faith in God, and we must do all we can to help our children turn out in ways which will make us all proud.

Experience the story of a thirteen-year old Black male from a loving, encouraging environment in rural Georgia. Place him in the projects of a typical big city where stories of defeat and death are more common than victories. Experience life in the inner-city ghetto through his eyes, then tell them!

"*It really boils down to this: that all life is interrelated. We are all caught in an inescapable network of mutuality, tied into a single garment of destiny. Whatever affects one directly, affects all indirectly.*"

Martin Luther King, Jr.
The Trumpet of Conscience, 1967

This work is dedicated first to Our Lord and Savior, Jesus Christ.

Second, to my father and mother, Annie F. and James Earl Loving, Sr., who have always been there for me.

To the countless folk who have helped when hitting life's "speed bumps."

To the many relatives and kin that I have been blessed to meet and share with.

To Dreanna Hurtt, who first loved Chris.

To Carolyn Gaither-Ellis, the midwife who delivered this book, my first baby.

To the youngsters who often are misunderstood and have no voice that many can hear.

To those who have enough heart to hear, "the Whispers of the Streets."

Table of Contents

Foreword

Well, these days I don't have much to do but to sit around these projects and watch these people lose their minds and souls. Not much more for an old fella like myself to do. Anyway, my granddaughter comes down here and brings me some food and she kicks the dust around a little bit and sits and talks to me. I think she sits here talking to me because she wants to make sure I eat the food she done cooked. She says she is not a very good cook, but I love it. I love it because she don't have to do it and sometimes an old man gets really lonely.

Anyways, one time this young fella brought her down here because she said her car was broke. She a pretty young girl, I think somewhere in her thirties or so, but ain't never had no husband. I hope these two get together, he turned out to be a nice guy. Yeah, I hope he or somebody marries the girl before too long.

So, while she's trying to make this place liveable, us guys was drinking and talking. He told me he was a teacher. I said damn because most men down here don't do much except try to be gangsters or winos or pimps or popping that stuff in their arms or just downright crazy. But ain't none of them crazy enough to mess with me 'cause I used to work in the slaughter house and knows how to cut so fast you'll be dead before you hit the ground.

While we was talking, he said he didn't know why many of his students acted like they were crazy. I told him that they wasn't acting, they got it real honest from they parents and by living in these ratholes. I got two talents, signifying and talking and listening to people. That's three, ain't it? So, all my neighbors talk to me from time to time and tell me about themselves, I mean private stuff. And what they don't tell me, I kinda fill in the blanks. Oh! I got another talent and that is telling...'cause I'm an old man and will talk you to death.

So while I was drinking with Earl, my granddaughter's friend that I hope will marry her someday, he got to be really interested. After a while, he said that somebody should write a book about want I was saying. I looked him in the eye and said you somebody, ain't you? Next thing I know I was talking him to death and he wrote this book.

It took quite a while 'cause he would come down here, drink the old man's liquor that he paid for and listen, take notes, and use this little tape recorder. When he was 'bout finished, I asked him if he would include a poem I wrote. It ain't got nothing to do with the story, but he said it was a good poem.

Well, I hope you find this story interesting and you learn something like I hope this young fella did. And thinking about it, from what I remember from school, your teachers might not like it too much, but it ain't a textbook, just the truth with a little yeast in it. And I hope you like my poem.

Oh! And my name is Harold P. Jones.

The Phone

Now my name it's Harold,
Harold P. Jones
And I ain't got no idea why I
got me this phone.
Being that I sit here all alone,
Got no idea why I pay for this phone.

Maybe, I is performing some kind of public service,
you see
Maybe that's why we together,
my phone and me.
When people get lost, they dying, or can't find their family,
who they call? You got it
Old by hisself me.

Hell no, I don't know Betty,
Tom, Slick or Sue
Don't believe I'd tell you
Even if I knew
All I know is after they disturb you
They don't even 'poligize when they through.
But what in the world can I do?

Well, next time you call, please just say hi
'Stead of saying, wrong number, goodbye.
Because after you hang up, I almost cry,
'Cause I got me this phone,
but I don't even know why!

1. *The Promise*

Even the very sun, who had been his friend back in Georgia, now seemed to hate him. It proved it by shooting its hot, angry breath through the bedroom window of this place, this hell where he was now forced to live, with his newly found mama, Dora Lee.

Thirteen year old Chris could not think of one reason to open his eyes in this big, stinking city. He knew that this would just be another day of boredom, dread and despair.

In this hell, there was no rooster to nobly announce the beginning of a brand new day, no chicks or chickens clucking loudly, laying eggs or scratching for food.

In this hell, there were no ducks honking, no grunts of hogs and pigs impatiently waiting to be watered and fed. There was no old dog restlessly waiting to be pet, watered, and fed.

God knows that he had not known how good life in the country was until he was forced to live in this place, this hell, this city!

A solitary tear fell gently down his light cream and coffee complexioned cheek as he reminded himself again that his grandmother was dead and gone forever.

Never again would his grandmother be there to fuss over him while making coffee, baking biscuits, cooking grits, frying bacon, ham, and eggs. And certainly, no one would be there to hug him, asking how he had slept.

No one would be there to say morning prayers with. Nobody would be around for him to even sing to before he merrily went out into the happy Georgia fresh air and sunshine to do his chores.

In the short time he had been here, Chris could not figure out what these people did. They just seemed to just hang around waiting. In their windows, on their steps, and on the corners, they waited. Like the crows and the vultures back home, they waited.

They waited for the mailman, the dope man, the policeman, the ambulance and the meat wagon.

Except the man next door, they didn't sweep their fronts or even pick up the trash. These people unwrapped their food, their candy, their cigarettes and stuff, and threw the wrappers on the ground.

There was so much trash on the ground that it looked like some strange crop growing. He had seen some men in bright yellow uniforms sweeping the stuff up. But faster than the weeds back home, the strange crop returned, seemingly by itself.

Although, Dora never asked as she really didn't care, Chris took pride in sweeping both the front and back of the low rise development in which they lived. He hoped that she would notice and tell him how proud she was of him. She kept the inside very neat and clean, but she "didn't live outside." So, that was that.

She was very happy, amusing, and witty when her friends were around. She really put it on when her boyfriend, Rommie, came to visit. But from the time it was decided that Chris would live with her, she made it quite clear that he was on his own.

Chris just wanted Dora to spend a little time with him, talk to him, cook for him, and maybe, make a little fuss over him. He knew she would never do for him like his grandmother did, but he held out the hope that ...well...

So, here he was in this strange, big city with no friends, nobody to talk to, and nothing to do. The only thing he had to look forward to was the fact that school would begin in a few days. He liked school. He would have something to do, and maybe, even make some brand new friends.

Only the long distance calls from his older sister, Christee, had sustained him through this nightmare. Idleness, despair, being threatened, beaten, and even worse, totally ignored by Dora were the only things that he could depend on now.

He had seen, even spoken to the very tall, lanky, dark boy named Marcus who lived next to him. The boy talked kind of strange, and spoke with a strong accent.

Across the court from him lived Sonia, a girl who was about his age and he thought she was so fine. Chris had met her and even had dinner with her the first day he arrived. Sonia totally excited and overwhelmed him.

His sister had encouraged him to talk to the man next door, Mr. Jacque and his grandson, Marcus, but warned him to stay away from ". . . that, that Sonia." Very disappointed, he asked, "Why shouldn't I be friendly with her?" His sister only replied that Sonia should have been Dora's child and changed the subject.

Sonia! How sweet! Chris only knew that he needed to get close to her, she really mystified and excited him. He never, ever dreamed that he would meet, talk to, or be with a young Goddess like her. Just to be near one so cute, so well built, so everything, was heaven.

Since he certainly didn't have a lot to do or even think about, he thought about her. His amorous thoughts were interrupted by the sound of his mother calling him. He walked slowly out of his room into the living room, where his mother was standing by the open front door.

"Me and Rommie is going to 'Lantic City to win me some money to get you and me some things. Food and something to drink is in the 'frigerator, and you know what to tell anybody if they come pass or call?"

Chris shook his head showing that he knew what to do, but that gesture aggravated Dora, big time!

"Look Chris, done told you 'bout shaking your damned head at me . . . open your damned mouth!"

Chris began slowly,"If anybody wants you, I am to tell them that you went to the store and you will see them when you get back."

Satisfied, she walked out the door without saying another word.

With absolutely nothing to do, Chris milled around from room to room. He tried television, but there was nothing on that interested him. Finally, he went to the kitchen and fixed something to eat.

He, then, went to the living room to watch television, but before he sat down, he saw Sonia walking toward her kitchen door, which faced his front door.

There were some men whistling and yelling at her. He was so angry that he wanted to confront them, but they were too big. From the broad smile on her face, she seemed to enjoy their attention. Before she disappeared behind the door, she added a little provocative wiggle, wink, and blew them a kiss.

Like wolves, they screamed and yelled their approval!

Sonia!

Chris settled down on the couch and watched an old western

movie, the kind that he and Uncle J.B. used to enjoy. A baseball game followed the movie. He fell asleep watching it and remembering all the good times, gone forever now that Grandma was dead and gone. He fell asleep with a tear in his eye and a prayer in his broken heart.

Suddenly, he was awaken by what he believed was his grandmother's voice calling to him! This was much too much for him, frightened and confused, he started to run right out the front door but hesitated!

Hearing the voice again, he ran out of the front door! As Chris cleared the door, he was stopped dead in his tracks, this time it was the voice of the lanky, funny talking boy next door.

"Whatiswrongmanyourhouseonfire?"

Chris heard him, but didn't understand one word of what he was saying or trying to ask. Startled and totally confused, Chris all but forgot the voice of his grandmother.

Chris squealed, "What? You talking to me?"

Marcus walked toward him, looked Chris in the eyes and repeated slowly,   "What is wrong, man, is your house on fire?"

Embarrassed Chris answered,"No, no I, uh, just had to get out of there . . . "   Marcus laughed,"Oh? You looked liked the very devil was chasing you!"

"It was my, I, mean, I just felt like running," Chris answered, embarrassed as everything.

Marcus looked at him curiously, but said nothing.

Fortunately, this was the beginning of a very close friendship between the two boys. Chris very quickly learned two things about Marcus. The first was that although they were the same age, Marcus was so much wiser. He was like a thirteen year "Old Man." He seemed to take things a lot more seriously than any kid that Chris had ever known. Second, Marcus didn't share Chris' admiration for Sonia. Her beauty, her charm, her raw sexiness didn't impress him the way that they impressed Chris and seemingly the whole world!

Marcus sensed that Chris needed a friend. So, he insisted that Chris come into his living room to listen to some of his grandfather's old albums. Some of the songs made them laugh, some were very sad, and there were others that neither quite understood.

The lyrics of a short song, *Spirit,* by a group named 'Earth, Wind, and Fire' caught the attention and imagination of Chris. The song suggested that everybody was on a path that leads to the light! He was immediately reminded of his grandmother as the song stated that someone was "...smiling down."

He was most impress by their suggestion that "*. . . in love..our spirits they will be one, they will be one.*" The idea that he would be joined with his grandmother made him feel better. But it troubled him to consider being joined spiritually or otherwise with people like Dora and her boyfriend, Rommie.

As the boys discussed the possibilities, Chris began softly crying. As he began to compose himself, he began to tell Marcus about circumstances surrounding his grandmother's death.

"My Grandma and my Aunt Glo were arguing about me and Dora. Aunt Glo was telling Grandma that it was about time that Dora came to get me, because I was thirteen and all.

Grandma made me go outside, because she didn't want me to hear what they were saying. Once outside, I hid close to the house so that I could hear what was going on. I mean, I had to know! All I knew was that I had a mother named Dora Lee that lived up here someplace.

I had a picture of her, but I didn't remember ever seeing her. They told me she was there about five years ago, but I was in school. By the time I got home, she had to left with her friend to go to Florida.

"Anyway, my big sister used to come down to stay with us every summer until a couple of years ago. Everybody said that Christee looked just like Dora Lee, only she was darker, and bigger than Dora Lee was at that age. The one thing that they always gave my sister credit for was not letting her looks go to her head like Dora Lee did.

My sister would work around the place, cook, and she even got a job one summer. These were things that they said Dora Lee would never do.

"Well, Grandma and Aunt Glo really had it out about my mother! Aunt Glo said with all the boyfriends that Dora Lee said that she had, with the money that she always said that she was getting from them, she certainly should have enough to take care of me!

Grandma laughed and said that my mother didn't have sense enough to take care of herself and that my sister musta had a guardian angel looking out for her 'cause she knew that Dora Lee was not.

She went on to say that my mother never finished school, never had a job, and if it were not for that Avory's father sending her to the city, she would still be down here in everybody's way. Grandma said that I was going to be somebody, and as long as she had breath in her body, she was not going to let Dora Lee mess me up with all the foolishness in the big, dirty, city.

"Then, Aunt Glo, who never cried about anything started crying, saying that my mother needed to take the responsibility of raising me, because Grandma was too old, had a very bad heart and everybody else had their own families to care for.

Grandma asked her how much it took to love and feed a little boy like me. Aunt Glo said that everybody loved me, but everybody had a place and my place was with my mother.

My Grandma said that she had promised God that I would be the new kind of colored man that He, and everybody else, would be proud of. After they fussed for a little while longer, Aunt Glo told Grandma that they would talk later.

"She didn't want her to get too upset. But on her way to her car, she saw me and at first, smiled and got into her car. Then she got out of the car and stood there looking at me kind of strange; and then, she ran over to me and hugged me so tight that I thought that she was gonna squeeze the life out of me!

"After she left, I wanted to go in the house and tell Grandma that I loved her and everything would be all right, but I couldn't! I couldn't! "

Chris began to cry as he had never cried before. He was crying, because he missed his grandmother who he loved him unconditionally, and because, he was so very miserable with Dora.

Marcus looked at his friend, hoping that he could say something that would help the pain go away. His words to Chris were the same ones that he remembered from the funeral of his own parents who were butchered in his homeland, South Africa. He softly quoted the priest, "When the beast first appears and does his best to destroy us and our spirits, it seems that his demonic deeds will last forever, but thanks to God Almighty, his presence and ill deeds will soon pass. Lean on Him and He will turn your dark todays into bright tomorrows."

Chris stopped crying as suddenly as he had begun, looked at his friend strangely and wondered aloud how a boy could be so smart.

Marcus replied, "Where I grew up we didn't have much time to be playful children, because it was really hard for Blacks in my homeland." He told Chris that death was the constant companion of his people.

Just as Marcus' father had done to him before he was murdered by the police, he grabbed Chris and whispered in his ear, in his native tongue what translated to mean, `Be strong, my brother, always be strong!' Chris, now composed, felt a real need to tell Marcus the rest.

"I started walking, then running around the yard trying to figure out what to do. I thought about running away, but I had no place to run to! I figured that running away might cause Grandma to have another heart attack like she had when my grandfather, Papa Benny, was killed in that car wreck!"

"Grandma sometimes got so sick that the doctor didn't even want her to get out of bed, but most of the time she would not listen. She would be doing stuff for that old dog and me. She would always make me do more than everybody else, because she said that she had promised Jesus that I would be somebody.

Then, she would sing this song about crossing the River Jordan, and say that she would not be here with me always, but she and her Sweet Jesus and Papa Benny would be looking down on me, very proud!"

Marcus interrupted, "You are very lucky to have had a grandmother like that. I wish that I could have met her. We should be real lions in honor of our parents and grandparents." Chris smiled and nodded in agreement.

"Well, after a while I went on in the house and Grandma was

sitting in that old easy chair of hers talking to that old dog. When she saw me, she made me give her a big hug and let me know that she knew that I'd been listening.

She told me that Glo might fuss a lot, but Glo would always be there for me. Always! But if Glo is supposed to be looking out for me, and Grandma, and Grandpa, and Sweet Jesus is supposed to be looking down at me, tell me, Marcus what the hell am I doing up here with Dora?"

Marcus answered by saying that things happen that we just do not understand, and my grandfather tells me there are things we will never understand.

Chris continued, "Grandma said that she was very tired and was going to bed, so we prayed together. Now that I think about it, she might have known that something was going to happen to her, because we prayed a real long time.

She mentioned some people I'd never heard of, and when we finished, she asked me to sing *Amazing Grace* for her. When I finished, she said that she was real tired, but Jesus was gonna take care of that.

"I felt real good after that and fell asleep watching television. I woke up real early the next morning. I wanted to get all the chores out of the way and fix Grandma's breakfast to show her how much I loved her so that Aunt Glo would not worry about us too much.

I washed up, got dressed to go outside. That crazy old dog was scratching on the door and whining, trying his best to get in the house. It was all that I could do to keep that old dog outside.

"Even as I was feeding the chickens and other animals, he kept on trying to get in. Everything seemed a little strange as the sun began to rise. I grabbed that old dog and put him in the barn so that Grandma would not hear him and come out to doctor him.

"By the time I got back in the house it was full light, so I got Grandma's breakfast together. It was not very hard, all she would eat was cereal, toast, and milk with a little coffee to give it flavor. I put it on a tray with a little flower from her garden. I hoped that she would not mind.

"I was feeling pretty good about bringing breakfast to Grandma, because most of the time she fixed mine! Anyway, her room was on the west side of the house so it stayed dark the longest.

I was a little surprised when I opened the door because there was a glow in the room. It was like a cloud of light in there, but it only lasted for a moment! It got dark again! I put the tray on the settee and turned on the lamp. Grandma looked so pretty, so peaceful, so still, that I knew that she was gone! I put my hand on her face, and it felt real cold!

"I heard myself say, `Mama, I brought your breakfast, please wake up and eat it!' But she could not wake up. I kissed her on the cheek, and called Aunt Glo. She hung up and called the ambulance.

Chris began to cry and shout, "I didn't because I knew she was gone!"

Then almost in a whisper, "They said that I should have called the ambulance first, but I knew that she was gone."

"The ambulance got there real fast, because the station is right down the street. Ben and Sally, who work the ambulance, were only in there for a few moments and they said that she musta have died in her sleep and there was nothing that nobody could do.

By this time Aunt Glo, Uncle Bill, their children, and some other people had arrived. Most were crying. Uncle Bill grabbed me and shook me real hard and said that Grandma might still be alive if I had called the ambulance first! Ben and Sally tried to tell him that she was probably died much earlier, but that didn't stop him from blaming me!

"During the confusion, Aunt Glo went in Grandma's room to say goodbye. Other people came and soon Grandma's room was full of people that were crying and praying. Ben and Sally put them out of the room and took her away.

"We were all very sad, but Uncle Bill was still mad at me. He started to beat me, but J.B. would not let him. Everybody told him that it was not my fault, but Uncle Bill kept on blaming me! Blaming me!"

By this time the tears were flowing.

The boys cried together.

2. *The Funeral*

Marcus left the room momentarily and returned with some tissue. Chris felt a little embarrassed as he accepted the tissue. Marcus was a real friend, and Chris needed a real friend to talk to about his grandmother's funeral. He finally had someone who would listen to him.

Chris began slowly, "They kept me away from the house most of the time, and when I finally got to go home her stuff was missing! I asked Aunt Glo where it was and she got mad and said that people act like fools when somebody dies.

Just about then we heard a loud noise come from the kitchen! It sounded like all the glass in the world was breaking! We ran into the kitchen, Aunt Alice and some woman that I had never seen before were standing in the middle of the floor just glaring like they were going to kill each other!

"Aunt Glo screamed at them, `What the hell is going on in here? '

Aunt Alice was so mad that she was crying, `This old bitch was in here stealing mama's good supper set, the one that me and Bill gave her!

The old thief said that mama said that she could have them if anything happened to her! Aunt Alice ran out of the room crying!

Aunt Glo just looked at the woman and asked, "Why?". The

woman didn't say anything, she just turned around and walked out the door. As Aunt Glo was cleaning up the broken glass, she told me to go get my clothes for the funeral, trying to hide her tears.

"As I walked to my bedroom, I heard Aunt Alice talking and crying to somebody in Grandma's room. I looked in there, but there was nobody in there but her.

She was talking to Grandma's bed, `They done took your stuff, Mama, I guess you know that your Sunday dishes are all broke to hell! Mama what are we going to do? Why did you have to leave us like this? What about Chris? What we going to do with him? Dora ain't here."

"Aunt Glo had heard her, too. She whispered to me to go get my clothes and walked in the room to talk to Aunt Alice.

The next time I saw Aunt Alice was at the wake. We were all sitting in the church. J.B. was playing the organ and singing real soft when that woman who was trying to take those dishes came in telling everybody how sorry she was.

Well, Aunt Alice took off after that woman before anybody had a chance to stop her! She smacked her so fast and hard that it seemed like the whole church shook! The woman hit the floor like lightening had struck her!

Before Aunt Alice could strike again, somebody grabbed her people held her back and she was screaming, "if I ever see you again, I'll bl . . . ' Before she could finish Aunt Glo put her hand over her mouth!

"Well, while they took Aunt Alice out of the church and apologized to the woman, I got a good look at Grandma. She looked so beautiful, just like I think an angel would look. I promised her that I would always remember and love her. And you know what? I swear that it looked like she smiled for a little while.

The rest of the wake was really peaceful. After a couple of preachers spoke and we were about to leave, J.B. asked me to sing *It Is Well With My Soul*, the song Grandma always liked to hear me sing.

I did and everybody cried and I promised Grandma that I would sing it for her when I saw her again.

"When we left, we went to Aunt Glo'S house. Everybody told me how well I sang and that Grandma would have liked it very much. We began to eat, and the grownups started to drink and talk about some of the crazy things that Grandma used to do.

Then, they began to tease Aunt Alice about smacking that woman in the church.

"Oh! I forgot! I met many relatives that I didn't even know I had. Meeting and talking to them was fun until somebody mentioned that I was Dora's son. Somebody asked why Dora wasn't there.

One man said, just laughing and winking, she was probably doing some business. Then many started to laugh with him! I was not sure what they were laughing about, but I did know that it wasn't a compliment.

"An old lady said that it was a shame that my mother could not stop being a big city you-know-what long enough to come to her own mother's funeral. A boy that I didn't even know looked at me and said that I was a disgrace to the family, having a mother like that.

J.B. told him to shut-up! Then some adults said that the boy had a right to his own opinion, and others started fussing. Aunt Glo made everybody shut-up!

"Finally, J.B. took me to his home. I didn't sleep too well that night, and I prayed that my mother would come and get me. That would show them."

"Maybe, I should have kept my big mouth shut. Grandma used to tell us to be careful of what we prayed for. Looks like I should have prayed to stay in Georgia forever.

"Anyway, the next morning Jerod, J.B.'s oldest boy, woke me up. He's almost twenty-five years old. Anyway, he told me to put something on and come to the kitchen because they wanted to talk to me in case things got really crazy at the funeral.

I got dressed when I could and went to the kitchen to see what they wanted to talk to me about. J.B. was sitting at the table drinking a cup of coffee and smoking a cigarette. Jerod was standing near the stove. He told me to sit and put a big plate of food in front of me.

I could hear the other children outside playing and turned my head toward the yard. When I turned back to look at J.B., I saw that he was crying. He looked at me and got up and hugged me.

"Jerod said he sort of knew how I must be feeling about Grandma's dying and all. They looked at each other and J.B. told me how he had felt a couple of years when my Aunt Inez died.

He told me that Inez and my mother were very close when they were growing up, and that Inez was the second prettiest of all Grandma's girls. He said that sometimes they would go out of their way to tease the boys that they went to school with.

"They flirted with every man they met. The only difference was that Dora sometimes went all the way. Every time Dora did something really bad, she told your Grandpa that Inez did it too.

Most of the time, she was lying, trying to save her own butt from getting a beating. Well, it didn't work too well because

Papa Benny would beat them both.

J.B. laughed, "Well, when Inez was about seventeen, she fell in love with the undertaker's son, Avory. Boy, was she in love with that boy! The rest of us didn't have a chance! I must admit that they were a swell couple, and everybody knew that they would get married someday."

This made Dora, who was about fifteen at the time, very, very angry and extremely jealous. You see, Dora was used to getting what she wanted and now she wanted Avory.

The only problem that Avory and Inez had was that he wanted to go all the way, and she had this strong thing about being a virgin when she got married.

Just about all the young ladies around here had this thing about being a virgin except them Johnson girls and Dora. So, when Inez would not, Dora let Avory know that she would.

At first, Avory would not touch her, being Inez's sister, you see. One Saturday, Avory and Inez were supposed to go to the movies, a real big deal in those days, because the only place that we could go was about forty, maybe forty-five miles away.

Inez could not go because she was really sick. Avory really wanted to see the show, so Inez told him to take Dora. They said that Dora acted like she didn't want to go, but finally went because there was nothing else to do. So, off they went in one of Avory's father's big limousines.

They didn't get back until early in the morning! Avory said that the car broke down, but nobody believed them. Papa Benny punched the boy in the face, and dared him to come near any of his girls again in life! Poor Inez was heart broken. She and Dora didn't have much to do with each other for months!

All this time Dora and Avory acted like wild folks. They went off and stayed and would sometimes get back drunk and crazy. Papa Benny got tired of fussing and beating Dora and just gave up on her. He ignored her and pretended that she didn't exist.

This went on until Dora got pregnant with your sister. She thought that she and Avory would get married, but Avory wouldn't have any part of it. He had thought about taking over his father's business, which meant that he had to go off to school.

He couldn't take her with him and knowing her, he knew he couldn't trust her to wait for him. Also, I guess he felt that she would be bad for business.

Papa Benny wanted to kill her, but you know your Grandma! They had to find something else to do with her. Avory's father was a decent type of guy, so they decided that she would go live with his sister in the city. She could have her baby and make a life for herself.

She stayed with his sister, but she wouldn't go to school or work or anything. She just about drove the lady crazy for the two years that she stayed with her.

Finally, Avory's father gave her some money to move on her own. He also set up some kind of trust fund for the baby. When your sister turns twenty-five, she will come into some real money. There are some other things that Dora was suppose to have done, but none of that stuff matters now.'

" J.B. said that he told me all that stuff about Dora because nobody else would. I was not responsible for the way my mother was and so that I could kind of understand why people were sometimes very mean to me. He told me that although I was not blood kin to him that he loved me like a son.

"Dora would not come down to see Inez when she was very sick and about to die. Inez wanted to talk to Dora to make her peace. The family wanted her at the funeral, but Dora didn't come.

When Papa Benny was killed last year in that wreck, she didn't even return the calls. Christee found a way to be here both times, but not Dora. They wondered about Dora, but there was nothing that anybody could do, but everybody loved me and my sister.

He said that sometimes people get so upset that they get mad at the wrong person. He said that I should remember that the people who were being mean to me were really mad at Dora. J.B. told me not to be surprised if Dora didn't show up for the funeral, and that my sister just could not be there.

I was looking forward to seeing her, because she had promised me that she would come get me when she became a star.

"Anyway, he told me to always keep my head up and never let anybody put me down. He told me to go in that church like a proud prince and when it was my time to sing, Sing! Sing like I was singing to God Almighty!

Marcus nodded, "Did you, my brother?"

Chris smiled proudly, "I turned the church out!"

Both laughed almost to tears!

Then Marcus looked at Chris quizzically, "Can you really sing that good?"

"Damned right!"

Pretending that he was holding a microphone, he began by bowing to Marcus and a make-believe audience, "Thank you! Thank you, very much! Listen, my next song, ladies and gentlemen, is 'Wildflower', a song made popular by a group called 'The Ojay's'.

Although he didn't know what to expect, Marcus applauded enthusiastically! He was rewarded with a very stylish and moving rendition of the song. Mr. Jacque entered, and he was pleasantly surprised and moved by Chris' voice.

Mr. Jacque was so impressed that he suggested that Chris see a friend of his, Reverend Govans. After he and Marcus finished congratulating and praising Chris, he reminded Marcus that they had to be across town soon.

He invited Chris to join them, but Chris declined because he felt that he was not dressed well enough nor had he taken a bath. They said their goodbyes, and Chris went back to his empty home.

He went to his bedroom, and jumped on the bed. He turned over on his back and gazed at the ceiling, remembering the funeral. The whole day had seemed like a dream, no not a dream but like a movie.

First, he remembered going to Aunt Glo's house with J.B. and his children. Then, there were the arguments over who was going to ride in the limousines and in which one. The undertaker, Mr. Avory, did what he could, but it was Aunt Glo, as usual, who straightened everything out.

Sitting in the third limo with people that he didn't know was not very comforting to him, especially since, they didn't seem to have too much to say to him.

So, he just looked out the window at the small streets in the small town that he knew so very well. He was surprised at the amount of cars parked at the church. Cars and people were everywhere! It seemed that the whole town had come out to bid a fond farewell to his grandmother!

The family procession included five limousines, several Cadillacs, Lincolns, and other luxury automobiles. Most of the family exited the automobiles with solemn dignity. Some nodded and even waved at friends and acquaintances. Some sobbed softly.

Remembering what J.B. had told him, Chris held his head

very high and followed the very slow procession into the overcrowded church. An usher grabbed Chris firmly by the arm and escorted him to the already crowded choir pit, where he had a clear view of his Grandma in the casket.

She looked so peaceful and so natural that he almost expected her to wake up and ask what all the fuss was about.

The long ceremony began with an upbeat version of *We Are Soldiers In The Army*, which was followed by a few words from the mayor, who was among the several local dignitaries who in attendance.

Besides the warm memories and praises he had for Mama Liz, who had at once worked for his family, he was proud that both whites and Blacks were present ". . . A true testimony to the harmony and goodwill of our loving community." Some applauded.

Chris didn't recall much of what happened during the funeral because it was so very long that sometimes his mind wandered. He was startled by Reverend Lewis' loudly proclaiming, "But the Fruit of the Spirit is love, joy, peace, long suffering, gentleness, goodness, faith, meekness, temperance . . . " As he was ending his sermon, the lady next to him alerted him that he was next!

He recalled becoming very nervous as Reverend Lewis was saying softly, ". . . and she will be in the house of the Lord, smiling down on us and keeping an eye on some of us, he smiled and nodded along with many present.

. . . And I know that she is with Papa Benny, waiting for us all to join them in the bosom of Jesus! ...Amen, and Amen! As most in the audience repeated the Amens, J.B. began playing the introduction to 'Amazing Grace' on the organ.   Chris walked slowly toward the casket, humming slowly and softly with the low mournful sound of the organ. Most present joined in and the church was filled with the sound of soft harmony, an occasional `Amen' and some open sobbing.

On cue, he began, "This is grandma's favorite, *A-ma-zing grace, how sweet the sound that saved a-a-a wretch like me! I-I once was lost but now I'm found, was blind but now I see.*"

Chris remembered the open, loud, cries of grief and pain. When he finished, there was not a dry eye in the church! Glancing over at J.B., he could tell that he was very proud of him. He, also, felt that his grandmother was looking down on him proudly.

A younger minister slowly walked to the pulpit weeping. He thanked God for the privilege of speaking a few words of comfort to the family and friends of Mama Liz.

The man told a very touching story of how he grew up on the wrong side of the tracks in that community. He said that he had always been in trouble, because he had hated himself and thought that he was no good. His family was no good either because everybody told him so.

"But Praise God, I met Mama Liz right down the street here when I was in the parking lot stealing everything that was not tied down. This lady made me put my ill gotten gains back. She took me aside and talked to me about the love of our Lord!

That woman convinced me that our time, the time for the colored man was at hand and that I should get myself ready!

`I left her so excited that I wanted to be somebody! But you know that Satan is always busy. My family, friends, and teachers brought me back to what I thought was real. How could a poor Colored boy hope to be anything but no good?

Well, they wiped out my enthusiasm, but I never forgot that lady. Well, after my third time in jail I figured that I was doing something wrong! Sometimes I have been just plain stupid.

Has anyone here besides me been so stupid, so blind that

they could not see the light? Many folks acknowledge that they had. Well, one very lonely night in my dirty, stinking cell, I remembered that lady's promise to me. She told me that it didn't matter how the world looks at you, my brothers and sisters. It don't matter how bad you think you are or where you come from.

Believe and trust in Him and He will guide you through those stormy seas. He will make a way out of no way! He is able! ...'

Chris remembered feeling very proud of his grandmother as he heard the minister continue.

`I started teaching myself how to read and write. When I got out, I went back to school. I worked my way through college to become a man of the cloth! My sisters and two of my four brothers who laughed at me at first are now college graduates, and we are praying for the other two.

Praise God, once we thought that the only way was to take from others, but we found that the only way is to give.

`Her promise to me is the same one that I leave with you. It does not matter where you start in life. It does not matter how people see you. Any fool can count the apples on a tree, but only God knows about the seeds in the apple!

So, in memory of Mama Liz tell some poor lost, soul how great he or she can be, he already knows how bad he can be. Thank you for allowing me these few moments to speak about what was on my heart."

The rest of the service was long and laborious and for the most part very boring. Finally, the service ended and the procession took a very long time just getting to the parking lot. Somehow, they managed to get the procession in order and headed slowly to the cemetery.

Unlike his ride to the church, the ride to the cemetery was

much more amicable. Those who rode with him expressed their heartfelt regrets for the lost that they shared, and they expressed their appreciation for his wonderful, soulful, and moving solo.

The older lady, who had been so nasty to him, suggested that he should come visit her in Atlanta and sing at her church. She added that he was a fine young man and hugged him!

There was quite a delay at the cemetery, it took a long time to get everything situated with the huge crowd, the many floral arrangements, and the typical heat of a June afternoon.

The sharp, crisp clothing and makeup had begun to whither. Many of the flowers had begun to lose their beauty. Most just wanted to get this thing over with as it was approaching three in the afternoon, and it had begun around 11:00 A.M.!

Finally, Reverend Lewis began what was to be the final grave side prayer. He was distracted by something up near the hearst! Most of the eyes followed his to a very stunning woman. She was wearing a white and gold coin-accented dressy shirt dress with sheer white stockings, white shoes, and a very large white straw hat turned up with a white bow.

Because the afternoon sun was at her back, just about everybody was squinting their eyes, trying to identify her. The bright sun outlined her statuesque body. She turned to give her escort her sunglasses. Who was this attractive woman?

As if to answer their question, she started gliding down the hill screaming, "Mama! Mama!" Her escort stayed with the car.

"That damned Dora," Aunt Glo moaned. Then, she turned to Reverend Lewis who hurriedly finished and disappeared in the crowd. The people parted like Moses' river, giving her clear access to the casket.

Her momentum was such that somebody grabbed her to prevent her from falling, but her hat slid off her head and landed next to the casket!

Her tearless crying didn't seem to impress anybody, and most walked away, appalled and disgusted. Some of the men who gazed at her were not too gently reminded to mind their business!

Chris wondered aloud about this pretty woman dressed in white. J.B., got misty eyed as he told Chris that the lady was his mother, Dora. He patted him on the back, told Chris that he would be near, and slowly walked away.

Chris stood there for a moment, looking at her! He remembered feeling like he was going to choke! What was he supposed to do or say?

3. *The Decision*

Leaving the cemetery, instead of talking about Mama Liz, folks were talking about "that Dora! " How could she come so late, dressed like she was going to a party, to her own mother's funeral? The nerve of her coming down here for God knows what with that nonsense in front of everybody!

Who did she think she was fooling with all that phony screaming and yelling? And only that Dora would have the nerve to be crying in front of everybody without tears!

"Poor old Mama Liz must be turning over in her grave! Bet Dora done got herself in trouble. Bet that guy with her is some kind of hoodlum. One thing for sure, you'd better believe that he's not her husband, maybe someone else's, but not her's. But you had to admit that she is looking good! Maybe, even better than she did when she lived here!"

Always the center of attraction, she mesmerized her sisters, brothers, relatives, and friends. She changed the mood of those in her company from sadness and sadness almost to a gaiety!

She had always been the most noticed, whatever the occasion so, why would this be any different? She had this way, a mystique about her that made the people who knew her generally forgave and enjoyed her, no matter how outrageous the act or action.

She was, well Dora, and most just accepted her as the type of carefree person that it would not make much sense getting or staying mad with for she certainly never seemed to care one way or another.

If nothing else, she had always been a distraction for her family and friends. Whenever things were boring or unbearable, one could always talk about, or laugh about the merry adventures of Dora. Other people had their eccentric heiresses, princesses, and starlets, but they had Dora!

Most felt that she was the most beautiful female that ever lived in that community. Some would argue in the world! Nature and time had been kind to her, she was perhaps more attractive than she was when she grew up there. One could hardly believe that she was in her mid thirties. She looked much younger!

Just look at her! Statuesque and curvaceous, five feet, eight inches with clear, smooth peaches and honey complexion! Large, dreamy, brown, bedroom eyes, Inviting lips on her oval shaped face crowned with thick, silky, black, shoulder length hair that she parted in the middle, a style that she had since she was about fourteen!

Besides being extremely attractive, personable and naturally charismatic, Dora did those little devilish things that many thought of but never did.

But for all of her obvious physical attributes and irrepressible charm the woman was and always had been extremely lazy and without any ambition in life, save finding someone with whom to charm or flirt. Dora was a prime example of wasted potential.

While she was soaking up all the accolades, Chris had wandered up to the shiny, new black sports car. He was curious about the car, but more so about the driver.

Chris was sure that his prayers had been answered and this

tall, dark, and strong looking man was hopefully his father, and that pretty mother of his were here to take him to the big city with them! The very prospect made Chris' heart beat faster and faster with anticipation, as he approaches the man and the car.

By the time Chris got to the man, he was all but out of breath! However, he managed to greet him with a big smile and a friendly, "Hi!"

The man bent over from his six-foot plus advantage, extended his hand and replied, "Hello, sir and how are you?"

Accepting the handshake, Chris responded, "Fine! What kind of car is that?" Very quickly the man responded, but Chris didn't recognize the name of the car. Chris decided not to ask another time fearing that he might seem stupid, and he didn't want to discourage the man from taking him away. So, Chris and the guy engaged in some small talk.

Finally, Chris just had to know. He knew what he wanted to ask, but what came out was, "Who are you?"

Not understanding what the boy was asking him, he replied, "I am Charles, Charles Hanson!"

"Hanson?", Chris repeated, obviously confused.

"Yes, Charles Hanson." Then he looked at the boy quizzically and gently asked, "Were you expecting someone else? . . . I mean, who should I be?"

"My father?" Chris responded without hesitation.

Wondering what he had gotten himself into by bringing Dora down to this place, he gathered himself and responded with an uneasy laugh, "No, Chris you are not my son, but we can be . . . uh . . . well, from now on you are my main man."

Undaunted, Chris fired another round, "Well, are you and my mother going to take me back with you?"

Confused, but knowing that there was a lot about this

situation that he didn't know, he responded with a very bland, "Let's wait and talk to Dora."

He surveyed the area looking for Dora and noticed that a bunch of kids were now rapidly approaching them. Some were running up the hill. As they got closer, they asked Chris the man's identity. One little girl got right to the point, "That your Daddy, Chris?"

Charles looked at the pained expression on the boy's face and answered for him, "I'm Chris' main man, his partner, Mr. Charles. And who are you, little girl?"

She didn't answer him, but turned to the others, smiling with an air of omniscience and triumphantly stated, "Told you, told you didn't I! He ain't Chris' father! Chris ain't got no father!"

Feeling extremely uncomfortable, Charles looked around for Dora for some help! When he spotted her, she was leading a crowd of very some angry and vocal people. A woman, who he was to later know as Glo, was seemingly taunting Dora, "Any fool would know better than to come to her own mother's funeral late as can be, dressed like a two-dollar wh. . . . "

She was interrupted by Dora's,"Still jealous, are we?" Dora flipped her head triumphantly and started playing the crowd for as many laughs she could. Some people laughed, while others responded with dismay and disgust.

The feeling which was expressed by glaring and frowning, didn't escape Dora. She just couldn't leave things this way! She could never have lived with herself if she let Glo get away with this! She felt trapped, angry, and frustrated! What could she do but defend herself?

Deciding to attack, Dora let out a barrage of extremely lethal sounding obscenities that shocked, dismayed and frightened everyone within the sound of her now very high-pitched voice! Her venomous verbiage could only have been worse if it had come from the far reaches of hell itself! Everybody and seemingly everything became dead silent as the two sisters glared at each other with sororicide in their hearts!

Gloria knew that pursuing Dora in this way could come to no good. From the diabolical look in her sister's eyes, she knew that the only sensible thing to do was retreat. She knew that Dora would die before she retreated. Gloria, also had to consider the innocent and the children.

Gloria turned her head slowly, signaling that she had enough. Many were disappointed at her retreating. However, those who mattered knew that she had done the right thing.

Sensing a victory, Dora smiled triumphantly. The irony was that it was almost totally unbelievable that those filthy words had come from such an angelic face. If he had not figured it out sooner, Charles now knew that he was definitely at the wrong place and certainly the wrong time!

While the folks were gaining their composure, Gloria said to Dora softly, "Well, aren't you going to say something to your son?"

Dora had never considered running into her son. Her face went blank and she didn't respond.

"You don't know, do you? How could you? You haven't seen him since you came down here and left him with Mama. Yeah, left him here until you got yourself straight! You straight yet, Miss Thing? Now tell all of us poor, ignorant country folks, which of these Georgia browned boys is yours?"

Accepting the challenge, Dora muttered something inaudible. She walked over and knelt in front of little Henry, kissed him on the forehead, cooing, "Here's my baby boy!"

Frightened, young Henry ran to his mother, Gloria, who glared at Dora. Sadly she said, "Now, that's really pitiful."

Dora stood there with a plea for help in her eyes, and her

youngest sister, Alice, responded by bringing Chris to her, "This is your boy, Chris." As Alice gently guided the boy to her, Dora felt her eyes began to tear.

She acknowledged Alice's compassion by slowly nodding and hugging her first, and then she hugged Chris.

As the crowd began to dissipate, Dora was doing her level best to convince the boy that he was, after all, very important to her. He was confused. Gloria was sorry for her part in the confrontation with Dora, and Charles knew for sure that he wanted to be some place, any place else.

J.B. and the undertaker, Avory, who had not witnessed the confrontation had been talking and walking toward the crowd.

As they arrived at the scene of dissipating crowd, Avory impatiently looked at his watch. J.B. suggested that they leave and go home. Nobody was happier than Charles, who saw this as an opportunity to make his great escape from this foolishness that he had somehow gotten himself into.

Dora, who had been kneeling in front of Chris, talking to him, hugged and kissed him again and slowly stood up. She walked over to Avory and spoke to him briefly, causing a smile on his otherwise stoic face. Then, she led Chris over to Charles and asked them to ride to Gloria's house together. She explained that she and Avory had some business to discuss.

Charles could not believe that she was going to leave the boy with him, but she did. So, he and Chris got in the car and slowly drove away. At the same time, Dora, who was now holding Avory's arm turned to Gloria and fired another round at her by asking,"You want to go with us?" Gloria didn't bother responding.

Once inside the sport's car Chris was impressed by the appointments, especially the electronic gadgetry. After answering quite a few questions about the car, they began some small talk about sports, music, school, and girls.

Charles was impressed by the boy's candor and wit. He told Chris that he didn't have a son, but if he did he would like him to be a lot like him. Chris smiled and told Charles that he wouldn't make a bad father either.

Charles, who was now reasonably relaxed, was telling Chris about some of his own childhood experiences, when he noticed that the boy was softly crying. Although Charles felt trapped again, he asked the boy the reason for the tears. Chris would not respond.

Then Charles asked whose funeral it was that they had just left. This took the boy completely by surprise, and he wondered aloud how could somebody go to a funeral without knowing the departed.

The only answer that Charles could come up with was that his mother was probably so upset that she didn't talk about it on the way. Dora had only said that she wanted to go home for a few days.

"It's not fair," the boy sobbed.

"Death never seems to be fair, but you got to remem . . . " Chris interrupted by saying that he thought that it was unfair that he didn't live with his mother, that he never even got to see her, and . . . Before he could finish, Charles stopped him by asking, "When was the last time you saw her?"

"I have a beautiful picture of her that she sent us a few years ago, but I can't remember the last time I actually saw her. Mama Liz says that she is the prettiest woman in the world, but she's not too . . . "

"I see . . . ", Charles interrupted, confirming to himself that as soon as he could he would rid himself of this woman he would. But he had grown very fond of the boy. He decided to spend some time alone with him and turned away from the cars that he was following.

He asked the boy to show him the way to the shopping mall or whatever they had here. Chris, still crying softly, gave him the directions.

After a short ride, they entered a very large shopping center which was much bigger than Charles had expected. They ate pizza, drank soda, and played some video games! The two had so much fun together that they did a little shopping. Charles completely surprised himself by insisting that the boy have a couple of shirts, a pair of jeans, a ball, a bat, and a glove!

The ride to Glo's house was fun! The two swapped stories, jokes, and Chris shared some experiences that he had with his grandmother, J.B., Aunt Glo, and the others.

Charles was absolutely and positively impressed with the boy's obvious wit, intelligence, and unassuming manner. He could really envision himself being close to the boy, but then there was Dora!

He wondered how he could ever deal with her again? Hadn't his loins gotten him in enough trouble? Wouldn't his best bet be to just go about his business? He knew the answers to the questions and reasoned that if the woman was any good at all, he would not have ever met her in the first place.

A woman as fine as she is would have been snatched up a long time ago. He knew from the moment that he met her who and what she was.

It was his fault that he was there in the first place, and it was up to him to get out of this potentially volatile situation as soon as possible. Yes, he knew that the party was over, and that he would leave her, the boy, and all the confusion right here.

As he slowly drove into the yard, he planned his escape. He felt that he needed to leave in a way which would preserve his dignity. He couldn't just drop the boy off and leave, although he knew that would be the easiest way.

As they got out of the car, they could hear the music, and laughter that seemed to come from everywhere. Chris grabbed Charles by the hand and led him into the house where everybody was partying back!

Dora was standing alone bouncing to the music and watching the people who were dancing.

"This is going to be real easy," Charles thought to himself, as he walked toward her nodding and speaking. Many people returned his greeting. " Easy, real easy," he thought to himself.

But, he was not prepared for Dora, who was, if nothing else, a survivor and master manipulator. As he approached, with a stoic expression, she returned it with a smile. As he drew nearer, she gently and slowly began to caress him and stroke his back.

When he began to talk, she gently placed her index finger on his lips to prevent him from speaking.

"Where have you and Chris been?" she probed softly. "If it had been anyone but you, I would have been very worried."

"Uh, to the mall. We had some food and I got him a few things."

Now holding him close, with her lips almost touching his, "I hope he didn't bother you too much."

"No, he is a wonderful boy, just like his mother is a wonderful woman."

"Damn!" he thought to himself, "I shouldn't have said that!"

Now, rhythmically swaying with him, to the music and kissed him on the neck, she thanked him for bringing her home. She told him that she really appreciated his spending time with her boy.

She told him that she had never felt as good with a man as

she had with him these last three weeks. She told him, with a very naughty and suggestive smile, that if she didn't know better, she'd think that she was in love this time, maybe, for the first time! Then, she playfully pushed him away saying that he was making her hot!

He allowed her to introduce him to everybody as her man. Despite his instincts screaming that he was being conned, the very possibility that she was being honest made him imagine the three of them as a trio, a family.

Now, the last thing that he wanted to do was to leave her! Sometimes you just get lucky! He began to think about how he would introduce her and the boy to his family and friends. He also had to consider how he was going to break the news at the office, but he looked at her and wagered that everybody would be so envious of him that he just might get one of those promotions.

She had the kind of appeal that could really help a man out, all he would have to do is to school her a little on what to say. Yes, Charles had somehow struck gold!

As Dora was leading everybody, mostly the men, in a dance called `The Electric Slide", Charles walked back to the kitchen and looked out the window at the children playing ball with the equipment that he had bought Chris. The boy looked so happy that Charles decided that he would get him in one of the little leagues. He was also deciding whether to send him to a private or public school.

Charles didn't remember ever having those types of paternal instincts, but he could not wait to be able to call this boy 'son'. He chuckled to himself and slowly walked back to the living room where they were finishing a high stepping fast dance!

Somebody played one of his favorite songs, *By The Time I Get To Phoenix,* by Isaac Hayes. He and his woman made eye contact, which made his heart beat very fast. Then she passed up a request for a dance and came to him with a very seductive, naughty look in her eyes that didn't seem to escape anybody in the room.

As they slowly danced, the warmth of her body and her very touch excited his every nerve. He could hold her forever! As they danced and Isaac was singing, " . . . *she thought that I'd never leave her, cause time, after . . .*," she asked him for the time.

"The time? "

"Yes, Baby, what time is it?"

Annoyed because she broke spell, he glanced at his watch, "It's about six - thirty."

Dora, who had been dancing so very close and smoothly with Charles, suddenly was completely out of step. Charles attempted to maneuver her back in the groove that they had been in, but it just wasn't working.

Opening his eyes, he saw that she was looking around the room. Suddenly, she led him over to a very attractive young woman whom she introduced as her next to youngest sister, Karen. Charles could see that they were sisters indeed.

Cute as she wanted to be! She was about the same height and build as Dora, but a shade or two darker with longer black hair that flowed past her shoulders. She had changed clothes and was wearing a starched blue shirt that almost completely covered denim shorts, which exposed her shapely, smooth legs.

As suavely as he could, he acknowledged her physical attributes, "I sure wish that my friends were here, they would not believe all the beauty that I am fortunate enough to be witnessing. You lovely sisters really make my eyes feel good! There should be a law against there being so many beautiful women in one family."

Karen smiled, blushed, and responded with a very exquisite, "I'm sure that you are being too kind. We could sure use some more gentlemen like you around here."

Dora suggested that they dance, and Charles was now ready to party! To his delight, the "Electric Slide" was being played! This was the one dance that he loved! As they were dancing, Dora danced over to him laughing and asked him for his car keys so that, she could get her luggage. Then she danced away.

Charles really enjoyed dancing with Karen and the others. He thought that although extremely attractive, the woman was a bit young for him. After they went through `The Slide' a couple of times, Charles retreated to the kitchen to fix himself a drink.

When he returned to the living room, Dora and Karen were talking, standing next to what appeared a bedroom. Well, Dora was talking and Karen was listening, with sort of a frown on her face. Finally, Karen shrugged her shoulders and seemed to reluctantly agree to something.

Dora brought Karen over to Charles and told him that she was going to shower and change. She also told him that Karen would be looking out for him, and that she would get him anything that he wanted. Dora turned away saying, "Don't you two do anything that I wouldn't do! " She laughed and disappeared behind the bedroom door.

Charles and Karen stood there, neither too sure of what to do. Finally, Charles excused himself and walked over to where the men were eating and drinking. They were talking about baseball, so it was fairly easy for him to join in the conversation.

They became so engulfed in their assessments of various players and teams that some of the women left. The others were talking about whatever women talk about and helping

Gloria to clean and straighten the house.

Night set in and the children came indoors, thirsty and hungry. J.B. had turned on the television and most of the men were watching a baseball game. Chris joined them and was telling them how well he had done with his new bat and glove. Charles was as proud as any father could be and was considering adoption.

"What the hell!," he thought, "I'm almost forty, in good with the company, maybe it's time for me to settle down. Dora, Chris and I would make a great little family."

As if on cue, Dora made a grand entrance into the room. She was enchantingly dressed in a black, gold-trimmed, form-fitting pants suit. Her delicately exposed cleavage was adorned with gold chains. High heeled black and gold shoes gave her the appearance of a Goddess. She looked so incredible that most could do no more than gaze at her.

Somebody played, *"Anyone Who had a Heart"* by Luther Vandross. Charles, as if in a spell, walked over to her and they danced. As Luther crooned *". . . would know that I love you, Anyone who had a heart..."* Gloria, standing by the window, said loudly, "I wonder what the hell he's doing here?"

Dora pushed Charles away gently and surveyed herself in the mirror and hurriedly walked out the door, leaving Charles standing there, feeling sort of stupid, as Luther sang *"... what am I to do?"*

After a few moments, she came back in the room with Avory in tow. She introduced him to Charles as an old friend who taking her to see some old friends that she had not seen in years.

Avory extended his hand and Charles accepted the handshake and lukewarm greeting. Avory's presence didn't seem to please many folks there, especially Gloria, who just glared at him.

Undaunted, he cleared his throat and benevolently announced that although there had been differences between him and the family, he was not going to charge them for the funeral except the expense of the limousines.

"After all," he continued, "Mama Liz was just like . . . and all of you are like family to me. I believe that my father would have wanted it this way."

He offered Gloria some documents to sign, along with a pen. On behalf of the family, Gloria thanked him while Karen ran out of the room crying. Dora looked quite pleased. Charles felt real uneasy about this development. After reading the documents, Gloria signed them and gave the copies back to him.

While all of this was going on, one of Avory's men entered with some bottles of liquor and beer.

"I hope that I'm not being very presumptuous by offering you good folks this small token. Please accept this in the spirit that it is being given."

Gloria mumbled something inaudible and went to the kitchen. J.B. grabbed Chris and walked him to the kitchen. The other folks either pretended to be watching the baseball game or pretending not to be paying much attention to the potentially explosive situation.

Avory, who obviously knew that he was hardly the most popular person there, softly told Dora that he would be waiting in the car, and nervously departed with his man close behind. By this time, Gloria was standing in the doorway glaring at Dora.

Dora kissed Charles on the cheek and assured him that she would return soon and that they would talk. Before Charles could respond, Gloria said very sternly to Dora, "I don't know about all that, but whenever you get back, you and I will definitely talk about you and Chris."

Dora looked at Gloria and replied, "Sure." She blew a kiss at Charles and reminded him that she'd be back soon. Charles looked at his watch, 10:30, and knowingly nodded his head.

Charles stood there, looking at the now deserted door, feeling very empty. Somebody offered him a drink and soon everybody was drinking and laughing again. The booze loosened everybody up, and they began to talk about Dora. Charles heard about the mischievous things that she had done as a child.

After the polite stuff, they began to share the real deal with Charles, including her relationship with Avory, her falling out with her sister, and the caustic relationship that she had with her father. As it got later and later, the crowd really began to thin out to the point that only Gloria, her husband, who was either sleep or drunk on the couch, Karen, J.B., Chris, who was fighting sleep, Alice, and Charles remained.

Finally, Charles and Gloria were the only ones that were awake. He decided that he would leave and spend some time in Atlanta before going back. He picked the boy up and Gloria led him to a bedroom.

Before they got him in bed, he was awakened by the movement. Charles and Chris had what Charles knew would be their last conversation.

He asked Gloria for directions to the interstate. Gloria stood in the door and watched the sports car cruise away, while Charles felt deserted and very lonely.

The morning breakfast was filled with lively conversation about Dora and Chris. Gloria's position was that Chris had to go with Dora, while J.B. was opposed to the move. As the morning wore on and the arguments went back and forth, J.B.

was convinced that Chris' going back with Dora would be best.

The prevailing thought was that according to Mama Liz's wish, Dora should have one last chance to be a mother to Chris. So, all that was left to do was to inform Dora, who had yet to return.

As the morning had passed and the afternoon was wearing on, most had become anxious about the whereabouts of Dora. Some had begun to suspect that perhaps the two had rolled out, which would not have shocked anybody. They were saying things like "... old flames never completely go out" and other pearls of wisdom.

At approximately 3:30 P.M., they returned. Dora popped out of the limousine, and blew a kiss at Avory who obviously didn't feel like facing the family.

The first thing they noticed was that she was not wearing the same clothes that she had left in, and that she had shopping bags from some of the more expensive shops in the neighboring town.

She walked in the house as if, she had been gone for only a few moments. Helping herself to some food and drink, she casually asked about Charles. The fact that he had left angered her.

While Dora was fussing and fuming about Charles leaving her, Gloria strongly suggested that she come in the living room for a little family talk. Sensing that she was going to get 'preached to' for going away and staying with Avory, she was prepared for battle.

She never dreamed that they would insist that the boy go back with her! "What the hell was she going to do with that damned boy! Where would he stay?" She pleaded, "I only have a very small apartment. You can't be serious!"

After two or three days of pleading, begging, and

rationalizing, Dora felt trapped and realized that regardless to what she said Chris was going back with her. The decision had been made, and it was final. She didn't like it, but now she had to figure out what to do with the boy.

On the fifth day, Chris found himself being kissed and hugged by everyone and seated in the back of Avory's limousine. With his mother and Avory up front, he felt very important. He was leaving everybody and everything he had ever known and loved.

Chris was on his way to the city. He had no idea what to expect. J.B. had warned him to be careful and always remember to pray.

"Prayer got me exactly what I wanted! I'm going to the city with my mother, Dora. Hope I'll see Mr. Charles real soon!"

Chris was one very happy child!

4. *Rommie*

Chris jumped off the bed and grabbed his ball and glove, his very favorite possessions. While walking through the empty rooms, throwing the ball and catching it, he tried to recall if Dora had asked him to do anything.

Who was he kidding? He knew that his mother wouldn't ask him to do very much except to stay out of her way.

So he walked down the street to the basketball court to watch the big boys play. One player was so much better than the rest that he could do just about anything he wanted with the ball. Chris was glad to see Sonia among the spectators.

After watching her for a while, it became quite obvious that she was a fan of one particular player because every time he touched the ball she got very excited and screamed his name, "Roy!"

This guy, the apparent crowd favorite, maneuvered down the court on a fast break by himself. He glided effortlessly around and through the opposition. After crossing mid court, he jetted toward the basket.

The very dark, massive athlete did a three hundred sixty-degree turn in mid air and slam-dunked the ball with such sudden force that those closest to the goal covered their heads. The ball hit the ground and ricocheted, it seemed, to the clouds. Everybody roared, "Roy! Roy! Roy!"

Even the opposition ran to him and congratulated him for that dunk! They threw him the ball again with all nine players surrounding him at the foul line. Chris heard and saw Sonia jumping up and down and screaming, "Do it! Do it, Roy!"

Despite some grabbing and attempts to hold him, Roy exploded from the crowd! He soared in the air like a huge black eagle, somehow managing to slam the ball backwards! After a brief awestruck silence, the crowd exploded with cheers!

Chris' mouth was wide open, he could not believe what he had just witnessed. He was now one of the thousands who were avid Roy fans.

After that everybody was so excited that they stopped playing! Roy was so good that there just wasn't any point to playing any longer. Many were now slapping Roy's glistening back, slapping him high five's, and just having a good time.

Chris decided to go speak to Sonia, but before he could get close enough she was sitting on Roy's knee. Chris decided that maybe he should play with the younger boys who were now on the court. He wanted to show them that he could run and shoot, too!

However, shyness and the fear of rejection kept him away. He sadly looked at the boys having fun on the court. He stood alone, looking at Sonia, Roy, and the rest who were having the time of their lives. Chris felt so lonely that he wanted to cry.

Dejected, he slowly headed toward the house. Once inside, he fixed himself a sandwich, grabbed a soft drink and allowed the tears to flow down his cheeks.

He thought about the day he arrived with his mother and Avory. After he and Avory had unloaded the car, Avory seemed to think that he was going to stay. Dora kept telling him that he would have to leave. As they were arguing, Chris went outside and sat on the steps.

Chris looked around and saw that the crowded projects were very different from the spacious country living to which he was accustomed. He could not believe the dirt, trash, and filth that surrounded this place. The fact that this would be his home scared him to death, and he prayed to return to Georgia.

A deep, demanding, voice interrupted his prayers, "You lose something? Why don't you find some place else to park your young ass?"

Chris looked up at this tall, dark, and angry looking man. Frightened and not knowing what to do, Chris ran in the house crying and screaming, "Mama, mama!"

For his efforts, he got yelled at and smacked. Dora, who had been fending Avory off, didn't like to be interrupted! She definitely didn't like being called Mama and she let him know in no uncertain terms that she was not " . . . going to have no bitch for a son crying and acting like a little girl!"

Before she could find out what Chris' problem was, the guy very coolly and calmly walked in as if he owned the place.

"Who is this clown? Dat his crumsnatcher?"

His instincts for survival well in tact, Avory asked the guy the amount.

"Seventy-five."

Dora who had become silent, nodded in agreement as Avory quizzically looked at her. He reached into his pocket and peeled off the money. After getting the cash, the diabolical grimace turned into a friendly smile. He warned Dora not to be late with his money again, smiled brightly and left.

Chris was ordered outside, while Dora took Avory to her bedroom to show her appreciation.

Chris wandered outside again, and was met by the heat and

stench of the projects. He sat and watched half-naked males and females of all ages, some talking, laughing, running, roaming, or just idle.

Avory came to the door, followed by Dora. She demanded money, but he was felt that he had done enough. He told Dora that he was going home and never wanted to see her again. Avory was so disgusted that he laughed nervously and walked out the door without saying anything else.

Avory nodded at Chris, shook his head and walked rapidly toward his car. Dora, standing in the doorway wearing a night gown, watched with indifferent silence.

Dora asked Chris to come in and put up his stuff in the room that would be his. She followed him to the room and helped him straighten it up. While they were working on the room, she told him what she expected of him, mainly to stay out of her way.

Chris having forgotten, made a bad mistake, and called Dora "Mama" again and she really went off!

She slapped the boy again and demanded that he call her Dora! She started screaming, "I can't deal with this! Who the hell they think they're sending this boy here with me? I really can't deal with this!"

Chris didn't know what to do. After she left the room, he sat on the bed. Dora stormed back into the room with a television.

"Use the plug over there," she shouted at him and again stormed out. Chris decided to stay put. A little later, he heard her storm out of the door, still yelling, "I can't deal with this! Hell no, this ain't even gonna work!"

Dora stormed across the court to her girlfriend's house, still cussing and fussing! She was so upset that her friend, Virginia, had to sit her down and give her a drink. Very calmly, she asked Dora what was bothering her so much.

Dora began by telling her about going to her mother's funeral and how unfairly she had been treated by her own family. She was especially upset with her sister, Gloria, who was responsible for her having to bring Chris here. Dora didn't mention Charles and Avory. She was at a total loss as to the reason that she had been treated so badly.

She complained, "What in the hell do they think I can do with some, some damned boy? Me of all people raising a male, ain't that a . . . " Dora stopped for a moment to laugh at herself.

"He could have stayed with them! Tell you what, if he gets on my nerves, I'll run his little ass out of here like I did his cute assed sister!"

Virginia laughed and reminded Dora that the boy was after all her son. Dora slashed back," Virginia, I don't see you going to the joint to see your son!"

Calmly, Virginia responded that she had done everything that a mother could do to keep her son, Little Al, out of trouble, but the boy decided to be a thug. She added that after that thing that he had done in school, she was finished with him. Anyway, she reasoned whatever it was, it had nothing to do with her and Chris.

"Listen Dora," she continued, "You're just upset because you didn't get your way this time. You need to cut that out. Tell you what, Rommie is giving a big party for some of his friends from New York.

It's going to be at that new hotel downtown, around the pool. Everybody is going to be there. He's rented the top floor in case somebody is afraid of water. But you know Rommie, he's just doing that to show off.

Girlfriend, I know if you stop feeling sorry for yourself, get dressed and go with us this evening, you'll find something interesting. You know what I mean, jelly bean?"

"Jelly bean? I haven't heard anybody called jelly bean in years! You're showing your age!" Dora laughed.

"So why don't you go home, rest up a bit, cook that boy a good dinner and bring him over here. He can go to the movies or something with Sonia."

"What if Sonia has something else to do?"

Virginia laughed and called her daughter, who was in the bathroom experimenting with her hair. Hearing her mother, she came down stairs fussing, "Sonia, Sonia, all I hear around here is Sonia, Sonia!"

Sonia's attitude changed instantly when she saw Dora. Much to Virginia's displeasure, more than anything else in the world, Sonia wanted to be like Dora. As far as Sonia was concerned, Dora could do no wrong and she was absolutely beautiful and knew how to deal with men.

Dora and Sonia had mutual admiration for each other. Dora wanted to be as young, and pretty as Sonia, while Sonia wanted Dora's free spirit and ability to attract men with big, fine cars and money.

They often spent time feeding each other's egos, which wasn't very difficult. They were both very conceited. Generally, they amused Virginia, who didn't suffer from that particular malady.

"Sonia, I swear, you are the finest young thing around here- besides me," Dora began. Sonia blushed, while Virginia playfully pretended that she was getting sick to the stomach and left to finish dressing.

"I want you to . . . girl, how big are you now? Seems like you done busted out a bit more since I last saw you!"

"About thirty-four or six D!"

"I believe I was sixteen before I was that big, and I was as pregnant as I could be. Anyway, I want you to do Aunt Dora a little favor."

"Sure, anything", hoping that it was something exciting that they would be doing together.

"I want you to kind of look out for my baby boy this evening?"

"Baby boy! ?"

Realizing that she had goofed by calling him that, she cleaned it up by explaining that a woman's boy is always her baby. She explained that she was going out with her mother and Rommie. She didn't want the boy being alone, although she could have cared less.

After conceding that Chris was too young for her to be seen with in public, they agreed that he would come over to have dinner, listen to a few records and then leave.

Dora asked Sonia to do another little thing for her. She suggested that Sonia call him to make the 'invite more personal'. They winked at each other and agreed that would be best. Dora added that she could help her with that basketball player, if she needed it.

When Virginia returned, they told her that Chris would be coming over for dinner and to spend some time with Sonia.

Dora got up, laughed and declared, "I know one thing, somebody's man is going to be in trouble tonight. It's been a long time since I've done the do my way! Catch you later!"

At about the same time all this was going on, Christee called and talked to Chris. She had just learned that Mama 'Liz's death.

She told Chris that she had been out of town trying to get a part in a play, but she didn't get the part and just messed around in Philadelphia for a few days and didn't have any idea that Mama 'Liz had died.

She told him that she would call him, but only when she felt that Dora was not around. They talked until Chris heard Dora returning.

Singing? Dora was singing when she returned and asked him if everything was all right, which really surprised Chris. He had expected her to continue her attack, but she was in a great mood. He was determined not to do anything to change it. Soon after she arrived, the telephone rang, and she asked him to answer it, and she sang and danced to her bedroom.

Much to his surprise and pleasure, the call was for him. A girl named Sonia wanted to talk to him! She explained that she was the daughter of his mother's best friend, and she wanted him to come eat with her that evening. Sonia added that they would play some music and get to know each other.

Chris was so excited that he was ready to run right out the door and told her so! She laughed and told him that she had to do some things first. They agreed on six o'clock. After they hung up, Chris was so happy that he began to sing.

Hearing him singing, Dora appeared to confirm that being with Sonia would be a great idea. She went back to her room singing again, but this time she was singing the same song that he was singing. Dora yelled through the door, "We sound real good together, maybe we'll go down to Eric's one night and win some of that money."

He looked at the clock and it was only about four thirty. Boy, was he impatient to go to meet this Sonia. While he was calming himself down, Dora came out of her room to tell him that she was going to sleep and not to make any noise or disturb her. She also told him that included any visitors or telephone calls. She gave him a key and told him to lock up when he left.

After bathing, dressing and messing around the house, six

o'clock finally arrived. A little nervous, he walked across the court to Sonia's. Virginia welcomed him to her home and the city. They engaged in a little small talk while Sonia laid across her bed anticipating a very dull and boring evening with Chris.

After talking with Chris for a few minutes, Virginia knew that Sonia was upstairs either stalling or waiting to make a grand entrance. So she finally excused herself and went upstairs to Sonia's room and demanded that she go entertain her guest. Although the girl had second thoughts about the whole thing, she felt that it would be best to go get this thing over with.

Sonia found a smile and headed for this dreaded encounter with this boy! Dora had once told her to always look good to the men, even if you ain't too interested, because you never know.

On her way to the kitchen she stopped in the bathroom to check herself out. Satisfied that she was looking good, she decided to go down and charm this boy to death! Arriving in the kitchen, she opened her mouth to speak, but words wouldn't come. Chris was truly cute!

Then she thought, "What did I expect? He is Dora's son." Finally, she managed to speak. Chris didn't even notice her hesitation, she was the prettiest girl that he had ever met. She was truly hot! Hot was the only word that he could think of to describe this beautiful girl! He felt things for her that he had never felt before, and he liked the way that being with her made him feel.

Chris was concerned that he would say something really dumb, and her only concern was that he was so very young, although they were about the same age! She laughed after a while and warned him that she hoped that he liked his food burnt, because she burnt everything even Jell-O.

Both laughed and Chris volunteered to help her burn up something, explaining that he had plenty of practice burning things for himself and his grandmother.

They indeed made out well. They cooked a complete chicken dinner that sent waves of delicious aromas throughout the house. It was so very delicious smelling that Virginia came down and joined them. They enjoyed a great dinner and fun conversation. Virginia got so caught up in the fun that she lost track of time.

She suddenly jumped up to get dressed, amazed at how the time had passed. She was mildly shocked when Sonia got up to clean the kitchen. Something she almost never did, at least, without her life being threatened. She was pleased as Chris helped her. She left them laughing as she went upstairs to get ready for the big party.

While cleaning the kitchen, they talked about school, music, and sports. Sonia was amazed that he knew and liked much of the same music that she liked, and he was surprised that she knew so much about basketball. After doing a job on the kitchen, they went to the living room and listened to music and danced.

Now, Sonia was completely surprised that he could dance so well. He just laughed, danced, and reminded her that he was not from Russia or some other foreign country. They were having so much fun that the time flew by. Neither heard Rommie knock on the door and enter.

"Hey, sweetheart! How you doing with your fine self?" Rommie asked with a big smile.

Sonia blushed and said, "This is Dora's young boy, Chris. Chris, this is me and my mother's man, Rommie."

"Hell, he ain't that young. Where's your Mama? Sonia ran to Virginia's room to get her.

Rommie nodded at Chris, "Yeah, you the young blood that was at Dora's? Was that dude your daddy?"

Chris slowly shook his head and softly said. "No, I mean, no, sir!"

"Good caused he seemed country or something, and a sure 'nough chump. Any man coughing up that kinda money is a chump in my book!" Rommie began complaining and made little jokes about how slow women were and Chris slipped in a polite laugh when it seemed appropriate. Rommie made Chris a little uneasy, in fact, he scared him.

Chris very soon discovered that Rommie loved to talk about himself. He talked about how rich he was, the people that he knew, his automobile, his jewelry, the women that he had known, and on and on. Although polite, Chris had absolutely no interest in what the man was saying.

Chris was not at all impressed by the way that the man was dressed. The black suit, the unbuttoned black shirt, exposing nine or ten gold chains, the black socks, and the black and white snake-skinned shoes made him look really grotesque to Chris.

The gold bracelets, the big gold watch, and the three gold teeth, one heart shaped, made him even more sinister to Chris. Rommie was not to be trusted as far as he was concerned. Chris was overjoyed that this man was Miss Virginia's boyfriend and not his mother's. His life was complicated enough as it was!

Bored almost to tears by the rambling of this guy, Chris was ecstatic when Sonia returned. He was, however, surprised to see that she had changed into a very revealing outfit, only a pair of denim short shorts and powder blue halter-top that accentuated her well-sculptured body! The size of her now braless breast astonished him.

However, the hungry, lustful eyes of Rommie made Chris very angry. He disliked this Rommie as much as he wanted Sonia.

"How old are you now, Sonia?," he asked, with a big toothy smile.

"Almost fifteen . . . ", she blushed.

"Here's a little something for you," he said with a big benevolent smile.

She accepted the ten dollars with a big smile and quickly shoved it into the pocket of her shorts, which was quit a task because they were so very tight. As she was tucking away her loot, he said in a more serious tone, "Now remember our date when you get sixteen." The two continued to talk, totally ignoring Chris.

His anxiety was broken by the entrance of Virginia who was absolutely beautiful. She was wearing a black A-lined dress with black stockings and shoes. Her dress was complemented by a single thin gold chain around her neck that held a small diamond that shined like a star on her honey brown skin.

Her finely curled, short cut black hair accented her round face. The small, simple diamond studded earrings, along with her soft smile, gave her the demeanor of a doll.

Genuinely impressed, Chris said, "Miss Virginia you look just like a movie star."

"Why, thank you," she answered, smiling.

"Looking good, ma," Sonia added halfheartedly, almost sarcastically.

Virginia's smile suddenly turned into a grimace. She ordered Sonia to go put some clothes on, she was not going to have her walking around men dressed like a tramp.

Sonia, now embarrassed, stormed out of the room. Rommie attempted to intervene on the girl's behalf, but was refuted so quickly and definitely that he tactfully retreated.

Virginia excused herself from the room and followed Sonia. They could hear Virginia telling Sonia that the very next time she pulled a stunt like that she would be sorry, very sorry.

They could hear Sonia complain about it being too hot in there, and she was only trying to keep cool. Unimpressed Virginia reminded her never to try that again.

All this seemed to amuse Rommie to the point that he was laughing almost out of control. Chris could not fully appreciate what was going on but regretted that Sonia was 'catching it '.

As Virginia entered the room, still annoyed, Rommie said that she shouldn't be so hard on the girl because it was hot. He also added that he'd offered her air conditioning, but she kept on refusing.

She countered by reminding him to mind his own business as far as her daughter was concerned and to stop messing with her head. She told him that she was not going to tell him again to leave Sonia alone. He laughed and protested that he was just playing, being friendly with the child. She ended that conversation by reminding him that she was a child, and how hard as it was to keep kids straight "these days".

Sonia walked into the room slowly, with the outfit that she had on before Rommie arrived, with a 'hurt puppy' expression. Virginia had to turn her head away to keep from laughing in the girl's face. Chris could feel the hurt that she was expressing. It made him sad for her.

Rommie could not control himself and laughed aloud, "You sure is right about that girl! With that look on her face, she could fool the pope, but we know that she's about as sorry as I am sorry about breathing!"

He turned to Chris and said prophetically, "Boy, you got a

mess on your hands. If I was you, I'd leave right now before them baby browns' kick your butt!" Both Virginia and Rommie laughed. Sonia pretended to pout a bit then she laughed.

Chris felt confused and uncomfortable, but he laughed to keep from appearing stupid. Virginia asked Sonia to turn on the fan, so Rommie can see how really cool it can be in here. Sure enough, soon the room was almost too cool.

Dora exploded into the room, wearing a red micro-mini, red stockings, red high-heeled shoes, and a shoulder length blond wig. With a big, confident smile on her lovely face she inquired loudly, "Did anybody here mention a party?!"

Her outfit was 'complemented' by gold sunglasses with rose colored lenses, several gold chains that seemed to dance in her deep cleavage as she moved about, an assortment of gold bracelets on one arm, a gold watch on the other and a gold bag!

"My Lord!" exclaimed Rommie, dropping his cigarette in his lap and jumping up to keep from burning himself!

"All right!", exclaimed Sonia with genuine admiration!

Virginia laughed, "Going hunting, are we, girlfriend?"

Dora, now in her world, exhibited her outfit by slowly gliding around the room. She stopped, looked at Virginia, laughing,"What's that word, um, sellabit?"

Shaking her head laughing, Virginia responded, "I think you mean celibate as in not having sex."

"No Girl, I mean sellabit, I'm so hot tonight that I might sell a bit and give a bit away!"

Virginia shook her head, still laughing. She didn't notice the look of lust on Rommie's face.

"Who is going to par-tee tonight? is me?", Dora proclaimed, admiring herself in the mirror.

Chris horrified and embarrassed, didn't know what to say. He felt it was wisest for him to say nothing. Seeing his mother look like one of those women in one of those dirty books or movies upset him to the point that he wanted to just die on that very spot!

All of those things that everybody at home had said about her were obviously very true. Being in his own private mental hell, he was oblivious to all the joking and teasing that was going on around him. Virginia asked Rommie if Dora could tag along. Without the least hesitation, Rommie not only agreed that she should go but insisted.

Still sorting out his feelings, he was hardly aware that the three had departed. He didn't even realize that Dora had kissed him on the cheek and advised him not to wait up for her.

Sonia was now saying something to him that he, at first, didn't comprehend. To add to his sorrows, she was telling him that it was getting late, she was very sleepy, and that he had to go. She assured him that she would see him soon as she all but pushed him out of the door.

The walk across the court seemed to take forever. He knew that he would be absolutely and totally alone. The image of Dora dressed the way she was caused bitter tears to fall. The fact that Sonia had dismissed him the way that she had, didn't help either.

What was he going to do? He considered running away, but where would he go? It would be too embarrassing to go back to where he knew or at least thought he knew that folks loved him. Trying to find Christee would be close to impossible. He resigned himself to his fate.

Reaching his front steps, he sat and tried to find something good about his situation. That too, seemed to be hopeless.

He surveyed the project. It appeared as desolate as he felt, but as he looked across at Sonia's door, his heart started beating with some anticipation. She was awake!

He could see her silhouette through the kitchen curtains. She didn't go to bed after all! All he had to do was to go over there and talk to her! She would be glad to have some company on a lonely night like this!

He got up the nerve to knock on the door, but before he could stand up he saw a very large figure approach the door. Because his eyes had already adjusted to the darkness, he recognized the figure as Roy!

It seemed like his very heart stopped as she opened the door and they kissed. Sonia let him in the house and the lights in the kitchen went out almost immediately.

Chris sat there stunned, gazing into the darkness. Finally, he got up and went inside this hell called home. He slowly walked to what was now his room of gloom and flopped across the bed and cried himself to sleep.

Although Chris was not aware of all the things that happened on that first day and night, he realized that life would be very different for him. The happiness and security that he had known in Georgia seemed so long ago.

Now, he prayed to return.

5. *Betrayed Trust*

While Chris was trying to sleep that first night, at least two plots were unfolding that would have a negative affect on his life without his ever knowing. Even if he had known, he would have been powerless to control or change any of the events.

After Roy entered the kitchen, Sonia stood in a chair, pulled him close, smiled, and kissed him long and deep. There was so much passion in that kiss that after a few moments, he pushed her away.

She laughed, led him to the living room and pushed him gently on the couch and with a naughty wink, continued kissing him.

In an attempt to compose himself, Roy opened his eyes to the darkened room which surprised him a little. He didn't recall her turning the lights out and tried to free himself from her grip. She was so tenacious that freeing himself became a monumental task, but somehow he managed while ordering her to turn the lights back on.

Breathlessly she protested, but complied. He asked her if he could take a quick shower, he had just come in from playing ball when she called him. When she hesitated he said he would understand if she thought that his taking a shower there would upset her sister. She had told him that she lived with her sister.

Knowing that Virginia wouldn't be home for hours, she told

him that he most certainly could take a shower. With a very sensuous smile added, ". . . and anything else that you want."

Sonia told him that she would go up first to tidy up a bit. Sonia happily ran up the stairs. She felt so grownup!

Since this was his first time in her home, he walked around the room looking at the various pictures that were displayed all over the place. He smiled as he looked at the various pictures of Sonia and this older, but very attractive woman who he assumed was her sister.

He recognized a picture of Dora who was a legend and young boy's dream, and he was no exception. He had seen and admired this attractive and mysterious creature often.

Suddenly, a cute picture of Sonia and Virginia caught his eye! It had an inscription on it that he had difficulty reading at first. He picked it up and walked over to the light to get a better look. It read, `Virginia and Sonia, "sixth grade Easter play" and was dated!

Horrified, and hoping that it didn't mean what it seemed, he looked around for other pictures of the two! There it was, a picture of the two with the inscription, `Virginia and daughter, Sonia at Hershey Park '!

Simple math revealed that Sonia was thirteen, maybe fourteen at the most, and a cold chill shot through his body! "How in the world did this happen to me? With all the women that I have to choose from, I picked this young girl?" he said aloud.

Disgusted, hurt, and afraid, he yelled up to Sonia to come downstairs. How he managed to get himself into this mess didn't matter. All that mattered now was getting him out of it. He heard himself screaming her name this time!

Sonia had straightened up the bathroom and was admiring herself in the mirror. She had opted to change into her bibbed overalls with no underwear and or blouse. She interpreted his ranting and raving as his growing impatience.

Sonia knew that she needed to get down there as quickly as possible, if for no other reason, to keep her nosey, nosey neighbors from knowing that he was there with her alone.

She surveyed everything, and things looked just fine. As a final touch, she unfastened one strap; so that, with one little move she would be all his. Ready, she ran downstairs!

When she saw him, she knew that something had gone very wrong. Her first thought was that her mother had returned, but that was impossible. She knew if had that happened, she and most likely Roy, would be stretched out on the floor by now!

Her question was answered quickly as Roy shouted, "Read this!" She looked at the picture and knew that she was cold busted!

He repeated, "Read this" and added sarcastically, "Yeah, read this if you are old enough to read!"

She slumped into a chair and made herself cry, while thinking, "What to do? What to . . .!" She jumped up and ran to the kitchen, while Roy was still in the living room ranting and raving.

He paced and fussed about her being a baby trying to be grownup and a liar.

"A thing like this could mess my whole life," he shouted. Realizing that he was talking to himself, he decided that it would be best for him to just leave and never so much as acknowledge that he knew Sonia.

As he walked through the kitchen, he decided not to say anything to her as there was nothing left to say.

However, Sonia had decided to go for broke and said with a very composed and calm voice, "I lied to you. Sure I lied, but

I think that you like me almost as much as I love you, Roy."

She stood up from the chair and continued, "I'm glad that you found the picture of me and my mother. But that picture makes no difference about the way that I feel about you."

Roy stood there motionless, and she sensed that he really didn't want to leave, and she became a lot more aggressive, "Do I act like a baby, Roy?" Roy didn't answer.

"Do I look like a baby?" she asked as she unbut-toned her strap and allowed her overalls to fall to the floor. She continued, "What difference do three years make if two people love each other?"

Although her math was intentionally a little shaky, Roy's resolve to leave had just about vanished and she sensed it.

Roy had completely lost control of the situation."Want a drink?," she asked as she grabbed a bottle of her mother's favorite whiskey and two glasses.

"Why don't you make sure that door is locked?," she said seductively, as she walked into the living room without looking at him. She sat on the couch hoping that he would stay, she just knew that if he did he would be hers and hers alone.

Moments later, he slowly walked into the room with her overalls. "You dropped this," he said, while placing the jeans delicately on the couch beside her. Sonia pushed them to the floor and gently grabbed his hand and kissed it.

They embraced, kissed and she poured a couple of drinks. Roy had never consumed any alcohol. His father had warned him that booze was absolutely forbidden.

However, he could not refuse her offer. She laughed as he choked and gagged after the very first sip, but after he sipped a little more, he began to feel totally uninhibited and good!

Sonia, who had been sneaking her mother's booze for quite

a while, just sipped hers and waited for his to "kick in." Soon Roy was so high that he was singing love songs to her. She laughed,"You damned sure can't sing."

Skillfully and tactfully, she slowly maneuvered him to the shower, and they showered just as she had seen on television. Washing each other created much more passion than she could have ever imagined!

After they had been to bed, the totally overwhelmed and exhausted Roy drifted off to sleep. Sonia sat up in the bed and watched him, very proud of the way in which she had handled the situation.

She could not wait to tell Dora. She, too, dozed off satisfied and not even caring if she got caught. She had a man!

Suddenly, the telephone rang, startling both of them. Roy jumped up, somewhat confused as Sonia went to her mother's room to answer the telephone. As she picked it up, she noticed that it was 4:30.

Fear struck as she recognized the voice of her mother! Her mind began to race. Had Roy put the night latch on and she was trying to get in? Did she somehow know what was going on and was ready to....?

"Baby, where are you?" Virginia sobbed.

"In your room, why?," she answered slowly, full of anxiety.

"Why? Why? Just do like I tell you, girl!" Virginia screamed. "Look in my dresser and see if you see some money," she said in a calmer voice.

Sonia did as she was told and returned to the telephone and told her that there was fifty or sixty dollars there. Poor Sonia's nerves were shot!

"Take the money, get dressed and go to the kitchen and wait until you hear a cab horn blow. Then come out with the money."

"What about Mr. Rommie?" Sonia asked.

Virginia took a deep breath and ordered Sonia to do as she was told as she slammed the telephone down. Scared to death, she ran to her room to get Roy out of there!

He was milling around the room, attempting to compose himself. The booze and Sonia had physically and mentally overwhelmed him. He was desperately trying to put everything together.

Roy needed to talk this thing out with Sonia, because he had never felt as out of control as he did with her.

However, Sonia didn't have time for all that, she began to throw his stuff at him and told him that he had to get out of there and fast! Panicky as they were, they managed to get dressed and she got him out of there posthaste!

Sonia sat at the table trembling, she had no idea what had happened. She wondered if someone had seen her and called her mother and she was coming home to kill her.

What would she do? She could cry rape if . . . no, that wouldn't work. She could say that . . . she just didn't know what to do! As time passed, she fell asleep with her head on the table.

The sudden, screeching voice of Virginia rudely woke and frightened Sonia so that she thought that she was going to wet her pants. Sonia was so afraid that it took a few moments for her to comprehend that her mother was asking her to explain being awake at that hour in the morning.

Sonia tearfully pleaded that she was only doing as she was told and extended her hand, with the money, as evidence.

Virginia apologized by hugging her daughter and saying softly, "I'm sorry, baby. I'm so damn mad that I can't think straight! Just go to bed now, baby, I need to sit here and think for . . ."

Sonia watched her carefully and guessed that whatever was wrong, she was not in any danger. Relieved, she kissed her mother on the cheek and left to go to bed. She was beat!

But as she was walking up the stairs, she heard Virginia open the cabinet and ask aloud as to the whereabouts of her liquor. Sonia thought that she was going to die! Her mind racing, she decided to go down and try to at least get the glasses out of the way before . . .

But she and her mother met in the living room simultaneously. They stared at each other for a moment, then Sonia asked if she had been called.

Virginia told her that she was talking to herself as both set of eyes spotted the bottle simultaneously, and they immediately looked up at each other.

Sonia feeling that her luck had run out, was desperately trying to conjure up an explanation, but her mother spoke first.

Thinking that her daughter was concerned about her getting drunk, tried to comfort her, "Don't worry, baby, I'm only going to have a couple."

Sonia just nodded and turned and walked out the room, up the stairs thinking that if anything else happened she would just have the heart attack, die and be done with it.

Just as she reached the top of the steps, Virginia standing at the bottom of the steps, asked her jokingly if she got Chris drunk before he went home.

Frustrated, sick and tired of being scared to death, Sonia could only muster up a very weak, "Mama?"

Virginia laughed an uneasy laugh, "I'm just messing with you, child," and walked away. Sonia went to her room, grabbed her favorite doll and asked if being with Roy was worth all this.

She fell off to sleep waiting for an answer.

Meanwhile, Virginia sat in the kitchen by the window smoking, drinking, and waiting.

As it became light, the soft summer breeze gently swept through the now still projects. The serenity was broken occasionally by the sound of early morning traffic and the opening and closing of doors of those who needed to be out early.

They lived near the end of the development, so you could clearly see the nearly empty parking lot. Her heart began to beat very rapidly as the familiar sight of Rommie's black, late model Cadillac glided into the parking lot.

Virginia wondered aloud how he was going to try to explain what he had done to her. She could see herself telling him not to bother and leave her alone! She could almost hear him try to convince her that he was too drunk or high to know what he was doing with Dora.

Virginia could just about hear herself insisting that he completely get out and stay out of her life. She went to the sink to wash the tears away.

She decided that she was going to be really cool and not even raise her voice. It was over and both of them needed to just leave each other alone, forever!

Virginia was not at all prepared for the events of the next few moments. First, Dora popped out of the car singing and twirling with a bottle of champagne!

Rommie ran around the car and grabbed the bottle and opened it! Dora leaned back on the car, while Rommie poured some champagne on her cleavage and sampled it!

Then she took the bottle and poured it over his head and over her own! They hugged and kissed for what seemed an eternity. Virginia was so unnerved that she was trembling with anger!

She poured herself another drink as the two playfully headed for Dora's home! When they reached the door, Dora handed him the key and kissed him on the neck as he fumbled, trying to open the door.

He finally managed to get it opened and walked in with a playful push from Dora. Suddenly, Dora spun and looked directly at Virginia's window and laughed!

Virginia too stunned, shocked, and hurt to even move. Helplessly she watched Dora disappear behind the door.

Completely shaken by the actions of Rommie and her "best friend," she could only sit there by the window waiting for one or both of them to come out.

She had no idea about what she was going to do, but she was sure that she had to do something. Getting drunker and angrier, she had illusions of beating them both to death.

Maybe she should hang them by their no-good necks, or even better, get a bunch of wild things, no rats to chew the hell out of them.

The hurt and anger just wouldn't allow her any relief, every time she dozed off, the pain of being used woke her.

Sonia woke to the sound of children playing outdoors. She looked at the clock which read 12:45. She sat up in her bed and told her doll about everything that had happened.

Her doll was very pleased and proud of her for doing all that she had done without getting caught. Her doll seemed to agree that Roy was very strong and handsome, and the doll wished that she could find someone like him for herself.

After they talked for a bit, Sonia decided to take a shower. Her shower turned out to be a very romantic fantasy as she recalled every blissful moment that she had enjoyed with her man and lover, Roy.

Hungry, she dressed and went to the kitchen to fix herself some food. She found her mother sitting in a chair looking out of the window. The empty bottle and the many cigarette butts gave testimony to the fact that Virginia had been awake since she had seen her earlier.

Sonia, still felling euphoric, merrily greeted her mother who turned to her and looked at her strangely. Virginia looked awful and a little scary to Sonia.

Virginia fumbled through some money that was on the table and ordered her to go buy her some cigarettes. Without hesitation she complied and returned rather quickly.

Completely disoriented, Virginia told the girl to go down to the bar where she worked to get her some booze and Sonia protested.

Bad move! Virginia slapped her and demanded that she did as she was told 'or else'.

Sonia knew better than to wait for the 'or else'. fussing and mumbling to herself, she wondered aloud about the sanity of her mother. She had never, ever sent her to the bar.

She didn't even like for her to even call her at the bar. Sonia knew that something was terribly wrong and hoped that Eric, the owner, would be there. He would know what to do with her.

Virginia has worked there as a barmaid for as long as Sonia could remember, and she knew that he had a thing for her mother.

Eric was, in the girl's opinion, 'all right', but he never seemed to appreciate her as a young woman. He never told her how good she looked as Rommie and many other men did.

He never seemed to notice how grownup she was, and worse of all, he never, ever flirted with her. He would only ask her about school, or movies that she had seen, or perhaps, some music that she liked.

Sometimes, he would give her things like pens, paper, and pencils. He even had the nerve to give her a computer for Christmas, which was in her room collecting dust.

Anyway, he always seemed to know how to calm her mother down and if she ever needed calming down, it was now!

She was relieved to find Eric at the bar talking to a couple of men. They immediately complimented him on his choice of young women.

Sonia loved it, but Eric burst her bubble by telling them that she was merely a child. They half-heartily apologized for their overtures.

Eric was very concerned about the girl's being there. He took her away from the still admiring men to find out what was wrong. Eric knew that the last place that Virginia would want Sonia was in that or any other bar.

Eric looked at her was suspiciously as she did her best to explain her reason for being there. Using great judgement, he called Virginia. After a very brief conversation, he placed the receiver on its cradle, looked at Sonia thoughtfully, and went behind the bar and grabbed a bottle and some beer.

His actions appeared suspicious to his companions who openly and gleefully questioned his morals. This obviously annoyed Eric, but the barmaid very quickly identified her as Virginia's daughter, which convinced them that their allegations were wrong.

The short ride back to her home was embarrassing to Sonia because he made her sit in the back seat. She always had to sit in the back of his car, even on those rare occasions when they were riding alone.

As they entered the kitchen, the first thing that Eric did was to tell Virginia how terrible she looked which surprised Sonia, because Eric never seemed to criticize her for anything.

Virginia, who was almost in a stupor, responded that he'd look bad too if he had been up all night.

"Well, why don't you go to bed, fool?"

"Why don't you mind your own business? " She responded angrily, as she poured herself a large drink and knocked over a chair on her way back to the window.

Eric picked up the chair and asked what she was looking for. She turned to answer, but glared at Sonia with such intensity that she interpreted her mother's look as her clue to leave the kitchen.

Curious, she went no further than the living room where she could safely find out what had happened to upset Virginia so much.

Turning to Eric while futilely attempting to light a cigarette, Virginia began her account of the events of the prior evening.

She began slowly, "My mother used to always tell me never to trust a female. You know that me and that Dora been friends every since we was in school. We were always together doing stuff to people, but we never messed with each other's men.

"I mean that was the thing that kept us so tight! Even when she would get in trouble for . . . doing things to other girl's boyfriend and getting into fights I always watched her back."

She laughed, then continued, "I even fought for her a couple of times 'cause she sure couldn't beat nothing. All that mouth she got and can't beat her way out of a paper bag.

But we were friends. The lady that she used to live with told me to leave her alone 'cause she was no good, I paid that sweet old lady no mind, 'cause Dora was my friend."

Virginia began to cry while telling Eric that Dora almost drove that lady crazy with all the wild things that she used to do.

The situation got so bad that somebody from Dora's home paid for an apartment when she was only about seventeen. She talked about some other things that they used to do there.

Virginia laughed as she told him how they tricked boys into baby sitting with Dora's little girl while they were out partying.

"Where is Christee?", he asked.

"She left Dora and went to New York, because of all the things that Dora did to her. Anyway, Dora came over here yesterday cussing and fussing about having to keep Chris, and . . . "

"Who is Chris?"

"Her boy who had been staying with Dora's mother until she died last week."

"I didn't know that she . . . "

"Will you stop interrupting me? Dora came over here mad because they made her bring her boy back here to live with her. She was afraid that the boy would cramp her style.

Well, me being her friend and all told her that Rommie was having this big party downtown for some of his friends from New York.

I asked her to go so that, she could get her mind off the boy. I also made Sonia be with the boy, because he was new in town and didn't have nothing to do. Not that she cared."

Eric interrupted her again, reminding her that everybody had warned her to leave Dora alone, and that she needed Rommie like she needed to be shot!

She began to cry again, continuing, "She came over here last night dressed in this red thing that showed all her butt! I didn't say nothing, because it wasn't me looking like no 'ho!"

"When we was leaving, she was bragging about how she was

going to take somebody's man! When we gets to the party, they were smoking that stuff, and some of them were doing some of Rommie's coke and that other junk."

Eric interrupted Virginia, reminding her that she had no business dealing with Rommie in the first place, because he was and would always be a no good small time hoodlum. Somebody's gonna put a bullet in his jive head putting him out if his misery.

He added that he was afraid for her, because if the shooting started when she was around she'd probably be killed too.

One of them from New York kept on asking me to give him a little play, even offered me some money to sleep with him. You know I ain't like that. So, I cussed him out and told Rommie.

I told Rommie, and showed him who the guy was, he walked over to him. I thought that he was going to punch the dude in the face because Rommie loved me and didn't appreciate him asking him to sleep with him.

Rommie talked to the guy for a little while, then came over to me and asked me to sleep with the guy as a personal favor, because I was the only one that he liked.

I couldn't believe that he was saying that to me, because he was supposed to be my man. I told him to go to hell, and he just laughed and walked away, "You better get real, baby, and get real fast!'

I couldn't ever remember being as hurt as I was then.

I went over to the bar and fixed myself a drink. I guess I knew that I had been fooling myself about Rommie, but I loved him.

Well, next thing I know Rommie, Dora and this guy is going into one of the bedrooms. I stayed away, because I was scared and hurt and the door was wide open.

Then, I saw some more people go in there, so I figured that they were doing some drugs. I wasn't too interested, because you know me, if I can't get it out of a bottle, I don't want it!

All of a sudden, I heard all this noise. You know, like they make when somebody is dancing really good!

People were crowded at the door, and I heard one of the women say that she wouldn't do that for a million dollars.

I was thinking that Dora had got herself so high off that stuff that she was in there stripping or some-thing. So, I went in there to get her.

I had to fight my way through the door, because it was so jammed and packed. When I got in the room, there she was on the bed, naked with some men pulling and grabbing and kissing all over her!

Some were on the floor with their clothes off! Rommie was on the floor too and I could see that his stuff was wet! I tried to get to him, and kill him with my very hands, but them guys that work for him grabbed me and carried me out of the room!

But I was fighting them so hard, hitting, scratching, and kicking that they soon let me go! I went back in there and Goldie was doing her while Rommie was kissing her in the mou . . .

Eric stopped her from talking. He was disgusted and Virginia was now so upset that she was shaking violently!

Despite his efforts she continued, "I got sick to my stomach and threw up all over the place. Then I went downstairs and called Sonia."

She concluded by telling him of their arrival and that she was determined to wait until one or both of them came out. She would at least have the satisfac-tion of kicking butt.

Eric tried to get her to go to bed before she got herself in some real trouble. He reasoned that neither were worth the bother.

Sonia was not really sure what to think, so she went upstairs to get advice and comfort from her dolls. Sonia didn't witness the fight, although she heard about it later. Her dolls had convinced her to mind her own business.

Meanwhile, all Chris knew was that Dora had come in, with Rommie, early in the morning. They made so much noise singing, laughing that they woke him up.

Then later, the noise of people screaming and yelling in front of the apartment woke him again. He got to the front door in time to see some man pull Virginia off his mother.

He looked to Rommie for help, but he was enjoying seeing the women fight. Rommie was having so much fun that he was disappointed when it stopped.

Chris thought that the fool was finally going to help, but Rommie merely watched them curiously, finished his drink, lit a cigarette, and casually walked away, singing.

6. *Hope*

Chris watched in stunned bewilderment as his mother crawled out of Virginia's grip. Some guy that he didn't know was trying to hold Virginia.

He made a human barrier between the wild and uncontrollable Virginia, and the seemingly hapless, defenseless Dora.

However, when Dora was safely out of Virginia's reach, she let loose with a barrage of obscenities. They were so vile that some people who had been restraining Virginia now agreed that she had the right to kill Dora, if she wanted.

Cooler heads prevailed, and Virginia was forced to her home struggling, kicking, and cursing.

Dora stood there profiling and styling in front of the crowd, who were obviously entertained by her antics. She didn't seem too concerned that her nightgown was ripped, exposing much of her body.

Finally, she decided to come in the house. This made Chris nervous. He thought that she might decide to kick his butt because it may have been the only one she could kick.

To his surprise, she was actually very friendly, especially after she carefully examined her face and found it undamaged.

She promised him a big old-fashioned dinner just like her mother used to cook, kissed him on the forehead and disappeared behind her door. She called out that dinner would be ready about six.

Chris was shocked and very excited about what seemed a change in Dora's attitude toward him. He decided to go out to be out of her way and not mess up the great dinner that she had promised him. So, he showered, got dressed, ate a little cereal, and quietly left.

Now standing on the front steps, he heard a voice call to him. He looked over to his left and saw a very dark, very thin, very tall youngster with very big dark eyes smiling at him.

Not understanding what the boy was saying, he asked the boy what he was saying.

"YesmynameisMarcuswhatisyours?," the stranger responded.

Chris had no idea what the boy was saying. Maybe he would understand if he were closer. He walked toward the youngster, who in turn walked toward him, smiling.

As they got closer to each other, the boy asked, "HimynameisMarcuswhatisyours?."

Chris realized that the boy spoke very fast, with a very strange accent, smiled and asked the boy to repeat what he was saying but slower.

The boy, now a little embarrassed, replied very slowly, "My name is Marcus. What is yours?"

"Chris," he responded with a quizzical expression on his face.

His very thick accent continued to be a problem for Chris. Marcus continued, "I saw you arrive yesterday, and I am very pleased to meet you, Chris, my friend. I live here now with my grandfather. Do you know him?"

Chris answered "No, I've been living in Georgia, but now I live here with my mother."

Chris asked him where he was from as he had never heard anyone talk the way he did. Marcus told him that he had been born in South Africa near the township of Johannesburg. Chris was curious and asked him some questions about living there under apartheid. Much to his surprise, Marcus told him that as far as he could see that there was not much difference between living in his U.S.A. and this U.S.A.

Marcus said that he didn't understand why American Blacks didn't try hard enough to be truly free.

To Marcus' dismay, the look on Chris' face was the same as the others who wouldn't or could not see the similarities of the treatment of Blacks here in the United States and his homeland.

The major difference, it appeared to him, was that many challenges that the Blacks experienced here were self-inflicted and could be resolved easier here than in South Africa.

His six months experience compelled him to drop the subject, he didn't intend to argue with this boy who might become his friend.

He offered Chris an orange instead and a guided tour of the neighborhood. Chris eagerly accepted both, and Marcus led him to his home to get the oranges.

As they entered, Chris noticed the many pictures of two young adults with Marcus. The pictures looked just like they could have been taken in Georgia.

Proudly, Marcus told him that they were his parents in South Africa. The man looked so much like Marcus that Chris knew that he was the boy's father, and the woman was very happy.

Chris was horrified when Marcus told him that the police had beaten and murdered his father and shot his mother in the back as she was trying to protect him.

Chris, at first, had difficulty imagining that the police could be as cruel and powerful as Marcus described them. But after thinking about it for a while, he was reminded him of the way that his grandmother had told him that colored people used to be treated by the sheriff in Georgia.

"Maybe," Chris thought to himself, "there is something to what he was saying about it being something like South Africa here."

His thoughts were interrupted when Marcus returned with two of the largest oranges that he had ever seen.

As the two boys were leaving the house, Chris regretted that he didn't understand much of what Marcus was saying, and he got tired of asking him to repeat himself.

Chris was getting really frustrated, but he didn't know what to do about it. Before they got out the door, the telephone rang, and Marcus excused himself to answer it.

Chris' first impulse was to leave, but he certainly didn't want to hurt Marcus' feelings, companions at this point were at a premium.

As he stood there, he saw Sonia leave her house. He wanted to say something to her, but he didn't know exactly what to say.

His dilemma was resolved when the effervescent Sonia saw him. As she ran toward him, her bright, animated smile on her pretty face caused his heart to race.

The very sight of her running to meet him made his heart jump and thump. However, no words came out of his mouth.

When she got within touching distance, she was confused by the fact that he was standing there like a zombie. She wasn't accustomed to that type of greeting and she definitely didn't like it.

Searching his eyes for an explanation for what she interpreted as a very cold reception, she asked, "You mad at me or something? "

He could only shake his head `no'.

"Well, how are you, boyfriend?", she asked.

"Boyfriend!!!" Could this mean that she really likes me?", he thought to himself, while uttering a very bland, "Okay, I guess."

She was starting to get upset with this young boy, "You just can't be nice to some people." Still smiling, she asked him if he liked what she was wearing.

Sonia twirled to give him the full effect of her a mid-ribbed blue blouse with blue designer stretched jeans, and blue designer socks and tennis shoes.

She was looked absolutely stunning to him, and he was astonished that her breasts didn't pop out from that skimpy blouse.

But much as he wanted to touch and hold her, he couldn't manage to say that she looked good or anything. While he was trying to figure out what to say, Marcus came out and spoke to Sonia.

They gazed at each other for a moment, and she looked at Chris who was now looking at the ground. He wanted desperately to say something kind, something clever to her, but he could not manage one word.

The three of them stood silent. Finally, she told them that she had to go.

Sonia looked at Chris, who was still trying to figure out something to say. She looked over at Marcus who was expressionless and said goodbye to them, then slowly walked away strutting her stuff.

She turned quickly and caught Chris admiring her. Satisfied, she waved and yelled to him smiling, "Later, boyfriend!"

Chris stood stunned as he watched her until she disappeared around the corner. Marcus sat on the steps patiently waiting for Chris to finish watching Sonia.

Chris finally joined him on the steps and was handed a couple of paper towels for the orange. They didn't say too much to each other as they enjoyed the succulent fruit.

This gave Chris an opportunity to survey the environment. He noticed the trees that were either dead or dying from the lack of care and water.

Looking down, he looked at the patches of grass surrounded by cracked, parched dirt in all the lawns except Marcus', which was well cared for and manicured.

The various articles of paper, bottles, and other junk on the cracked pavements and on the other lawns gave testimony to the general tribulation of the area.

Looking at the projects which was composed of dull red bricks, broken or missing storm doors with rotting wooden window frames in desperate need of repair and painting. It made them surrealistic and caustic.

In open windows people were looking about with blank expressions on their faces. There was an abundance of younger children running, jumping, fighting, cussing, and fussing.

Older men and women were wandering about aimlessly or sitting on steps, chairs, or boxes while teenagers roamed about some with "ghetto-blasters."

He looked upward and for the first time noticed, what he was to find out later were the high rise projects.

He could see absolutely nothing that would even remotely cause optimism except here at Marcus'. Although, Marcus' home was obviously in the same area, it was an island of hope in a sea of tribulation.

The melancholy on Chris' face of prompted Marcus to ease his mood by telling a joke. Although he tried, it was, according to Chris, the very worse joke that he had ever heard.

However, it finally had the desired effect as the boys laughed about how bad the joke had been. They talked a little about Sonia but Marcus didn't seem to be too interested in the subject.

This confused Chris, but he dared not ask the reason for fear of the answer. After they had finished their oranges, Marcus took the peelings and the rest of the trash inside to dispose of it. When he returned, they decided to go for a walk.

As they walked, Chris felt as depressed as the environment seemed. An old man dressed in an old army jacket and khakis was standing in the doorway of one of the houses next to the corner.

He started waving and yelling to Marcus. " Hey, jungle boy, come here, come here!", he shouted.

Although the man's yelling and waving unnerved Chris, Marcus smiled, grabbed him by the arm and led him to the old man. Chris felt uncomfortable, but he didn't resist.

"How are you today, sir? " Marcus greeted the man almost reverently.

"Real good for an old man!", he responded cheerfully, with the stub of an unlit cigar in the corner of his mouth.

"Who's your friend? I don't seem to remember seeing him before."

"This is Chris, sir, Miss Dora's son", Marcus responded.
"Chris, this is Mr. Clarke."

"Well I'll be damned! I never thought that I'd see you, boy. Your mama all right? I saw her this morning. She best stop trying to fight, especially people like that Virginia!", he chuckled.

Chris didn't respond, the old man frightened him. Marcus answered for him saying that he was sure that Miss Dora was fine.

"You all right, boy?", the old man asked Chris.

"Uh, yes, I'm fine."

The old man looked at him curiously, then spit in a can, saying, "You sure you are all right, boy?"

Chris nodded.

Suddenly, the old man grabbed Chris and turned him around, scrutinizing him.

"Let's see, you about five feet, three inches. You weigh about one hundred fifteen pounds. You got your mother's mouth and eyes, but your nose, face, and skin color are just like your father."

"My father?!", Chris resounded with such force that he startled both Marcus and the old man.

A little embarrassed, Chris looked at the old man, then at the ground and asked him if he really knew his father.

This was a real shock to him because nobody, ever, ever mentioned his father.

"Could this crazy old man really know what he was talking about?", he thought to himself.

As if the old man knew what he was thinking, he responded, "Yeah, I know your father, a good old boy, but I guess that you don't and I ain't gonna get into that right now. But I will say that he is a fine man. Too bad Dora ain't got no use for no hard working fine man."

Chris wanted to insist that this old man tell him something about his father. Nobody had ever given him even a hint that the man even existed.

He now had hope that he did indeed have a real live father. He hoped that the old man would volunteer the information but he didn't.

Instead the old man grabbed Chris by the hand and told him that he wanted to show him something inside his house.

Chris was sure that he didn't want to go in the man's house, but Marcus gestured that he should accept the invitation.

He followed his host and Marcus into the house and was immediately surprised that it was so well kept. The living room was dark and cooler than it was outside.

As his eyes became accustomed to the darkness, he saw that the room was full of pictures that were old but well preserved.

They all featured Black military personnel. Seeing them caused Chris to feel that he was absolutely correct by not wanting to enter the home of this old man. He was now convinced that he was crazy.

The old man turned on a lamp and walked up the stairs without uttering a word, while the eerie illumination from the dim bulb caused the pictures to appear to be watching Chris.

This feeling generated so much anxiety in the boy that he wanted to run as fast and as far away as he could.

"From the time that Jessie Owens showed them Nazis up in the Olympics by running circles around them Godless bastards to the time that Joe Louis was embarrassed by that Max Schmeling in `36 by getting himself knocked out, we Negroes wanted to get a little piece of that damned Hitler and the rest of them Nazis," the old man bellowed as he slowly walked down the steps.

He was now dressed in his old but very clean and neatly pressed U.S. Army uniform. The man even had a holstered pistol and a rifle in his hands!

If Chris had been a little apprehensive before, the sight of this man with completely unnerved him.

However, Marcus' obvious admiration for the man quieted his fears. As the old man cleared the steps, he continued, "But we all knew that Joe could bust Schmeling's damned Nazi head wide open.

In 1938, he knocked that so-called superman right on his

super ass.

In '41 when them Japs bombed Pearl Harbor, we was as mad as anybody else, but we couldn't to do much about it."

As if to answer Chris' unasked question, he continued, "Our own government, them white folks, didn't much care too much about us Negroes being in their armed services.

They didn't think we were smart enough. Many old boys that I used to run with was flatly turned down, because they could not pass them tests, you see.

The ones that got in got to cook, scrub, and serve them white folks and I sure as hell was not going to do none of that.

But we loved that old Roosevelt and when he signed that Order 8802 a whole bunch of us got in the service.

But you see, I didn't trust them too much, and there was a lot of money to be made with all the work that the war caused. We were living the life, with a lot more money than we knew what to do with.

I just met this old girl that came up here from New Orleans. Well, I thought that she was dirt poor and came up to make some money and find a husband.

She was the prettiest thing that we ever seen around here, and she and I started courting almost as soon as she got off the bus, he chuckled to himself.

Her name was Antoinette. She had the softest light, real near white skin that I had ever seen even on white folks, long black shining hair, and a very pretty smile, you see.

She loved to laugh, and I did as much as I could to make her laugh. If she wanted a clown, I damned sure was going to be one.

She always spoke in a near whisper in that half French way that they speak down there in the French Quarter down there. Sometimes we didn't know what the hell she was talking about.

But she was so damned pretty that I really didn't care since she was my girl. Hell, after a couple of weeks of being together, she started talking that talk to me and whatever she was saying sounded so good to me that I was agreeing all over myself!

She got so excited that we didn't go to see the show like we was suppose to and spent the night together. We made good music that night, if you know what I mean?

That was the summer of '43, and I was so happy that I didn't know what to do with myself. The next morning she told me that she had to send her Mama a telegram to let her know that we was coming down so she could meet me and show me off to her family.

That's when I realized that the woman was talking about marriage! Well, I tell you that I was scared to death, because I never thought about marrying her or anybody else at the time, you see!

But she was such a pretty thing that I said to myself, "Boy, as ugly as you are, you ain't going to do much better."

So, I agreed and told all them fellas that I was running around with. Well, you would have thought that I was planning to steal from their mothers by the way they acted!

They all told me that I was crazy and that I should take some time to find out about this woman!

I got mad at them fools, because I knew that they were jealous. So, I told them where to go.

My real boyfriend, Lester, took me to the side and told me that there had to be something wrong with the young woman since she was up here all by herself.

He also told me that they would never let her marry me, because they didn't like my type of Nigger down there!

Well, I got so mad that I punched him dead in the mouth!

Ole Lester never lifted a finger at me, just reached in his pocket and gave me his pistol.

He told me to take it with me if I was dumb enough to go down there and mess with them Creoles. I knew that Lester had to know what he was talking about, but I was going to marry this woman no matter what!

I took her down to where my folks lived, and they took one look at her and were scared to death! My own mama told me to get away from her, before I got myself into some real trouble!

I didn't want to hear that either, so I got me a car from one of my boyfriends who was running the numbers, told him that I was going to Atlantic City because I knew he would let me have it to go there.

Boy, I caught hell traveling with that young woman down South, because them crazy white folks thought that she was white.

I damned near got lynched a couple of times, but she convinced them that she was Colored and that made everything okay.

Well, we finally got there and when she took me into her Mama's house, the woman had a fit! I mean, I ain't never been called so many kinds of black Niggers in my entire life!

I knew that I was in trouble when that crazy old woman called her names that I hadn't heard before nor since and went upside her head with one of them iron pot lids!

When the girl hit the floor all busted up with her mama screaming and cussing and throwing shit all over the place, I decided to pop that old bat right in the mouth woman or no woman, mama or no mama!

But before I could get my hands on that old 'ho, about thirty-eleven big, half white stevedore Negroes busted into the room and proceeded to kick my very ass!

They whipped on me until they got tired! While they were beating on me, that old crazy woman was screaming, `kill 'im! kill `im!

I don't mind telling you that I thought that they was going to kill me!

Suddenly, it got real quiet and I looked up and this old white man was standing there, dressed in some kind of black uniform with all this gold trimming and buttons.

He never raised his voice, but you could tell that everybody respected him. He said something to them in that Creole, and they all got shame-faced and started walking out with their heads hung down.

That old woman was explaining what had happened. He listened carefully and patiently, nodded, said something to her and she left the room; but not before she gave me a final dirty look.

Some of the prettiest young women that I had ever seen came in and attended to the girl.

While all this was going on, the old man gently helped me up and offered me a handkerchief to wipe the blood and tears from my face.

The old man suddenly stopped talking and left the room. The boys were deeply moved by the old man's story and hungry for more.

Soon he returned with a couple of soft drinks for the boys and a couple of fingers of whiskey for himself.

He offered them a seat on his sofa and continued, the old man offered me a seat and said something in Creole to one of the girls attending to Antoinette. She nodded and left the room.

He looked at me through his sad, blue eyes and asked me if

I was all right. 'Hell no, I'm not all right worth a damn.'

He looked at my busted up face and started laughing and said that asking me if I was all right was the most insensitive question that he had ever asked in his life. Then we both started laughing.

Anyway, he told me that his daughter had run away, because she had been messing around with this white boy who was the son of one of the big shots in town.

When she told the boy that she was a Mulatto, he told her that he couldn't have anything else to do with her, things being like they were there in New Orleans.

So, she just ran away and the first time that they heard from her was when they got the telegram informing them that she was getting married and coming home so that, they could meet her fiancee.

My friend, you are not who my wife has in mind to marry our daughter and they overreacted.

Hell, I didn't have nothing to loose, so I came out and asked him how come he was married to this crazy Negro woman instead of white one.

I could have passed out when he told me that he was about as Negro as me and about as white as any white man.

He told me all about the history of the Negroes and whites in New Orleans. He told me that some whites were Negroes and some Negroes had ancestors like the Beauregards, Bourbons and Contis.

These names didn't mean nothing to me, but he assured me that you couldn't always tell whether a body was white or Negro by the color of his skin.

He said that during the Civil War, some Negroes wanted to fight them ungodly Yankees. They were turned down, because some white folks were scared of being shot in the back.

He said that he believed that old stupid white pride was the real reason that they wouldn't let Negroes fight. They would have had to admit that they were as good as whites if given a chance.

He showed me a beautiful sword and a fancy Confederate army cap that he said belonged to his grandfather.

He said that them idiots would let a few Negroes parade with them dressed in full Confederate uniform but wouldn't let them fight.

The boys looked at him in total disbelief, and the old man could sense it. He challenged them to go to the library and read all about those things.

He himself eventually did as he was not sure that the old man knew what he was talking about.

You know, I was listening to this guy, and I wondered why he spoke so well. He talked like some of the important white men that I heard speak, like the lawyers in court.

Just about then, the young woman that he had sent away returned from the kitchen with two real tall pretty drinks and gave them to us. I was always sorry that I didn't ask what it was because it sure was good and cool.

Anyway, he told me that he was a college graduate, had studied at Tuskegee Institute. He told me that he had a many a dream of how he was going to change things with the education that he had earned.

Then he started to weep and started using some of that Creole talk that I didn't understand, but I did understand that he found out that his skin color prevented him from being what he had dreamed and worked so hard to be.

Then he changed on me and asked me why I was not in the service, and I laughed and told him that was the last place for a Colored man.

The man could really paint a pretty picture with words. He told me about the Negro pilots that were being trained at Tuskegee, the 99th Pursuit Squadron.

He said that he would give his very life to be a part of that squadron. He went on and on, and I began to believe for the first time in my life that I, too, could be somebody.

I left there feeling that the military was my ticket to freedom! I left New Orleans feeling that I could conquer the world, and all I had to do was to kill me a few Nazis.

I had to leave that old girl down there, but I could just see myself returning with a uniform full of stripes and bars and ribbons and sweeping not only my woman, but her mama right off their feet!

Marcus interrupted by asking to go to the bathroom, and while he was gone Chris was shown pictures of the men of the 99th Pursuit Squadron.

Chris was impressed and felt very proud. He had never heard of or even imagined that there had ever been Black fighter pilots.

The old man showed him many pictures and told him of many accounts of Blacks who had distinguished themselves during World War II.

Chris wondered aloud why he had not heard of these heroic men, and the old man explained that they didn't want him to know.

When Marcus returned, the old man continued, "Well driving all the way back here by my damned self I had plenty time to think about life and the little I knew about it."

I decided and promised God that I was not going to be just another ignorant Negro drinking, gambling, hustling, and waiting for death to take me out of my misery. He started laughing!

That ole boy that I had borrowed the car from was sure glad to see me. He was beginning to think that me and the woman had run off with his car, you see.

Anyhow, I was determined to be somebody. So I went down to church to meet somebody that could help me out. That's when I started courting Miss Daisy Mae Lewis with her stuck up self.

She was not too good to look at, but she was smart as hell. She had gone to some school down there in Atlanta and was a school teacher down at the Negro school that used to be down the street.

She liked me, because I was a real sharp old boy, and she was so, uh, well plain looking that I made her look good, you see! The boys laughed.

My boyfriends used to kid me about this woman, but I didn't care because she was teaching me how to read and write a lot better than I would have without her.

We was a pair, the school teacher and the hustler! She was real good at teaching, because after a while I was talking so different that my boyfriends started accusing me of trying to talk like a white man or that I was funny, you see.

I taught her a few things too about hustling and being out in the streets. We had to be careful in the streets, because in those times teachers were suppose to be like nuns, and none of the places that I took her were too good for her reputation.

One night, I took her down there to the club to see Billie, Billie Holiday and while we were sitting there she spotted her principal. She almost shit on herself, she was so scared!

She wanted to leave, because she said that the man could have her fired for just being there. Just as I had got her calmed down, he saw her and started frowning like he was her daddy or something.

When I saw that, I got mad! I wanted to bust his head wide open, but I knew that if I did and got locked up I wouldn't have been able to get in the service, you see.

I looked around the club and saw some of my boyfriends. One of them, Big Ed, was a collector for one of the biggest number runners in town.

He was big, ugly, looked like a gorilla and just loved to hurt people. He didn't need much of a reason, he just loved it and everybody knew that even if he killed somebody nothing would happen to him as long as the person wasn't white.

So, I told this nervous woman to just sit there and I would straighten this thing out. I went over to Big Ed and explained the situation to him.

I offered him ten dollars, a whole lot of money at that time to talk to her principal. He wouldn't take the money. `Reds, I'll take care of this for free, because I don't like him anyway.'

Well, I thanked him and went back to Daisy Mae, and told her that I had fixed things. She was so square that she didn't believe that I could deal with this guy that she thought was a God or something.

She didn't drink hardly nothing at all, but she was so nervous that she downed mine and begged for more. Being the perfect gentleman, I let her drink all she wanted.

Well, Mr. Principal and this other guy that I could tell was his girlfriend, if you know what I mean were sitting there drinking and talking during the intermission when Big Ed and a couple of the club's bouncers invited themselves to their table.

After a while everybody heard this `Yip!' like the sound that a hurt puppy makes. They snatched him and his friend up out of those chairs and started dragging them out of the bar. Daisy Mae gulped down her drink and mine.

Now boys, I'm not telling you that's the way to handle a situation, but that's how it was in those days. Anyway, after a little while Big Ed and those other guys came back in and gave me the high sign.

So, I knew that she was not going to have a problem with him!

7. *Love?*

"Well, Billie came back and finished her show, and she was especially good that night. In fact, everything was just perfect. Billie sang this love song that got me real anxious for a woman!", chuckled the old man.

"Now, you see, even though I was spending a lot of time with the teacher lady, she was not the type of woman that a street person like myself ever thought about, uh, spending the night with.

Her face was real plain and she didn't do nothing to make it look no better to me. She wore them old dresses that covered her legs so that you couldn't see nothing but her ankles most of the time. Under them dresses she wore all these slips and stuff; so that, you couldn't tell or even guess what her body was like.

"To make things worse, she walked like she was a soldier or something, you see, real stiff!" He laughed again, and this time his laughter was so infectious that the boys began to laugh with him.

Then she always wore these tops made so that you couldn't even tell if she had tits, and I always been a tits man. So, you see, I was never too interested in her as a woman, you see.

"So, when the show was over, I was going to take her back to Miss Betty's boarding house and go to the after hour party and meet my street woman, Mary."

She was built like a brick shit house and didn't mind showing off all of her curves! I was in a big hurry to get rid of old Daisy Mae so I could go down and get me some loving, you see!

The thing that I had not figured on was that the old girl was as drunk as a skunk, and I couldn't take her to that boarding house like that, you see.

"So, I took her to my place so that she could sleep it off and I could go to the cat house", he blushed.

I mean the, well, anyway I stuffed her in a taxi and we went to my place.

She was singing and laughing and cursing. I had never heard her use any bad language, she used to get on me for using them kind of words. She was pulling all over me like I did them fancy girls.

"I started to punch the driver in his face, because he knew who she was and thought that her acting like that was the funniest shit he had ever seen.

But my hands was busy fighting off this woman who had gone completely crazy, pulling all over me like she was an octopus.

"When we got to my place, I had a little apartment not far from here at the time. She jumped out of the damned taxi and started parading up and down the damned steps like one of them fancy women from down the place. I paid the fare and hurried her inside so that nobody would see her!

"When we got inside, she started singing this real dirty song about two people fu . . . , uh, I mean making . . . , uh, sleeping together! I just stood there with my mouth wide open! I never even imagined that she knew anything like that!"

"She looked at me with that look and asked me if I had something to drink. While I was getting my bottle and a couple of glasses, she sang another of those songs. I didn't know what to do now!"

"She started laughing as I handed her a drink. She sat me down on the couch and sang the very same song that Billie did at the show, but as she was singing she started to slowly taking off her clothes."

When she finished taking off all of that stuff and throwing it all over the place, I almost passed out. She had the most beautiful bodies that I had ever seen!

That night, my whole life began to get a little out of control, because when she finished with me I was completely whipped and madly in love.

"I had never been as worked over by a woman in my life as I was that night! ...and all along I had considered myself as being quite a lover, you see!

After that I gained new respect for them plain girls, especially if they were from down south somewhere!

"Then all of the crazy stuff started happening. Soon she started dressing different, I mean more stylish, moved out of the boarding house and bought herself a house.

I found out that her daddy had plenty of money. Then, she started running my life, but since I was in love, I really didn't care.

She started correcting my speech, and had me reading all these damned books.

She told me that her future husband, me, was going to be somebody that she and the children that we was going to have was going to be somebody that everybody could be proud of.

"Then she told me that I was going in the service so that I could get off the streets and make something of myself.

Like a fool I started getting ready for the test, because she convinced me that Colored men didn't do well on those tests, because they were not properly prepared.

"Well, one book that she made me read was *Paradise Lost* by Milton. It talked about the human mind.

There is a part of the story that I want you boys to always remember, it's something like . . . *The mind is in its place and in itself can make a hell out of heaven or a heaven of hell.*

Those words have got me through a lot of shit in my life. Well, . . .

Chris interrupted, "What does that mean?"

The old man responded by looking at Marcus and asking him if he knew what it meant. Marcus replied that he thought that it meant that wherever a person finds himself, he can make it a heaven or a hell.

The old man laughed and went to the kitchen and brought back a lemon. The boys watched him cut the lemon and accepted the slices that he handed them.

He began, "Life can be like this lemon, taste it! Now, from the expressions on your ugly faces, I can see that you would agree that it is bitter."

"That's how life can be really bitter, but you don't have to be bitter because life is sometimes. All you have to do is to add some water and some sugar and what will you have?"

In unison, the boys smiled and responded, "Lemonade!"

"That's right, you see, when life gets a little bitter for you, add a little sugar and water. Make it better for yourself. Do it in your own mind. Never let the circumstances that you cannot control, control you, you see!"

Both boys took time to consider what the old man Kingsley had said and agreed that was a good way of looking at things.

He continued, "Like I was saying, in the fall of 1943, I went down there and passed all the tests that they could throw at me.

We had even cooked up this lie that I had graduated from some high school in her hometown where her uncle was the principal and that I went to college across town, you see.

She figured that they would never check on it anyway and that I would always have that on my military records.

She was right because even today I can prove that I graduated from high school and went to college thanks to Uncle Sam's records of me.

"I had two good 'going away' parties. The first was down at the church that my father and mother raised me in. They were so proud of me for going in the service, and they were really proud that I was courting a woman like Miss Daisy Mae Lewis!

She gave me a big party at her house, but she wouldn't let my friends come because she said they were a bad influence on me, you see.

The funny thing was that the principal that I had worked over was there too.

"You would have thought they had always the best of friends by the way that they were always in each other's faces just laughing and joking all night!

He introduced me to some of the most important Negroes in town and told them how proud he was of me, with his bald head, fagot self.

I could have thrown up all over the place with all the junk he was saying about me. He also took the time to announce that Daisy Mae was being promoted to vice principal, because she was such an inspiration to the community and the school."

He noticed that the boys had finished their soft drinks and proclaimed that he was buying drinks for the house and went to the kitchen to retrieve the refreshments.

While he was away the boys agreed that they could listen to the old man talk forever! He returned with some chips, soft drinks, and a couple of fingers of whiskey for himself.

"Like I was saying, I was surprised that she was getting to be vice principal and all, and that she was getting buddy-buddy with all the big shots, you see."

So, there I was again, seeing myself coming home with stripes, and bars, and metals all over the place, but now back here instead of that damned New Orleans.

Well, with all the excitement I got drunk that night and the next morning I woke up in her bed all by myself.

"I could hear her in the bathtub singing and I was on my way in there to get me some farewell loving when I spotted the principal downstairs on the couch sleep.

I didn't think much of it, because I just knew that he didn't like women, you see. So, I just went in the bathroom to get me a little loving.

Old Daisy Mae wouldn't let me touch her. At first she said that she couldn't, because he was there downstairs and she didn't want a little love making mess up her promotion.

"Then after he finally left, after breakfast, it was too late. I had to catch the damned train.

"Well, down at the train station my family, some friends, and many other folks were there to see me and the others off!"

There was much hugging, kissing, and crying that morning, I tell you. The first ride was sort of a short one except we got held up with something that got on the tracks, but finally we arrived in New Cumberland where they had this long, long, long train full of people and equipment headed for basic training.

"Then they spent a long time getting all the men where they were suppose to be, you see, the whites in certain, certain cars and the Negroes in the others."

It was a real mess, but we finally got started. He chuckled and poured himself another two fingers of whiskey.

We started cheering like fools when that train finally got started! Well, the old train crept along so long that many of us were starving to death, but we were so excited about killing Nazis and being heroes that it didn't matter at first!

"Some boys had fried chicken and stuff, but they made the mistake of being polite and offering the rest of us their food! So, it didn't last to very long.

Some of us had a little whiskey and that didn't last very long either, you see. As the evening started setting in, we were getting so hungry that we could have eaten each other.

"We had our own Negro officers and sergeants, and they were busy as hell trying to keep us under control. It was so sad that it got to be very funny, you see.

Some old boys were ready to quit and jump off the train, but were reminded that they were down South and them sheriffs would have loved to shoot them some runaway deserting Negroes.

"Even if the sheriffs missed them, they stood the chance of being lynched by some of them crazy white folks, so quitting and jumping off the train had little appeal to most of us, especially me, because I had some experience with them crazy white folks.

Later we found out that some soldiers both Negro and white did jump the train, and as far as I know a couple of the Negroes have never been accounted for.

"I hope to God that they made out all right! Anyway, we got really quiet, and I couldn't help but think about a song that I had heard Miss Billie Holiday sing called *Strange Fruit*, about Negroes being lynched.

"Finally, the train stopped nearby Birmingham, Alabama at this restaurant called Thompson's of Birmingham, I believe. Well, we got really excited when we were told that we were going to get our first meal on Uncle Sam, and that we could order anything that we wanted! Damned we were hungry, and some old boys had never eaten in a restaurant; so they were doubly excited.

But our excitation was killed real fast, because we saw them march them white soldiers down there first. It looked like there were a million of them.

"Then after about a million years, they marched us down there. That's when I knew that I had made a big mistake, because we could see them white folks marching in and out of the front door from the train.

But when we were marched down there they marched us to the back of the damned place. We were a little upset, but we were so hungry that we could handle that shit!

The people had these long tables for us, and it didn't even look like any place that I had ever eaten before."

The old man paused and wiped some tears from his eyes as the boys sat there in reverent silence.

Through his tears he continued, "While we were waiting to order, one of them old boys was looking for a place to relieve himself and just happened to look through them boards that they had built to separate us from the white folks."

All of a sudden he started screaming, "Nazis! Nazis! Look at them Nazi bastards!"

"Before you knew it, we were all at them damned boards looking at some Nazis eating like kings in the area reserved for white folks.

We were so mad that it was a miracle that we didn't start a riot. We were so mad that many of us wanted to kill anything white.

Our captain calmed us down to the point that we didn't mess up nothing, but we sure damn were not going to eat in that place.

After a while when nobody would order nothing, he told us that if we were not going to eat that we would just get back on the train.

"So, we went outside to march back to the train, and by this time the man that owned the place came out screaming that the captain had to sign the food voucher, even though we had not eaten."

He refused and that old white bastard went running inside the restaurant. We cheered, because we thought that we had done something. Then all hell broke loose, almost!

"The very sheriff showed up with some old boys with shotguns and shit, demanding that he sign the voucher.

The captain made us get on the train while he, the sheriff, and the white officers argued about the situation.

Well, it was decided at first that the train was not going to move unless the voucher was signed. Then, somehow, it was decided that they would lock him up until it was signed, which meant that he would be left behind.

They took him away, but the train didn't move. I don't know what happened, but after a while he returned and we left.

"Our resolve to kill Nazis died a lot that evening, because as one of the old boys said, `Hitler ain't never called me a Nigger.'

We were additionally angry when we found out that he had been ordered to sign the voucher.

"Well, we got to the basic training camp, most of us were a little upset, but you know after a while most of our minds and souls were on all that marching, and shooting, and all the other stuff that we had to do.

Our major relief, besides trying to figure out how to kill our sergeant, you see, was mail call. That Daisy Mae had written me maybe two letters a day, at first; but she couldn't believe that I didn't have the time to write her as often as she would write me, you see.

"Then, one day I got the chance to call her at her home, you see. Of all things, that damned principal answered the telephone.

I didn't think too much of it until she made some lame excuse about it being too late to talk to me because she had some work to do.

Now, I was real suspicious and jealous, you see. Here I was in this damned army and my woman was home with this part man, part woman; and the worse part was that there was nothing that I could do about at the time.

"Finally, basic training was over, and I was a brand new private first class. I had earned a couple of ribbons, so I thought that I was on my way in the army.

Hell, I even liked the way it looked on paper and the way it sounded, 'Private First Class Kingsley Clarke'!"

"Well, they had this sort of graduation for us and Daisy Mae came down to see it, you see. After it was over, they gave us the leave that they had promised us and old Daisy Mae and I went to this little motel just off base and we made a son.

We didn't know it at the time, you see. But later when I found out that she pregnant, I felt that my life was set. She kept on worrying me about getting married so that, the child would have a father.

So, well, I liked old Daisy Mae and marrying her did have it's advantages and I decided to do it.

"Well, about that time they had decided that I was best

suited to be a M.P. Military Police, was just about right for me, because I liked to boss people around and those uniforms made me look real good or maybe, I made the uniform look real good, he chuckled!

"I was getting real good at this M.P. stuff. By the time I was to get married, I was a corporal which gave me a little rank and some power, you see.

So, I was coming home to get married and be a big shot in front of my family, friends, and her folks who had not meet me yet.

She had been a little slow with the letters, because she was now a full principal, you see. At least that's what she said.

Anyway, here I am coming home to my bride to be and as happy as a . . . well, I was real happy.

"I should have known that something was wrong when she didn't meet me at the station, but I didn't pay that much mind.

I caught a taxi and went to see my boyfriends and show off! Boy were they impressed, especially after I told them a bunch of lies about what I was doing in the army, you see.

After I went to see my mother who was praising the very Lord all over the place after she saw me. He laughed with the boys. My father was proud too, but he didn't say too much, you see.

"Anyway, I called her and she asked me where I was. Being in a real good mood, at first, I didn't pick up the very panic in her voice when she said that we had to talk.

Then, it hit me, "Talk! Hell, talk about what? I was home to get married, get me some loving and go on to my next base, you see, 'Talk??'"

"Well, when I got to her house, there she was with old William, the principal! They were so nervous that they were sweating, although, it was real cool that evening.

I grabbed her to kiss her, and she turned her head away at the last moment so fast that I kissed the back of her damned head.

Old William looked like he was going to wet his damned pants, he looked so scared. She asked me to sit down, because she had something to tell me and hoped that I would understand.

She told me that William was a 'homosexual'. I believe that was the first time that I had heard them called that as we had other things that we called them. The boys looked at each other.

"Then she told me that his, uh, well, private parts didn't work like it should. I told her that all that was interesting, but what did it have to do with me?

Then she told me that he was what the Negroes in this city needed to educate their children. I said, "Fine, but what did that have to do with me?"

Then, she said that she believed that educating the child was more important than me, she, or him. She started talking about sacrifice and a whole lot of other stuff. By this time, I was so damned confused that I was getting mad, you see!

"While she was talking, he got as busy as a one legged man in an ass kicking contest and was working his way out of the room. She knew that all this was getting out of hand, so she told me.

She said, "Kingsley, we decided that in order for William to take his place as a leader in education, he needed to be married and maybe have a child! So, although I love you and always will, I decided to marry him."

Boy, I wanted to kill something, and by this time, he was nowhere to be found! She went on explaining that craziness, and was surprised that I didn't see the logic in it. She went on to explain that we could always be lovers, because he couldn't fulfill that part of being a husband.

I was so sick that I just turned to leave. Then she grabbed me and asked me to spend the night, because he wouldn't come back while I was there!

She also told me that we could always be lovers and on and on. I was in love with her, but none of that made any sense to me.

Not knowing how to react or what to do, the boys sat there motionless and silent, while Kingsley poured himself another two fingers of whiskey.

He looked up at the boys and continued, "I left there and went down to the cat house and found old Mary. She had some more miles on her, but it was to be my wedding night and if I was not going to get married, I sure damned was going to have a honey moon!"

Kingsley stopped talking and sort of gazed into nothingness. Marcus' curiosity had peaked to the point that he had to ask what happened.

"Well, a few months later, she wrote to tell me that we had a fine boy, she named him . . . well, after her grandfather to keep down the suspicion.

But all of that went for nothing, because one of his influential friends happened on him and some young stud. Soon, everybody knew him for what he was and he couldn't stand it. So, he blew his brains out rather than face people.

Daisy Mae blamed herself and had a nervous breakdown, and they had to carry her off to the hospital. She was never all right and died there a few years ago.

"I would go to see her, but she never recognized me. She thought that she was still teaching school and I was some kid that had to stay after. She treated everybody that way.

The boy was raised by her sister and husband who treated him like their own. When they thought that he was old enough, they let him meet me. He still comes past to see me from time to time."

Kingsley poured himself another two fingers and asked the boys if they were hungry. Although they were quite hungry, both denied that they were out of politeness.

After a little gentle persuasion, the boys admitted that they could use a bite or two. The three decided on burgers and fries.

Kingsley gave them the money and off they went to the neighborhood fast food joint to get the food.

As they walked, they talked about the story that Kingsley had shared with them and speculated on what happened next.

They were so anxious to hear the rest of the story that they ran to and from the store.

7. *Resignation*

After the boys had returned, the three sat in the kitchen munching on their feast of burgers, fries, and drinking sodas happily but silently.

Chris became aware of the fact that Kingsley was watching him carefully and was enjoying watching him eat.

Marcus who could not stand the silence asked Kingsley what had happened after spending the evening with Mary.

Without the slightest bit of hesitation he began, "The next morning, I was sitting in a restaurant around the corner from where I had left Mary, you see."

I was there minding my own business, you see, when one of my big mouthed boyfriends came in and asked me as loud as he could speak, "What time you going down to get your neck broke?"

Breaking your neck meant getting married, you see. Most of the people in there knew me, at least, well enough to speak to me, and they made a big fuss over my getting married!

I was too mad and embarrassed to tell them that I was not marrying Daisy Mae on that or any other day, because at the time I had decided never to see her again, and I had strongly considered never coming home again!

I was so down that I was wishing that they send me overseas so that one of them Nazis could do me a favor and blow my dumb brains out.

I kept all that to myself and accepted all of the congratulations and well wishes from everybody. One old boy slipped me a little drink out of his handy flask.

Finally, when things calmed down, I left the waitress a big tip and left. Somebody had already paid for my breakfast.

I walked around for a couple of hours trying to figure out what to do with the rest of my leave. I was so hurt that I knew that if I had stayed in town I would have gotten in real trouble real fast!

So, I went home and talked to my folks, and that evening I was on a train headed for Fort Benning in Albany, Georgia where I was ordered to go.

It was the deepest south that I had ever even thought about or really cared about going, but orders are orders.

The couch that I was on was full of Negro soldiers, fresh from basic training and from their talk in a real hurry to go kill themselves some Nazis and some of them Japs on the side.

But some of them old boys, especially from down south were even more determined not to take no more stuff off white folks.

Many had to run away to join the army, and once they had learned that they were men who put their pants on the same way that everybody else did, they were not going to be treated like animals ever again.

They claimed that they were 'ready to kick some white ass' on their way to killing the other enemy, if any of them got them wrong, you see.

That's when I met this big, dark, distinguished looking Negro sergeant! He looked like a ... well, he looked like he was born to be in charge. Even without the uniform and stripes, a man would have guessed that he was the man.

He looked like he could have been in one of those movies that were so popular to us at the time, you see. I forget his name, but while the others were raising hell on the train, he was reading a book.

I was shocked, because it was a book that Daisy Mae had made me read.

The man noticed me kind of watching him, and asked me what the hell I was looking at with a smile on his face.

At first, I could not tell what the smile meant, but after I mentioned that I had read the book that he was reading we started to talk.

We talked a little about the book, but he would not let me spoil his reading by telling him more than he had read, you see.

He turned out to be very easy to talk to, you know, just like an old friend or older brother. Soon, I was telling him all about Daisy Mae and the way that I felt.

After I had worn his ears out with my sad story, he told me that I was much better off without her, and stop looking back!

He told me to always look forward and never, ever look back. I felt a whole lot better after talking to him. I wished the hell that I could at least remember his name, and I often wonder how he made out. I saw a man around town that looked like him, but . . .

While we were sitting there talking, the train stopped somewhere in North Carolina and they were getting off to eat, you see.

Well, he invited me to join them and since I didn't have any big plans, I did. We marched over there to this restaurant along with some other GI's, both Negro and white.

His squad was the sharpest out there, I mean that they were so crypts in everything that they did that all seemed to watch them with pride and maybe, a little envy!

They made me feel real proud to be a Negro in the armed service, you see. Those jokers looked so good that some others yielded to let them go in before them.

Well, my pride died when we got inside, because the first thing that I saw was this big ugly Jim Crow curtain that was used to separate the Negroes from the whites.

I remember lowering my head in shame, because I had some experience with that kind of shit before in Alabama. Well, my appetite had gone and all that pride that I had went with it, too.

I had turned to leave when I heard all of this commotion, yelling, and cheering.

I turned to see what had happened, scared to death! Because I knew that something real awful had happened, but I swear to Sweet Jesus that I saw something that I never ever even imagined could ever happen.

Praise be to God, they tore that damned curtain down and were standing there at attention! The boys noticed a tear in Kingsley's eyes.

I have never felt so proud in my life, and when I looked at the sergeant, he was just smiling. He looked at me and winked! Damned that felt good! Well, things settled down and we ate real good that evening.

Now if you think that they showed off marching to the restaurant, you should have seen them march back to the train! Real Black knights they were that evening with the evening sun shining on them!

When I see those civil rights people, I always think of that bright day. Not too long after that or maybe I should say too soon after we got back on the train, they arrived at their destination and left me on the train.

I was real sorry to see them leave and real sorry to see the sergeant go. We shook hands and wished each other well, but I always wished that I had thought about getting his ... well, I didn't and maybe that was best. Hell, ain't nothing that I can do about it now, is there?

The boys nodded in agreement.

Well, that was the slowest train in the very world, because it stopped just about every mile to pick somebody up. This was getting on my nerves until this pretty young woman got on somewhere in South Carolina. She looked so fresh and so innocent that I could not keep my eyes off her.

I don't know if she noticed, but she sat right down here beside me. We started talking and after a while we were just like old friends. She told me that she was going to stay with some relatives down in Georgia near Albany! Now, I got real excited! We started making big plans, and again I felt good about women and this woman was making my heart sing!

We finally got to where she was getting off, and she asked me to be sure to come see her. Come to see her! I got right off that train with her which surprised her and almost sent her Grandpa and Grandma in shock when they found out that she was the reason that I got off the train in the first place.

They didn't know what to do with me, because we were deep ... I mean, way deep in the country. So deep in the country we were that her folks were picking her up in an old work wagon pulled by a mule. I knew that I had made a big mistake, and the next train was not due for about a hundred years, he laughed to himself!

They decided that I was not too bad, so they invited me to go along with them. I still had a few days left before I had to report to Fort Banning, and a pocket full of money.   That mule was the slowest creature on God's earth, but that slow trip gave me an opportunity to see how life was down their in

Georgia, you see. Well as that animal moved in slow motion, I saw many Negroes working them fields.

Boy were they in them fields mostly picking cotton, and it was hot as I can ever remember being. I was glad that I didn't have to pick any of that stuff!

Well, I was sitting on the back with my feet dangling like this here, you see. So, I could only see things kind of backwards. I can still remember those old dusty roads with all them dips and curves. Old Grandpa had to move out of the way of the traffic that came the other way, and sometimes I got hit in the head by branches of trees, that old girl would laugh every time I got hit.

Well, we passed one of them chain gangs. I don't know if they still have them or not, but seeing those Negroes being worked to death on them roads gave me some deep respect for the law down their in Georgia.

It took us until late afternoon to get to their farm. It looked like hell to me, and I was sure that I had made a big mistake woman or no woman. There were a whole bunch of folks there, and they had prepared a feast for this young woman.

The food was great! They had chicken cooked several ways, pork, fish, stews, corn, greens, grits, tomatoes, corn bread, biscuits, and a whole lot of other foods. They had pies, cakes, watermelons, berries, figs, and homemade ice cream.

All this stuff was real fresh, because they grew most of it. They had dogs, chickens, cats, pigs, cows, that damned mule and many other creatures all around they place. Both boys nodded as if they had first hand experience on farms and that type of feasting. Anyway, I ate like a hog and everything was fine until they tried to figure out who I was related to. For some reason that was real important to some of them. To make matters worse, I didn't know the girl's name. Georgeada was her name! To make a long story short, them old backwards country people shamed me into working myself to death, made me sleep in the barn, conned me out of a lot of my money, and I never even got a kiss. I was so far back in the woods that only Jesus could help me find it, if for some dumb reason I wanted to find that hell hole. As a final lesson, I had to walk back to the place where they picked me up, because when I decided to leave they told me that the damned mule was not feeling too good. So, they gave me some meat, biscuits, and directions and sent me about my way. Well, I walked and walked and walked and walked and just before dark, some old boy gave me a ride to the deport which was by then only a couple of miles away. Tell you one thing, no hike, exercise or nothing that the army threw at me was as painful as that walk. So, I suppose that they did me a big favor by . . . Hell No, they just got me. But, I finally learned my lesson about female women . . . that is, we men have and will always find a way to help a female woman make a fool out of us if we do not watch ourselves. That's the truth!

"I was down there in Fort Benning when Daisy Mae wrote me and told me about the principal blowing his brains out like I told you this morning. Then, when I was in training to be a M.P., she wrote me to tell me about the birth of her son!

I never will forget that letter, because now she was mad at me and told me to stay away from her and her son, because if was had been any kind of man I would not have let her marry the principal in the first place.

Well, I decided the hell with it, because I sure damned was not going to take the responsibility for that. Anyway, it was not long after that I learned that she had gone off her rocker and had to be locked up in that hospital where she died like I told you this morning.

While all this stuff was going on, I was getting rank by being one of the Army's bounty hunters. I was assigned mostly to catching deserters which was real easy, because most of them old boys didn't have no money or nothing.

All I had to do is to go to his hometown and eventually, he would show up and I would lock him up.

"I really liked my job, because mostly everybody respected me. I felt really important. I had found out that I was somebody, you see. I guess that another thing it did was to keep my mind off Daisy Mae, the kid, and just about everybody else. Wasn't that long before I made sergeant, and I was in charge of mostly taking P.O.W.'s and other prisoners from fort to fort, and from prison to prison. Most of the time it was real easy, because I was now an NCO which meant that usually all I did was tell other people what to do. I was a real big shot. I got to travel all over these United States, and got to stay in some pretty good hotels sometimes, eat in some real good restaurants, and sleep with some of the prettiest women in this country. Yes sir, I had it made. . .   "Did you ever have to shoot anybody? " Chris asked with youthful enthusiasm.

"Most of the time them old boys were too scared to start anything, and since they were handcuffed most of the time, if they got out of line I'd just punch them like that (he showed a couple of rights) or pop them upside the head with my stick or sometimes when I was really feeling mean, I'd just kick them in the ass!

I only had to shoot two of them old boys, one Negro boy and one of them crazies from down there in Mississippi.

The Negro kid was a deserter and I caught him at his girlfriend's house. He had left his company, because he had gotten one of them "Dear John" letters.

When I got there, he was mad at the whole world, you see.

I was feeling real sorry for him, because the woman was really talking shit to him as I was leading him out!

I would not cuff him at first, because, like I said, I felt real sorry for him. He had a couple of stripes, and I knew that he was going to lose them and have to pay the very devil, you see.

Anyway, she called him some kind of stupid something, and like a flash of lightning he pulled a knife from somewhere and wanted to cut her very heart out! Although, I understood what he was going though, I could let him just kill the woman.

So, I drew my big old .45 and ordered him to drop the damned knife! He had this real strange look on his face, and told me to go on and kill him. He started screaming. He didn't want to live without this woman.

Well, I was between the two of them, and she was screaming for me to go on and shoot the `dumb Nigger' and was calling him all kinds of, uh, things. Well, with a real crazy look in his eyes he lunged at me and I shot him!"

The boys gasped!

"But I was a pretty good with that .45, and I just shoot him in the leg. He couldn't ever use it again, but like I said, I felt sorry for the poor boy. I didn't see no need to kill him, because I knew that he was trying to get to her and not to me. That thing hurt me too!

After I got him all straightened out, I had to take some time off! God knows that I didn't want to hurt him. That was right before I made sergeant, and like I said, we were mostly taking prisoners around the country.

Well, we had delivered some old boys out there in Arizona. Damned it was hot out there, and I went to this little saloon to have myself a beer. There were some soldiers in there shooting the bull and drinking that beer. Everything was fine until this red neck spotted me! He didn't have nothing to do, but to fu..., uh, mess with me!

"Now, I knew that he was a damned fool, because between calling me a bunch of African monkey Niggers. He said that he had been in 'this man's army for five years'.

I noticed that he didn't any stripes or nothing on his sleeves. He said that the reason that he could not get any rank was because of all the coons in the army. Now, I had on my full uniform with my gun, stick, and any fool could see that I was a M.P. and a sergeant, something that you just didn't mess with. But did that stop that fool?"

"No?" the boys answered in unison.

"That damned beer or maybe the devil himself told that fool to keep on messing with me. His buddies tried to stop him, but after a few tries, they gave up and just watched, you see. I decided that I was going to finish my beer and leave, because I didn't want to have to mess with this fool.

I wouldn't even look at him, because all I wanted to do was to drink up and leave. Well, I felt this something go past my head, and when I turned my head I saw that it was one of them darts that they use in those games.

When I saw that I jumped up and was going to kick his very ass! He leaped behind the bar, and the rest of the people started hitting the floor, the very floor. So, I knew that there was some kind of gun back there, so I drew mine and ordered him to come out with his hands where I could see them.

"That fool came up with a sawed off shotgun, firing except somebody had forgot to put some shells in the damned thing. As it clicked, I fired right into the bastard's chest! Twice!

The force of the two bullets slammed him back against the wall and he fell forward on his face! By then, I was all on top of him kicking the shotgun away from him.

Do you know what his last words were? Not waiting for an

answer, his last words were 'Did I get the Nigger?' just before he took his last breath and died.

Somebody called the sheriff and somebody else called the base. At first, they tried to pin a murder charge on me, but after questioning the drunken red necks from the bar, they changed their minds.

A captain, maybe from his hometown, was determined to see me burn for it, but there was nothing that he could do. Everybody in the place told the truth.

I didn't know it at the time, but that was the moment of decline of me in the service.

"Like I said, I was really feeling like I had found what I was going to be doing for the rest of my life. I had planned to stay in the service until I retired, then go off somewhere with a pretty young woman and live happily ever after, you see, like in them damned fairy tales. Hell, but that fairy tale stuff just ain't true. It was early in 1945 when things started getting crazy on me. I had gotten myself a couple of more stripes and everybody was feeling like we was about to finish them godless Nazis off, you see. Well, there were a whole lot of Germans around, P.O.W.'S and some civilians that we had to baby sit. By that time, I was spending most of my time out West and there was not a whole lot of Jim Crow things happening, at least where I was. Anyway, I heard about Many Negro M.P.'S having trouble with segregation while transporting and guarding them Nazis. You see, in some places when they stopped to eat or go to the rest rooms there were these 'white only' signs and shit all over the place. It made no difference to those racist bastards that these Negroes were guarding prisoners of these United States of America. They would rather have a white anything than a Negro. Anyway I had started to bullshit myself into believing that I was somehow different, because by this time I was Master Sergeant Kingsley ... (tears began to run down his face which he wiped off, then continued) ... Yes sir, I was a big time master sergeant, loved and respected by everybody in this man's army."

He showed the boys the pictures around the room of many men that he had served with, some of them were dead and the rest, well, he had not seen or heard from in years. He had no idea about where they were now. They were all proud men of color, and the proudest Was Master Sergeant Kingsley Clark. There were other pictures, newspaper accounts, and artifacts of that era that he proudly shared with the boys.

He told them that they would never hear about the many contributions that Negroes had made in the military during that or any other time. He told them that he had spent a life time reading and listening and learning about his people while other Negroes were out their making money for 'Whitey'.

Very bitterly, he showed them an article identifying 'The 100 Most Influential Black Americans' whom he denounced as the 'the 100 Most Acceptable Slaves in America', which was easier for Marcus to accept than Chris. Kingsley advised them to read and learn as much as they could about Negroes in America and to never forget who they were or they would be lost. He looked at Chris sadly and said something that caught him totally by surprise and confused him, "Someday you might be asked to keep all this, please keep it and remember!"

"Like I was saying, I started believing that things would be fine for me as long as I kept my nose clean, you see. We had a whole bunch of Nazis that we were guarding, you know, like in jail. One night I was in town drinking me a little beer and a couple of fingers of whiskey, and this young white corporal came up to me and said that there was something real strange going on there. Well, being all G.I. and M.P. I asked him what he meant.

"He told me that there was a table over near the back door that three of our Nazi prisoners were sitting and drinking with some civilians. I could smell the beer on his breath, so at first I dismissed it as bullshit, you see. After he kept on insisting that they were suppose to be locked up at the fort, I walked over to do a little investigating.

"Very casually, I made my way over to where they were sitting and sure enough I recognized one of them Nazis, because I had taken him to be interrogation a couple of times. He was a friendly enough old boy and had tried to joke with me in broken English. Did I mention that I always wore my uniform? Don't matter except, well when I recognized him I showed my pearly whites and spoke to him.

"I'd be damned if it wasn't him, because he smiled and spoke to me in that broken English. Soon as he did that I drew my pistol and ordered everybody to get the hell up and put their damn hands where I could see them. They looked at each other and slowly stood. I damned near blew one of the civilian's heads off as he wanted to show me something that was inside his suite coat. I'm no fool, so I told him that if he put his damned hands inside his coat I'd kill him. He froze and I ordered them all against the wall while I was figuring out what to do next, you see. Next thing I knew I felt this sharp pain at the back of my head, then total darkness.

"I woke up in a hospital with all these things stuck in my arms! I was like in a daze, but I tried to speak to the nurse who ran out of the room. Before I knew what was going, some men rushed in the room with one of them yelling at the nurse. Before I could even speak this guy in a white coat stuck a needle in my arm, and I was gone again! The next time I woke, I didn't say shit, I looked around the room and knew that I was in a hospital detention center somewhere, but why? Also, there were two of the biggest marines in there that I had ever seen. It was like a nightmare, and I just wanted to wake up!

"Later, and I don't know how much later, I woke up in a different room. It was a much nicer place, and as I looked up I saw a fan. It was hotter; or at least, I was wetter than, I mean I was sweating a lot more. Anyway, I would not move my head, because I seemed to remember that I was not suppose to move my head. I could not clearly recall the reason, but something awful was supposed to happen if I moved my head. So, I decided to see as much of the room without moving my head, but as I surveyed the room with my eyes I saw a young nurse, a pretty little thing, sitting beside my bed reading a magazine.

"Because we looked like we were by ourselves, I sat up and it was real easy. Then, I realized that I no longer had them needles in my arm and no restraints. Restraints? Why in the hell did they have me all restrained? They only restrained hostile prisoners or crazy people. Crazy!?! What the hell was going on here!?   "Well, I decided to speak to her to try to find out what was going on, you see. As I was about to speak, I remembered holding them damned Nazis . . . against the wall when suddenly everything went black!

Putting together all the pieces to everything that I could remember and being a big time master sergeant and M.P., in this man's army, I had everything figured out!

"Them damned Nazis had captured me and were holding me some place. Spies! A whole nest of spies! My duty was clear to me, I needed to find out where I was being kept, than get some help and turn the tables on these bastards. They didn't know who they were messing with . . . they had messed up and captured the U.S. Army's M.P. Master Sergeant Kingsley

Clark and they would have hell to pay for making that big mistake! Real big mistake!

"I just knew that I was going to be one gold-plated war hero with a maybe some kind of presidential . . . Kingsley suddenly began to cry openly and profusely, with made the boys very uncomfortable. I was true to my flag and country, you see. I would not tell them anything but my name, rank, and serial number.

"At first, they were amused with the way that I would not tell them nothing. But in my mind they were so good that they kept telling me that they were also American military personnel and that I had accidentally uncovered a very sensitive top secret project.

They tried to convince me that they had over reacted to me and never should have treated me the way they had. They were apologizing all over the place, but I was much too smart to believe that junk!!

"Well, they sort of left me alone and allowed me to do almost what I wanted to do. They told me that I could call anybody, anywhere that I wanted, because what they were telling me was the sad truth. But I could not and would not believe that they had done all that to me.

Anyway, on May 2, 1945, the real truth kicked me right in the ass, the base was like a madhouse, because the Germans had surrendered.

"I had wasted all that time not believing what was true that was that my country didn't trust me, although I had worked my Black ass off for it. Nothing that nobody has ever said or done has made me want to do a damned thing for it. They finally broke down and gave me my discharge along with a healthy pension, because by this time I had convinced them that I was crazy.

From the time that I got back here I have devoted my whole life to reading, learning as much as I could about Negroes in these United States of America.

"I have not worked a day since my discharge. I never bought a car, house, or nothing. I totally resigned myself to not doing nothing for this country that betrayed me.

Now, many folks have tried to convince me that I was wrong to drop out, but this is my Black ass. I'll do what I want with it! "

The boys didn't know what to do or say to this angry, old man and were silent. Kingsley became so upset and agitated that he put them out, and they left silently and quickly.

8. *Sweet Rommie*

Once outside, they decided to go down to the basketball court. Marcus was not as enthusiastic as Chris, but he went along. They talked about Mr. Kingsley with compassion and concern, but there was something about the old man that confused Chris. He asked Marcus what the old man meant by "someday I might be asked to keep all that stuff and remember."

Marcus answered by telling him that it is always wise to listen to and learn from your elders. Maybe, he was talking directly to him because that was the first time he had talked to him.

Although Chris was not totally satisfied with Marcus' explanation, he certainly didn't have a better one. So, he let the matter drop.

They reached the basketball court, just in time to see Roy make one of his spectacular shots. The crowd screamed, yelled, and carried on as if they were a crowd at a major sport's event.

Everybody knew that Roy was somebody very special with a one way ticket to stardom, and most hoped that they would be remembered by Roy when he became a really big celebrity.

Chris was so caught up in the excitement that he jumped to give the taller Marcus a high five. As if to leave no doubt about who was best, Roy stole the ball from his opponent, and performed his 'patented 360 degree slam dunk'!

What made his 360 appear so awesome was the fact that he bent his knees; so that, one could see the bottom of his basketball shoes which he had painted his initials, 'R.G'. Roy walked over to the guy and said something to him that caused both of them to laugh. He then walked off the court hugging Sonia who had run to the court to meet and greet Roy with a big hug and kiss.

Everybody was to be impressed and happy for Roy, except Rommie who was gazing at Roy with a diabolical grimace on his face. Standing there in a black sweat suit, black designer tennis shoes, and enough gold to open a pawn shop. He was flanked by his two 'business associates', Snake and Tom. He said something to them. They, too, glared at the boy.

Rommie was distracted by some young boys on bicycles approaching him to give him money. With the most homicidal expression he could manage, he motioned for them to give the money to Tom.

Tom patiently counted the considerable money and nodded to Rommie, who in turn nodded to Snake who led them to a black sport's car. Snake carefully distributed small packs of cocaine to the kids who counted behind him and left on their bikes.

While this was going on, Tom gave the money to Rommie who counted it and stuffed the large roll in his pocket. He motioned for a young girl who was eagerly standing near him to go to his car.

He ordered Tom to meet him along with Snake in an hour at the 'place'.

As he was about to get into his car, he noticed Chris. He looked at him with a concerned expression on his face and called out to him. Chris saw and heard him but choose to ignore him.

Snake, Rommie's bodyguard and enforcer, eased up behind Chris and was about to grab him. Suddenly, like a bolt of lightning, Marcus placed a well-aimed, forceful full karate kick to the man's forehead!

From the ground, Snake shook his head to clear it and jumped up with a very large pistol in his hand pointing it at Marcus and screaming!

Marcus stood his ground defiantly, looking the homicidal Snake straight in the eyes. Those who were near urged Snake to leave the boy alone, not to shoot him!

With a snarl on his face, it seemed certain that he was going to shoot Marcus. Rommie, now, standing next to Snake quickly surveyed the crowd that had gathered and being perceptive to the temperament of the crowd, he snatched the large weapon from Snake with a philanthropic smile on his face.

The much infuriated Snake protested that "no punk kid could kick him in the . . .". Rommie's glare quieted Snake. Giving him a moment to calm down Rommie loudly proclaimed that the boys were his personal friends, and that if he ever saw them in any trouble he was to 'look out for them'.

He grabbed Snake by the head, still smiling whispering in his ear that he didn't give a damn about the boy, but killing him in front of all those fools would be very bad for business. Think!

Still smiling, he looked into Marcus' eyes and told him to be sure to tell his grandfather that he never forgot a friend.

He, then, put his arms around the boys' shoulders and led them toward his car. Beaming with self importance, he told the boys that he was truly sorry about the 'little misunderstanding, but everything was fine now'.

He explained that Snake was like a trusted, trained dog and

didn't think before he acted, but warned Chris that he should have answered as they were family.

Marcus shook free. With a very sincere, surprised, and hurt expression on his face, Rommie told Marcus that he was like family, too. Rommie added that he and his grandfather 'went way back'.

He was now talking to the back of Marcus. Marcus walked away from him with disgust. He had a total lack of respect or fear of him and the dreaded Snake. Chris, drawing strength from his friend, glared at Rommie and Snake, then turned and ran to join Marcus.

He thrust the weapon in Snake's chest, and called him a few derogatory names. Frustrated and needing someone to abuse, he opened his car door, glared at the smiling young girl, smacked her, and threw her on the front seat of his car.

Those that witnessed his actions were visibly disgusted with his behavior, but none volunteered to help the girl as he sped away. Rommie was 'the man'.

As Rommie drove through the projects with the young girl as if he were nobility surveying his dominion, he was still visibly upset and annoyed.

The girl had dried her eyes as rapidly as she could as she didn't want to blow getting the money and free cocaine that she knew would be hers after she did the 'do' for Rommie.

At a traffic light, he grabbed her by the head and kissed her. She pretended to be excited by his touch and began slowly rubbing him on the chest. He began to smile as he knew that all of young the young girls loved to be with Sweet Rommie, a fact that he was very proud.

While enjoying all of the attention that he was receiving from the girl who was now kissing and hugging him as much as she could in the confines of the small automobile, his thoughts drifted off to Roy and Sonia.

Somehow, some day, some way he was going to sleep with that young freak, or he was going to die! Already he had put together a plan to get rid of that damned Roy.

By the time they reached "the place," Rommie had begun fantasying that the girl, whose name he had now forgotten, was Sonia.

He very gently and suavely escorted her past the first room of the apartment into the very large and dark bedroom which featured a very large water bed. He turned on the stereo, and the room was filled with music that was too slow and too old fashioned for her taste.

Although this whole thing was much more than she cared to deal with, she was very careful not to let him even guess that she was dissatisfied. She didn't want to mess up getting enough money from him to buy a pair of jeans, and maybe, a blouse that she had seen at the mall.

She really wanted to look good at the party that she was planning to go to later that day. Although she was fifteen, Tysia was much too streetwise to mess his thing up. She had no problem, at all, with his continuously calling her Sonia.

After sitting her on the bed next to a large marble night table which was bare except a single edged razor blade, he said something to her that he thought was very romantic (she thought it was stupid) and retrieved a bottle of expensive champagne from the portable refrigerator. Balancing two glasses from the well stoked bar in his other hand, he slow danced himself over to the bed where she was sitting.

He was singing along with a record by the late Marvin Gaye, *Let's Get It On* which was only vaguely familiar to Tysia who was by now totally bored but smiling as she knew what the real deal was with him.

As he placed the bottle and glasses on the table, he leaned over and kissed her gently on the cheek. He, then, reached over to the headboard and turned on the light to the built-in aquarium that immediately caught the attention of his otherwise bored guest.

She crawled across the water bed to get a better look at the colorful fishes as he watched her lustily.

As she gleefully admired the fishes, he reached under the bed and retrieved his 'good stuff' which was much purer than the stuff that he sold to the chumps.

With a razor blade he carefully, almost ceremoni-ously, made four rows of the cocaine. Satisfied with his handy work, he gently picked up the bottle of champagne and popped the cork which startled the girl.

He smiled and announced that it was party time as he tightly rolling two fifty-dollar bills to be use to snort the cocaine.

Although she certainly was aware of her sole reason for being there, the moment that she regretted was now upon her; however, the sight of the two fifties excited her. Boy, if he would only give her those fifties she could . . .

He interrupted her thoughts by strongly suggesting that she take off her pretty clothes; saying, as if he cared, that they would get all messed up. As she stood and undressed giving him a little show, he puffed on a cigarette while admiring her firm, smooth body swaying to the music.

When she was completely undressed, he choked a little on his cigarette which embarrassed him a little.

Then under his careful directions, they sipped the champagne and snorted the cocaine through the fifties which he, with an air of kindliness, announced belonged to her.

She was so ecstatic that she grabbed him and kissed him rolling him on top of her! After a few moments, he got up, took off his clothes and joined her in the bed for what was jubilation for him!

The best that she could do was to keep her mind on the hundred dollars. One hundred dollars was all she could think of as she completed her tasks.

When she finished her shower, Rommie was still sleeping in the middle of the bed where she had left him. She hurriedly checked her pockets to be sure that the two fifties were still there.

Satisfied, her only desire was to get out of there before he could awaken and demand seconds or thirds. Tysia was anxious to get those jeans, the blouse, and maybe, something for her boy friend.

She quickly dismissed the later idea as she reasoned that he could ask her where she got the money, and she didn't want him to think that she was a whore or nothing.

Suddenly, she heard the front door slam with Snake calling out to Rommie. However, upon seeing her, he toned down and asked her for a little play. She was concerned that he was going to try to do her for free like he did many of Rommie's girls.

Not only would she be doing him for nothing, but she knew if Snake did her Rommie wouldn't have anything else to do with her.

This was a major concern, because Rommie paid better than anyone else as he was the man. Her fears were well founded as Snake started to undo his pants and demanded that she come to him.

However, she was extremely fortunate as Snake's loud voice woke Rommie who was now in a very, very bad mood.

He jumped out of bed and came in the room screaming, "Did Tom come with you?"

"Yeah, he's out there parking the car? "

"Well, leave the bitch alone and go tell him to bring his ass in here!"

"But Rommie, let me . . . "

"Get Tom!"

Tom, who had overheard as him was entering the room, calmly asked Rommie what he wanted. Tom always had a calming affect on Rommie. Many felt that Tom not Rommie should be running things.

Rommie ordered him to take the girl across town much to the outspoken displeasure of Snake. He also told him to stop past Dora's and tell her to be ready to go to Atlantic City in a couple of hours.

He looked at the girl and told her that if she ever told anyone that she was there he would turn Snake loose on her. Frightened, she assured him that she would not tell nobody nothing.

She turned to say goodbye to Rommie, but he was intently talking to Snake. She felt that it would be better to leave him alone, so she and Tom left the two talking.

Impatiently Rommie grilled Snake, "What about getting that crazy-assed Little Al out of that joint? Did you do it?"

"Yeah Rommie, all it took was a little coke and a little cash. He's been out a couple days. Done told you the other day, Rommie."

"Did you tell him all the shit that I told you to tell him? You fix him up?"

"Rommie, I done, did just like you told me, but why you want to go through all that shit for one 'ho? Damn, you could . . . "

"Snake, you just do the hell what I tell you to do, and don't ever tell me what the hell I could do. I could do any damned thing that I want to do! You understand?"

Meanwhile as Tom and the girl were leaving, Tom wondered why Rommie didn't just call Dora. Did Rommie somehow know? He reasoned not as he was sure that Rommie would have killed him.

The girl noticed that Tom was giving a signal in the direction of two men sitting in a very plain sedan, but she dismissed it as none of her business.

10. *Rommie's Rage*

Tysia was annoyed with Tom as he paid very little attention to her. She liked Tom enough to do him for free, but he never said anything to her.

She noticed that he was very concerned about something behind him as he kept looking through the rear view mirror. Every time she would try to start a conversation, he would respond only with a slight smile and grunting sound or not at all. He seemed to be nervous.

Finally, he asked her where she was going and pulled over to the curb. He gave her twenty dollars, telling her to get out and catch a cab. She thought that he was very stupid as the cab fare from where they were could not have been more than a couple of dollars, but she took the money smiling as she got out of the car.

Tysia flattered herself by thinking that maybe he could not trust himself with her, and he didn't want any trouble from Rommie. She would never tell.

As he pulled off, she noticed that the same plain sedan was still following him. But, again, it wasn't any of her business.

She decided to walk home and save the twenty as it was only about six. This would give her enough time to go shopping on the way home and be ready when her boyfriend would be coming to take her to the party.

He was too young to drive, and he didn't have an apartment like Rommie's. But he would do as a boyfriend until she could do better, maybe Tom.

"Just don't jerk us around," one of the detectives said sternly to Tom who had met them around the corner from where he had dropped off the girl. Tom assured them that Rommie would be picking Dora up later that evening, and Rommie would be alone with her.

He also assured them that she was definitely expendable in case they had to use force. After confirming the address, they sent him about his way.

Once gone, they called their supervisors who dismissed them and told them that they would handle it from there. They in turn called the Assistant United States Attorney to let him know that they had a major player, a pusher, ready for plucking.

He was thrilled, because this type of high visibility arrest could do nothing but enhance his career. He in turn made a couple of telephone calls so that, other agencies could share in the glory of the arrest.

His only regret was that he realized that the local police had to be involved. So be it.

Meanwhile Rommie was drying himself from his shower and yelling at Snake. Snake had asked him why he was so pissed with Roy.

"Rommie, why you sweat what Sonia and Roy do? Sure, she fine, but there is a bunch of them young fine young freaks out there. You "The Man", you don't even have to care 'bout them."

Rommie glared at him, "I don't give a damn about Roy, Sonia, Dora, Tom or you! Do you understand what I'm saying?"

Snake just stared and listened.

"When I was the greenest kid out there in the streets, I was a cold sucker. I liked people and I thought that they liked my ass, too. But shit happened to open my eyes to shit, and now I don't even care 'bout nobody but me.

"All of them can go to hell as far as I'm concerned. Them kids that take and sell my shit, I hope they all die. Die like dogs. They're just like them kids I used to know when I was their age.

When everybody, my friends turned their backs on me, I decided that I had to something and quick. Roy's mama, Juanita, taught me the golden rule, he who got the gold, rules."

"The only," Rommie became so agitated tears began to flow down his face, "like all she had to do was like me a little bit. Her husband, that jive-time preacher, Mike, uh, Reverend Govans, was supposed to be my friend, but he married her."

Rommie picked up and started throwing things, almost hitting the now scared Snake in the head with a lamp. Rommie snorted a little cocaine as he continued his diabolical plan that would take care of Roy, and leave him completely clean.

He asked Snake if he had arranged to get Little Al out.

The now shaken Snake answered,"Man, I done told you a few minutes ago I took care of it!" What you cra..."

"We get to him, I mean, do he know?"

"Sure, he knows," Snake responded.

"Well, didn't he freak out on that principal? He damned near killed the man with his fists, because he thought that the man was doing the do to Sonia?", Rommie laughed.

"Yeah, that was some funny shit, because at the trial he found out that he was wrong about the man. A lot of good that did, because he'd already kicked the man's ass but good. But you know that damned kid, he ain't 'wrapped too tight' and once he thought....," Snake continued.

"Damned all that, did you do like I told you?"

"Yeah, he knows that Roy is pumping Sonia. We put a little yeast in it, made it sound real bad, if you know what I mean. Made it sound like he's pumping her like he would a boy, and if I know that crazy bastard, he'll be kicking ass, big time. Little Al might even kill the sucker."

Rommie laughed, "Yeah, he's dumb enough to kill for that freak sister of his. You ought to see the way that he used to look at her. His own damned sister, I tell that he is one sick dog. But that's okay, 'cause if you do like I tell you, I'll pay all their asses, Mike and Juanita and that damned Virginia who showed me that she wasn't about me."

Rommie snatched his gun off the bed and shoved it against Snake's head, "You do this right on and I'll put a little something in your pockets. But if you don't, I'll blow your damned brains all over them projects. You know what I mean?"

Snake got the point.

"If you ever call me crazy again, I'll show you crazy! When my shit gonna get here?"

"Tonight!"

Rommie slapped him on the back laughing, "Tonight? Well get it done, and I'll see you tomorrow. I'm going to get dressed and take Dora to Atlantic City right now. I feel lucky! You will take care of that little thing for me?"

Nervously laughing, Snake assured Rommie that he would take care of it. Rommie glared at Snake with the gun still in his hands.

"I swear to God they ain't never gonna lock me up. They gonna have to kill me first, and I'll take some of them with me. You know what I mean?"

As Snake was leaving the room, Rommie was dialing Dora's number. He told her to get dressed because they were going to Atlantic City with some friends. He warned her to be ready when he got there.

He was mildly surprised that Tom didn't meet him there. He dismissed it quickly, thinking that he may have stopped somewhere with the young freak. "That damned Tom," he laughed to himself.

He sang a happy song while dressing, he was sure that finally he would pay Michael, Juanita, and Virginia back. He knew that Sonia would be his personal bonus, and when he finished with her he'd turn her out. He glanced at his watch, it was 6:12.

"Good!", as he called Fred, asking him to meet him on the parking lot.

"We can be in A.C. by 9:30, 10:00 with my old freak, Dora."

Snake nodded and walked toward the next room. Suddenly, Rommie started screaming, "Don't shoot me no more! Damned! They done killed me!"

Snake drew his gun. He ran in the room where he saw Rommie glaring down at the floor. "They didn't have to shoot me so much. Who is that bitch?"

Snake whispered, "Rommie, who you talking about?"

Rommie never heard Snake. He continued to gaze at the floor whimpering.

Suddenly, he stopped, looked at Snake with his gun drawn, "You can't kill me. They done already got me. You know what I mean?"

"You all right, Rommie?" the unnerved Snake asked.

"You just do like I told you and stop talking like my mama."

Rommie looked at him sternly and walked out the door without saying anything else.

Meanwhile Chris and Marcus were sitting on the steps talking. Chris was awestruck by the way that Marcus had handled Snake. Realizing that Rommie and Snake would not soon forget, they both agreed that they should stay away from the basketball court until things cooled down.

The boys talked, joked, and played for a couple of hours until remembered that Dora was going to cook for him. It was a little after six when he went home. Both agreed to meet each other after dinner.

Disappointment struck Chris right in the face as he entered his home. The first thing that he noticed was that there were no aroma of cooking food stirring around the place, only the bitter sweet aroma of incense which Dora loved.

Dora met him in the living room where she was hopping toward the front door and trying to put on one of her shoes. When she saw him, she asked him whether or not he had seen Rommie. He answered by asking her when.

With a look of scorn of her face, she retorted, "When? When you came in the house or even better, stupid! Before you walked in here, did you see Rommie in his car outside?"

"No, Dora I didn't see him or his car when I came in", he answered slowly.

Looking at him in order to determine if she should get in his ass, she inquired, "Was that hard, stupid?"

Chris decided not to respond and forced himself to hold back his laughter as she nearly fell a couple of times trying to put the shoe on, while hopping around the living room.

He thought about asking her about the dinner that she had promised him but felt that would only lead to a useless fight. So, he slowly walked into the kitchen and poured himself a soda.

As he was enjoying his drink, he heard the voice of the

dreaded Rommie flattering his mother to death and kissing her making noises of ecstasy.

Chris was frightened as he could hear Rommie asking about him. Then, Rommie asked if he had said anything about him.

Dora totally unaware of and not really caring about the implications of his question merely said, "No."

Rommie asked her to hurry up; so that, they could get to A.C. and win a lot of money.

Dora called Chris to the living room where she told him that she and Rommie were going to Atlantic City as Rommie looked at Chris sheepishly.

He began to lead her out the door when she suddenly stopped and turned to look at Chris. "Shit! He ain't had nothing to eat, Rommie."

Rommie pealed a twenty off of one of his rolls of bills, winked, and placed it on the coffee table. He glared at the boy and started toward the door, this time leaving Dora.

With all of the compassion and motherly love and concern she could muster, she advised him to get something hot and hurried out to catch Rommie.

"Enjoy your damn selves," Chris said dryly to the now empty door.

11. *Tom's Plot*

Chris felt so hurt and disappointed that his mother did not keep her promise about cooking him dinner that he could have just died. He felt the moisture of the tears running down his joyless face. Again, he considered running away, but what good would that do? Or more important, where would he go?

"Someday she is going to be really sorry for this," he thought to himself. A solitary tear flowed down his cheek as he had no idea when that someday would be.

His anguish slowly turned to hunger, but he was determined not to use the twenty. He was just miserable in that house all by himself. He thought about going over to Marcus' to eat dinner, but dismissed that idea as the prospect of going there to bum a meal would have been too embarrassing.

Surveying the refrigerator turned out to be an exercise in futility as there was nothing unfrozen that he wanted.

He slowly walked out of the kitchen to the front door where he sadly watched his neighbors going about their business. He was so very hurt and dismayed that he was beginning to make himself sick with self pity and despair.

The deafening silence in the house was broken by the shrilling sounds of the telephone. He started not to answer it as he just knew that it was some guy trying to get to his mother.

But even that would be better than sitting in the empty house starving to death with nobody to even speak. His heart started to beat a little faster as the telephone rang for the forth time as it was possible that Sonia was calling him.

Suddenly, it became so important for him to answer the telephone that he almost totaled the living room lamp getting to it. All of his despair turned to instant joy when he recognized the voice of his sister.

"Well, Chris, this is the warmest reception that I have ever gotten from a gentleman," she responded to his greeting. "You really must be doing well there with Dora, and I must confess that I am pleased . . . "

Totally overwhelmed by despair and disappoint-ment, Chris began to cry and beg his sister to come get him. He told her about all of the things that had continued to go wrong between him and Dora.

She painfully listened to his account of Dora's obvious neglect and indifference toward her brother, totally understanding and identifying with his plight. As she patiently waited for him to finish, her tears flowed as from a river of dread.

However, somehow she managed to keep him from sensing her anguish and fear for him as she knew first hand that Dora was quite capable of extreme cruelty and willing to inflict a great deal of pain. For both of their sakes, she decided to change the subject by asking him whether or not he had made any friends.

She was happy to know that he and Marcus had begun a friendship, but disappointed that he was infatuated with Sonia.

She kept the later to herself as she knew the girl well enough, she thought, to feel that there was nothing that Chris had that the girl would need or want. Therefore, there was little chance that she would do anything that would really harm him except maybe hurt his young feelings or break his heart.

She was not at all surprised that Dora was now dating Rommie, but warned him to stay as far away from him as possible. She comforted him by telling him that she was working very hard to try to find a way that they could be together.

Before she hung up, she advised then demanded that he take the twenty and buy himself a good meal at the neighborhood carry out.

After talking to her brother, Christine looked around her one-bedroom efficiency very anxiously. She had hoped and prayed that she could somehow be an instant success, but she now was painfully aware of the fact that success came to those who were prepared and paid their dues.

She knew that she would have to work very hard in order to be able to care for herself and Chris. She prayed for her brother's happiness and safety. She prayed that somehow, some way, and someday her mother would see the light and behave like a reasonable human being and responsible mother. She drifted off to sleep softly crying.

Meanwhile Chris considered her advice and decided to go and spend the twenty. Walking into the neighborhood soul fool restaurant, he noticed several video machines. He wanted to play, but there was a crowd of yelling and cursing teenagers playing them as others watched.

The owner was safely behind the security barrier unaware of the boy's presence as he was more interested in the television.

One of the boys spotted the twenty in Chris' hand and instantly decided to take it. Not wanting to take the chance that the boy who was about half his size could somehow fend him off, he whispered to his cronies that he wanted them to watch his back while he robbed the boy.

One of the thugs recognized him from the basket-ball court and told him that he could mess with him if he wanted, but he should get his ass ready for Snake to kick it as the boy was something to Rommie.

The courageous soul grunted, but decided that robbing the kid was not worth risking dealing with Snake for twenty dollars as he knew that Snake had killed a kid for two dollars.

Chris, who was not aware that all of this was going on, finally got the guy's attention and ordered enough to almost spend the entire twenty much to the dismay of the thug.

Also without his knowledge, he had established a reputation that would safeguard him for quite a while, even after, Rommie would have no power to protect him or anyone else.

The hot early evening air was filled with electricity, excitement, and danger! On his way home with his two bags full of food and drink, he was exposed the sights, sounds, and smells that are unique to the inner city.

There were people of all ages aimlessly wondering around looking for something to do. The drug addicts milling around on the corners waiting for their connections.

Young women and men were working the streets looking for tricks. Young couples who seemed to be so very much in love going wherever young lovers go. His ears got tired of the ceaseless wail of emergency vehicles hurriedly going about their missions of mercy.

Police cars speeding up and down the crowded, dirty streets attempting to bring law and order to the chaos. Walking through this island of degradation and despair, the only island of hope and friendliness was his spotting his friend Marcus and the always smiling Mr. Jacque on the bus stop near his home.

He was so happy to see them that he almost dropped his food and drink. His delight was short lived as he was told that they were going across town to hear a close friend, Reverend Michael Govans, preach at a church across town.

He turned down their invitation Tom join them as he felt that he was not dressed well enough. Although they did their best to convince him that his attire was appropriate, he declined the invitation.

He bid them a fond farewell as they boarded the bus and left him standing on the corner. He slowly walked past a young woman who seemed to have been watching him, but he dismissed it as his imagination.

He went to his lonely home to watch television and eat his food. He hungrily ate and drank in his room until he almost made himself ill. Bored he drifted off to sleep.

Chris had no way of knowing that Rommie had left his car on the parking lot as he and Dora had doubled up with another couple. He, also, did not notice the car either to or from the restaurant.

A person that had seen them was Tysia who knew of the infamous Dora and wanted to take the place of the old bitch who was Rommie's main woman despite his lust for young girls.

She was sick and tired of her life as it was with all the hassles. She lived in the next court with her mother, eleven year old brother, and two year old daughter, who was at best a pain in the ass to her.

She had become pregnant at what should have been the young, tender, and innocent age of twelve. She had no way of knowing who had fathered the child as she had been extremely sexually active at that early age.

Because she had herself been a neglected child, she always

seemed to be alone and hungry. Having to take care of herself without any supervision at all, instead of learning the lessons that a young girl should at school and from her parents.

She found that there were numerous males of various ages who were more than happy to spend time, money, and feed her in exchange for sexual favors.

Her pregnancy had been a mystery to her as she had never connected it to sex, although the doctor and the social worker at the clinic each did their very best to explain her pregnancy to her. She never totally comprehended the process.

Although physically advanced for her age, she lacked the intellect, knowledge, and maturity that would have at least helped her to understand what had happened to her.

Her pregnancy had been a rough one as she would not remember or care to get the prenatal care that she needed as she was always too busy or tired to go to the clinic. Therefore she did not diet or exercise properly as she had not taken the pregnancy very seriously.

Because she had very little knowledge in terms of what to expect, she almost delivered while at home. Her contractions were to her a very scary, strange, and painful stomach ache.

Only the intervention of her neighbor who was now the baby's de facto parent prevented her from delivering at home which probably saved the lives of both her and the baby.

The delivery was difficult, and Tysia lost her ability to have other children at what should have been the playful, innocent, tender age of thirteen.

The fact that she could not have any other children was of no big deal to her as sex to her was just something that was done to get what you wanted, nothing more.

Actually, sex did not at that time nor did it now have any really personal satisfaction for her, but it was her way of making it. It was her way of supplementing the welfare checks that she managed to spend usually on herself very quickly.

Her mother was always too busy trying to get her next fix to be too concerned about her except on check day. She in turn did not have a lot of time or love for her daughter who spent most of her young life with a kind neighbor who never had children of her own.

Anyway when she saw Rommie and that old bitch, Dora, climb into the car with the other couple, she was filled with hate and envy for Dora and wished that the old bitch would just somehow get out of the way. Then, maybe she would be Rommie's main woman?

She felt that if she were his main woman, he would take her away from where she was living and make her live with him. Or maybe, he would take her away and put her in her own place.

Whatever he would do with her, she felt would have to be much better than they were for her presently. All she really knew was the fact that she was usually very lonely and unhappy.

Also, at the same time Rommie was leaving for Atlantic City, Tom was sitting in Eric's bar drinking and hoping that his scheme to do away with Rommie was working.

He was extremely nervous as he knew that his chips would be cashed in instantly by the very capable Snake if something were to go wrong, and Rommie would find out that he had plotted against him.

So, he sat and waited and drank and sat and waited and drank to the point that Virginia thought about cutting him off. Since he was Rommie's main man, she decided that she really didn't care if he drank himself to death.

To make matters worse for Tom, an old nemesis of his and

Rommie's lifelong competitor, Goldie strolled in place. As usual, she was accompanied by two very attractive, young women, one on each arm. As usual, she was wearing very tight black leather pants with various large tasteless, gold ornaments around her neck and on her arms and fingers.

A very large woman with very smooth dark skin and blond hair which would have been comical if it were not for the fact that she always seemed to be extremely volatile, needing little or no reason to kick asses, especially if, her potential victim happened to be a man.

She always seemed to have a scowl on her face. Her face which was not that attractive to begin with had a very deep, jagged scare that began under her left eye then back toward her left ear and around her neck. It was her badge from a battle to the death that she had a few years ago when she confronted the late Pickles who had been the big drug lord of the area.

It seemed that the two had disagreed about some money that he claimed that she had owed him. Perhaps sensing that Pickles was getting a bit old and soft, she told him that he would just have to try to take the money out of 'her big, black ass'.

According to those who had witnessed the confrontation, Pickles was at first amused by that fact that this 'stud bitch" was talking trash to him and tried to calm things down by granting her additional time to 'get his money together'.

By this time a large crowd of people, most of whom were afraid of Pickles, had gathered and were anticipating his cutting her throat with his infamous pick-like knife.

Well, she snarled at his benevolent offer and punched him in the face. Before she could react, he slashed her in the face and around the throat with his weapon! She screamed and fell to the ground with a resounding thump!

As a gesture of total contempt and a warning to the

witnesses, he spat on her motionless body and turned to walk away. One of his bodyguards, the very sick and sadistic Snake, wanted to fire a couple of rounds in her head, but Pickles laughed, "There ain't no need in wasting good bullets in 'that stud's . . .', which were his last words on this earth!

Obviously, she had either fainted or passed out when she was cut, because suddenly, she jumped up firing her pistol point blank into the back of the bald head of Pickles!

It appeared that he was dead before his body fell to the ground as his eyes were still open with his brains splattered all over the sidewalk. His loyal cronies, who while he was alive, often put their personal safety in jeopardy for him, where now like vultures picking his lifeless body for what they could get!

Rommie, who was his right-hand man, took the car keys, ran, jumped into Pickles' car, and sped away. He knew that Pickles had a lot of cash and drugs in the car. So, Rommie instantly promoted himself to being 'The Man'.

Anyway, the police had no problem finding out that the almost butchered Goldie had killed Pickles. She ultimately went to trial and received a relatively light sentence of five years. She felt that Tom had 'snitched' on her, but she was not sure enough to deal with him.

Knowing that her allegation was true made him uneasy as he knew that if she ever found out that he was indeed the one, he would be a dead man! He also knew that she would be his executioner, and that he would be helpless against Goldie!

So, there he was worried to death that something would go wrong with his plot to get Rommie out of the way. Now realizing that even if he did take over Rommie's turf, sooner or later Goldie would have to 'off' him.

To add to his anguish, an off duty vice cop, a friend of Eric's, happened to come in the bar and sat right beside him! They talked briefly about a recent baseball game, and the guy drank a beer and departed as Eric was not there.

Goldie, who never missed an opportunity to make Tom's life miserable, ordered and sent him a drink - a bloody Mary! He had all he could stand! He staggered out of the bar with Goldie laughing at him! He went to his car and at there for a moment, trying to gather himself.

Unfortunately, he decided that he wasn't quit high enough to deal with all the pressure that he felt. Although he very rarely got off on the drugs that they sold, tonight was a night that he needed a little something extra.

First, he rolled and smoked a joint while listening to the radio. After smoking and listening to the music, he began to feel aggressive. He reached under his seat and grabbed his pistol as he had decided that he was going to deal with Goldie and get it over with!

He started his engine and moved his car across from where she had parked so that he would be able to ambush her as she got into her car!

"Damned right!" He said to himself as he parked and checked his gun. Needing a little edge to carry out his diabolical plan, he decided to get a little bit higher, so he 'fired himself up' by injecting some cocaine in his arm.

He did not know that the stuff that he had picked up for Rommie was as pure as it was until, . . . well, he felt a strong rush and then, nothing . . . nothing at all. Tom became a statistic, another O.D. victim.

Meanwhile, Goldie, still in the bar having big fun with her girls, was not aware of the fact that she was only hours away from being 'The Man".

12. Sometimes They Come True

Chris was now restlessly sleeping, wishing that he was somewhere, anywhere else! Suddenly, he heard a crashing sound that seemed to be coming from the front room.

At first, he decided to ignore it. But then, his curiosity got the best of him, he decided to investigate. Still a bit groggy, he opened his bedroom door and started toward the front door. From seemingly nowhere a large hairy hand covered his mouth and simultaneously a huge arm lifted him from the floor!

The apartment was filled with men and women with flashlights and drawn weapons. As he struggled, trying to free himself from his aggressor, he realized that the man was a policeman!

He could see the big yellow letters, F.B.I., D.E.A., and POLICE on the backs of the men and women who were searching the place.

Satisfied that the boy was alone after a very rapid but a thorough search of the place, they put away their weapons, and turned off the flashlights. One turned on the lights in the living room, and signaled an "all clear" on their radios!

Naturally, poor Chris was frightened out of his wits as he had no idea what was going on! The officer who had grabbed him was aggressively asking him, "Where is he? Where is he?"

Chris could do nothing but cry. Through his tear soaked eyes he could see the young woman that he had seen watching him on the streets. Somehow, her very presence comforted a little. Then he realized that she reminded him of his Aunt Karen.

She walked over to him smiling. She asked the officer who was now holding him firmly by the shoulders to release him as she knelt in front of Chris. The officer hesitated, however, he released him rapidly when she looked at him sternly saying, "I'm not going to repeat myself!"

Now looking Chris directly in the eyes, she softly asked him if he were okay. Chris shook his head. She apologized to him for being treated so roughly. She explained that they were only doing their job. She asked him if he knew who they were, and he, again, shook his head.

Still smiling, she reached in her pocket producing a picture which she showed him. Although he instantly recognized it as Rommie's picture, he said nothing. "Now I know that an intelligent, handsome young man like you can do more than shake your head," she said with a smile on her face.

Still frightened, he blushed but could not manage to say anything to her. The others began to get restless and warned her that they were just wasting time talking to him. One mentioned that the suspect could return while they were there and the whole operation could get risky.

She gently but firmly reminded them that she was in charge of the operation and suggested that he go outside with the others and stay alert as the suspect could be returning soon.

Then turning again to Chris, she asked him his name to which he replied, 'Chris'.

She asked him a few questions and his answers led her to

believe that he was very contemptuous of the suspect. She, then, told him that it was important that they talk to the man that he knew as Rommie, and assured him that they had no desire to hurt him or anyone else.

Frustrated by the way he had been treated by Dora and at this point not caring that Dora would probably kick his butt for snitching, he confirmed not only that he knew the man, but he began to tell her much, much more than she really wanted to know.

She listened to his verbiage patiently, and he finally told her what his wanted to know. He told her that his mother and Rommie were driving to Atlantic City, she jumped up with a concerned look on her face as she knew Rommie's car was on the parking lot.

Concerned, she asked him if his mother drove. He replied by telling her that his mother did not have a car, and he had never known her to drive.

She gestured to the remaining agent who hurried to the door speaking rapidly on his radio! Whatever he was saying was inaudible to Chris, but it caught his attention.

She wiped the remaining tears from his now very calm face, the lady said to him softly, "I know that what I'm going to ask you will be hard for you to do, but please consider not saying anything about us being here. We consider this man very dangerous, and I'm afraid that he may harm you or your mother if he knew that we were here."

Chris wanted desperately to please this lady and promised not to say anything. Appearing satisfied, she thanked him for answering her questions and assured him that he had done the right thing. She smiled and winked at Chris, then joined her fellow agent who had the door open for her. After another quick smile at Chris, she quietly closed the door behind her.

As they walked away from Chris' home, she looked around the projects recalling aloud that she, too, had grown up in a similar development. Her companion, a white male was surprised. She told him that she hated projects for what they did to people, especially, the kids who had no choice in whom their parents were and where they lived.

Not wanting to comment, he asked her if she thought that the boy would tell that they were there.

Very sadly she replied that she had no way of knowing, because although she was certain that the boy was not very fond of the suspect, he was his mother's boyfriend.

She looked around and said to him that they were watching them.

"Who?"

She smiled knowingly and replied, "Yes, they are watching us!"

She decided that they should wait as she felt that he would be returning soon. Chris was sitting in the living room wondering what to do.

Chris had no way of knowing when his mother and Rommie would be returning from Atlantic City. Rommie had decided that he needed to be in town that evening and was annoyed with himself for even suggesting going anywhere.

He had been wry of the business that he had chosen, and extremely anxious and distrustful of the people that he had to deal with on a daily basis.

He was tired of having to watch everybody all the time and had devised a way that he could keep on making money without all the hassles that he was now facing.

Underneath his cool, daring exterior and deep in his cold calculating heart, he was deathly afraid of the sadistic, homicidal Snake. He knew that Snake loved inflicting hurt, pain, and grief without provocation.

However, he was more concerned with Tom who was much better with calculating the profits, making deals, and the total business than he could ever be. How long would Tom be satisfied to be number two? The constant and lingering fear of his was an allegiance between Snake and Tom.

They could rip him off, wipe him out, and dump him in a dirty, filthy dumpster somewhere! Rommie knew that if it did happen to him, nobody would even care or even miss him.

Business, he knew, would go on without him as it did when Pickles got his, and that scared him almost to death! He would give anything for a good night's sleep without having to worry about getting murdered.

He had put together a plan which would have given him two options. The first was to get his hands on enough cash to open a bar, a real nightclub. He could get himself some women, fix up a joint that had failed and make him a good living.

The second option was to get his hands on some serious cash and blow town forever! Getting himself a place somewhere and do any damned thing that he wanted, when he wanted, and how he wanted would be the perfect life for him!

He finally choose the bar business, because he truly felt that he had no place else to go. His plan was so clever, so foolproof that his only regret was that he did not think of it sooner. Damned if he was going to end like Pickles and the countless forgotten ones that came before him.

Tom always picked up the stuff. He and the girls would step on it enough to make it go a long, long way with the chumps and the kids who did not know about quality.

Now, this time, tonight, Rommie had arranged to get some really pure cocaine that he was going to sell to some independent dealers at a huge profit, and still have enough for the chumps.

He planned to use the money from the kids and chumps to give most of it to Tom and Snake so that, they could take over. He would use his money to open his nightclub. He would be done with Tom, Snake, and all them other fools.

Rommie knew that once Goldie found out that they not he was in charge that she would fire their asses up and take over everything which would be fine with him because he knew that his sister would not bother him.

The key to his plan was not to let Tom know that the cocaine that he was picking up was pure. He had paid the people some up front money; so that, the money that Tom would give them would be the balance. That way Tom would not get suspicious. Because Rommie did not want anything to go wrong, it was imperative that he made sure that he was around so that the drugs would be cut and distributed properly.

When he got in the car with his friend, Fred, his link to the nightclub that he wanted to buy, he was confronted by their excitement to go to Atlantic City. Very calmly, he told them that he really could not go to A.C. because he had to be in town very early in the morning.

He offered to treat everyone to dinner at one of the city's newest and finest restaurants. As disappointed as they were about going to Atlantic City, the prospect of going to the restaurant with Rommie treating was more than an acceptable alternative.

As Fred drove toward the restaurant, without any apparent malice in mind, he said to his date, Glenda, "Well, now you don't have to come up with an excuse not to go to work tomorrow." Both laughed.

Not to be outdone, Dora snuggled up to the now pensive

Rommie and proudly proclaimed that she did not have to work for anybody as her baby, Rommie, gave her everything that she needed. She went on to add that she had never and would never work for nobody, because a good woman did not need to work.

Glenda could not believe her ears! Fred pretended not to hear her, and Rommie, who was obviously absorbed in his thoughts, did not even hear Dora's statement.

Dora's statement infuriated and disgusted the proud, hardworking, and independent Glenda to the extent that she quietly asked Fred to take her home. Fred, whose only motive for being with the infamous Rommie, was to close the bar deal for which he would make a huge profit, asked her to do stay for his sake.

She smiled advising him that he owed her a big one. Relieved, he turned up the volume on the radio to prevent further conversation between the two women.

Fred felt that perhaps his acquaintance was going through some sort of drug withdrawal as he could see that the man was beginning to perspire profusely although it was cool inside the car.

"Damn!," he thought, "I sure as hell don't need for this fool to overdose in my car!" He started to say something, but he decided not to as he knew that he would be risking his relationship with Glenda.

Finally they arrived at the restaurant where Fred glided his car through the driveway. The attendant opened the women's doors, an action that really impressed culturally starved Dora. She flirted with him with a seductive gesture.

Glenda glared at her, and the attendant ignored it. The attendant with very quick, crisp steps was on the other side of the car opening Fred and Rommie's doors simultaneously.

As Fred was about to get out, he saw the startled attendant take a quick step backwards. Rommie who had been in a trance like state reached for his gun when the door was suddenly opened.

Rommie slowly covered his gun with his jacket and smiled at the guy. The attendant regained his composure, waited for Rommie to get out and closed his door. Rommie gave the man a twenty-dollar tip and walked toward the women. Neither of the women saw this occur as it happened so quickly! The very embarrassed Fred followed the visibly shaken Rommie as the attendant sped away with the car.

The snobbish maitre d'hotel could not for the life of himself locate a table for the four of them until Rommie slide him a very large tip. As the maitre d'hotel lead them to their table, his facial expressions and gestures suggested that he was totally under-whelmed with Dora's attire which he would have described as late evening "slut."

The otherwise Black feminist Glenda got a fiendish thrill out of his actions. The maitre d'hotel attempted to sit them at a table by the kitchen out of the way of the more acceptable clientele, but much to his disgust, Rommie quickly objected and was given a prime seating. Dora's attire became the immediate topic of conversation of the patrons.

Dora misinterpreted the glares that she was getting as genuine admiration. Glenda and Fred were embarrassed for her, they hoped that no one was there who would recognize them.

After they ordered their drinks which they all needed desperately, the distressed Rommie began to share his concern by saying to them, "Any of you ever have a sort of dream while you were wide awake?"

Fred and Dora looked surprised, while Glenda had by now

prepared herself to not to be surprised by anything that Rommie and Dora might say or do.

"Look!" he said in an excited but low tone, "I keep seeing myself getting shot! I mean like in one of those movies!"

The ever sensitive Dora laughed, Fred lowered his head, and Glenda was at this point convinced that she was dining with maniacs.

"Seriously," he protested, "Sitting in your car, I could see myself getting shot and falling on my face! Man, it seemed so real! I could see all these people looking down at me!"

"Maybe, Rommie, it was something that you ate, drank, or ingested in some other way," Glenda suggested.

He insisted that he hadn't had anything and seemed to be annoyed that she did not believe him. Fred intervened by suggesting that maybe he had been under much pressure and perhaps all he needed was a little rest.

Dora was posing for and flirting with an older patron dressed in a flamboyant dinner jacket who was gazing at her lustily much to the disgust of his obviously younger date.

The waiter brought the drinks, and the still shaken Rommie gulped his down and ordered another.

"And I always see this young woman standing over me with a blue jacket and a smoking gun in her hand!", Rommie continued.

Fred laughed and suggested that maybe it was merely a case of conscience that was bothering him. He continued by suggesting that Rommie buy Dora a little gift and his little problem would go away.

Rommie responded by suggesting dryly that maybe he should spend a little more time at home with his wife.

"Wife!," Glenda laughed, "Boyfriend, if your wife is . . . wife! ..Look, if you spent your time with your wife instead of with this . . . uh, ladies like Dora maybe you would not be having them damned daydreams, or nightmares or whatever in the hell you are having."

Fortunately, Dora missed her comments as she was now distracted by an evening gown and wondered aloud how she would look in it. She suggested that she and Glenda go shopping one day. Glenda laughed.

They finally ordered, and Fred took advantage of the moment to discuss the bar deal with Rommie. Fred asked Rommie whether his wife would consent to having her name on the license, reasoning that it would make the transaction easier.

Dora, who was now paying attention, said that she not his wife should be on the license as she was more wife to him than his wife.

"That's not a great idea as you have no visible means of support and the board may rightfully wonder where you got the money, Dora.", Glenda replied.

"What the hell do you know about a damned bar? You own one? Or are you just jealous that you don't have a man that would put a bar in your name with your funny-looking self!"

Fred impatiently responded for Glenda by advising Dora that besides Glenda being his best friend, she was also his lawyer. Rhetorically, he asked her if she had ever heard of the law firm of Sander, Bowman, and Brooks.

He went on to proudly say that she, the Bowman in the firm, was the founding partner. He continued by telling her that getting Rommie in the bar business was going to be difficult at best, and that if anyone could pull it off, Glenda could.

As annoying as the evening had been, he wondered if dealing with Rommie was worth all of the nonsense.

"I guess that if I was a funny looking, skinny, no dressing

bitch like her, I'd be a damned lawyer or something myself!", the classless Dora retorted.

Rommie laughed because he could not even imagine Dora being anything but what she was!

Glenda had enough and got up from her seat and walked toward the door. Fred jumped up to follow her, but Rommie grabbed him by the arm protesting that they needed to finish talking business.

Fred at this point realized that dealing with Rommie had been a mistake on his part and that his greed was jeopardizing his relationship with Glenda, who meant a lot to him.

With this in mind, he said very sternly to Rommie, "Let's consider the deal dead and please, sir, don't ever call me again for any reason!"

As he snatched away from Rommie, he thanked him for the dinner opportunity. Rommie sadly watched what he thought was his only real chance for peace and longevity walk out the door.

Dora realizing that their dinner companions were not returning, took full advantage of the situation by sampling all of the meals. Rommie again could see his demise which frightened him more and more as the scene became more and more graphic.

Still, there was the young attractive woman with the gun smoking. He for some reason heard her calling, no yelling his name. She did not yell Rommie, but his complete name.

The last time that he had heard his complete name was in court. Rommie heard it again, but this time it was so loud that he was sure that everybody heard it!   Rommie leaned back in his chair watching Dora greedily gulping down as much of the food as she could. As he watched her, for some reason he started remembering the happy days of his youth, hanging out with his two buddies Mike and Jacque.

Then he thought about his mother who had died when he was about eighteen. He wondered if she somehow knew how he had turned out.

Rommie, at that point, faced the fact that he was nothing more than a small time thug and eventually they were going to kill him. He suddenly realized that all he had ever been was a chump. Rommie was so upset that he almost cried.

He was going to play the hand out tonight, then put as much distance between himself and this town as he possibly could! But the first thing that he was going to do was to take this greedy bitch home and work some of that food off her. This would be the last time he'd see the worthless whore!

After Dora had her fill, Rommie paid the sizable check and requested doggie bags for the remaining food much of which was untouched. The waiter more than satisfied with his gratuity, diplomatically suggested that he would arrange for a cab for them.

Moments later, he came back to them to advise them that their cab was waiting. As they were leaving, the waiter asked them to return when possible. After they had departed, he told the some inquisitive ones that she was a rock star and quietly laughed to himself.

"Sure is funny that the classless get respect with fame!", he mused to himself.   Rommie was again uneasy as he rode in the cab with Dora. It seemed that everybody and everything was watching him. Suddenly, he began laughing, which startled Dora, and he announced that they were going to have a private party!

He ordered the cab driver to stop at a liquor store where he bought a very expensive bottle of cognac and a bottle of the scotch that Dora liked.

For some reason he felt the need to party! And party he was going to do until he had to go and deal with his business. He thought about talking her to his place but decided against it as she might try to kill herself snorting his private stock of almost pure coke.

Dora said something stupid which caused him to laugh and completely change his mood. When they arrived at Dora's even the sight of the kid did not bother him. He could never figure out his reason for disliking Chris but did, and that was that.

The now horny pair was very temporarily annoyed by Chris who was trying to tell them something about some woman. Finally, Dora went to the kitchen to get some glasses. While she was in there, she noticed some telephone workers outside her yard, but she promptly dismissed it after she checked her telephone.

She returned to the living room with the glasses and turned on the stereo. All was well until Rommie reminded her that he had to have his sniffer to drink his cognac.

Undaunted, she sang her way back to the kitchen. Again she noticed the telephone people, but there were more of them than before. Again she dismissed it!

Returning to the living room, she was greeted by a big, long, deep kiss from the now very horny Rommie. After a little dancing and fore play, she temptingly asked him to have a drink while she freshened up and put on the short, red silk nightie with the matching silk robe that he loved to see her wear.

Filled with anticipation, he walked over to the stereo and selected an old album featuring the late Otis Redding. He sang his favorite song, ` Sitting on the Dock of the Bay ' along with the album.

Suddenly, he heard his name just as he had in his

premonitions! At first he thought that he was having another one, but very clearly from outside he heard a female voice ordering him to come out with his hands over his head!

Dora, who was in the shower, did not hear the voice. Chris heard it and jumped under the bed! Sonia heard it, but did not react immediately as she was having a high volume discussion with Roy. The neighbors heard it, and many started heading toward the excitement anticipating a shooting!

All of the officers were strategically positioned, surrounding Dora's home, with their weapons drawn!

The woman's voice caused Rommie to panic; it was the same one that he had been hearing all day!

Dora, who had completed her shower, was primping to the tune of some very loud music and was still not aware of the potential danger to Rommie!

Rommie lifted the bottle to his shaking lips and swallowed so deeply that he choked! He composed himself and looked in the mirror to make sure that he was looking good! Somehow, that was important to him!

"Jerome David Johnson, this is your last warning! I have in my possession a federal warrant for your arrest! I am therefore ordering you to come out with your hands above your head!"

The very thought of a woman ordering him to surrender was much too much for the very proud womanizer Rommie to stand! Women just did not talk to him that way!

Easing toward the door, he caught a glimpse of the woman in a partial crouch. She was just left of the walkway. Instantly, he put together a plan!

He guessed that there would be two to four of them out there. So, he'd stick his head out to see where they where, fire a shot at her then pretend to surrender. Then, he would dive to the ground and fire up the rest of them! They did not know who hell he was! No bitch talked to him that way!

He took another gulp of his cognac, threw it to the floor, and opened the door to fire a couple of rounds! Unfortunately for Rommie, he threw the bottle straight down and slipped as he opened the door!

The first shot that he fired went above the heads of the agents through Virginia's window not far from where Sonia was talking on the telephone. From several advantage points, the various agents opened up a lethal barrage of fire on Rommie!

His body slammed back into the door frame, and his now lifeless body fell face forward on the sidewalk. On his way to the ground, he fired a shot posthumously, wounding an officer. The female agent, who was closest to his body, kicked his gun from his now lifeless, worthless body!

Rommie's premonition had come true!

13. *Not Me!*

Special agent Dyanne Hopper stood over Rommie's body doing her best not to cry. She was not grieving for Rommie, but for the fact that another Black man had to be killed like a rabid dog! She knew too well that there were many who would argue that he and others like he had no other viable alternatives, because they were black, poor, uneducated, and hopeless.

Dyanne could not and would never accept that as fact as no one, she felt, was more of an unlikely candidate for becoming a special agent with the F.B.I. than she.

She was not an ordinary special agent, but one in charge of planning and implementing several sensitive and dangerous operations. She was the product of a poor, very poor single mother whose husband, her father, had been killed in a nickel and dime crap game.

She knew that her mother had done all of the dirty jobs that nobody else would do to raise her and her five sisters and brothers.

She could never remember, as a child, having enough to eat or clothing to keep her frail body warm in the winter. But they were taught pride, dignity, and a hard work ethic that carried them through the hard times.

This and a great belief in God Almighty prevented her and

the rest of the family from becoming victims of the ghetto. So, don't dare say to Dyanne that they can't help themselves, because she saw herself as living proof that they or anybody could do anything that they wanted to do, if only they were willing to work at it!

Dora heard the loud, resounding gunfire while in her bedroom. She knew that Rommie was in there being killed either by the police or some ambitious dude wanting to be "the man." She hoped and prayed that it was the police, because she knew that sometimes when "the man" got hit everybody around him got hit!

Then, she smiled a smile of relief as she remembered all of the telephone workers that were outside and now knew without a doubt that they were the police!

She slowly walked onto the living room and peeped out the window at all the police and spectators. The female agent standing over Rommie caught her attention, and for some reason, the woman fascinated her. She just could not keep her eyes off of her. There was something about the woman that fascinated her.

Meanwhile Chris crawled from under his bed and cautiously walked to the living room where he saw Dora looking out the window. He just stood there so as not to disturb the unpredictable Dora. However, the fact that she was calmly gazing out the window calmed his fears that he and his mother would be all shot up.

Sonia, who had been frightened out of her wits by the bullet's bursting her kitchen window and whizzing by her, had stopped screaming. She picked up the now dead telephone that she had dropped and cursed she realized that Roy had hung up!

As she was cursing him for hanging up the telephone, he was

on a dead run toward her! He was very afraid that something had happened to her.

She was too through with Roy as she stood on her steps watching. She could see Rommie stretched out in front of Dora's house with a woman with the initials F.B.I. on the back of her blue jacket, standing over him with a pistol in her hand.

She knew that he was dead as she saw many in the crowd shake their heads as they looked at him on the ground.

The paramedics, who had arrived at the scene, checked for his nonexistent vital signs and placed a blanket over his torso and head. The others were attending the wounded officer. Sonia observed all of this with keen interest as many of the men (police, F.B.I. agents, and paramedics) were cute.

She hardly even noticed or paid much attention to the near panicked, exhausted Roy who had run the entire considerable distance to be at her side.

He was only mildly interested in the chaos surrounding them. His only interest was Sonia. After several futile attempts to talk to her, he once, twice, three times attempted to leave.

Remembering that Rommie had some kind of relationship with her, he conveyed his condolences thinking that she was remorseful because of the demise of Rommie.

She looked at him sharply responding, "He used to be my mother's boyfriend. He dead not me!"

As she turned away from him to continue to watch all the exciting happenings, he gently grabbed her arm. She immediately snatched away proclaiming aggressively and loudly that he did not own her!

Having had enough, he slowly walked away, completely and totally unnoticed by Sonia. He cursed himself and promised himself that he would never ever be that girl's fool again.

Again, he realized that he had no business messing with that child. Again, he knew that he could not wait to feel her touch.

Tysia had heard the shots and had seen people running around the corner, while sitting on her steps with some guy. Whatever was going on was a lot more exciting than the broke dude who was worrying her to death.

Much to his surprise, she jumped up and ran around the corner to see what was happening. She arrived on the scene about the same time that the paramedics arrived and caught a glimpse of Rommie as the paramedic was covering his face.

She began to moan as she thought that her only real chance to leave the projects was sprawled out on the walkway dead. Damned him! She wept, feeling totally helpless and hopeless.

At this point and time, there was very little emotion as the demise of Rommie was very predictable, expected, and dismissed as business as usual in the drug trade.

Many were even predicting possible successors to Rommie! Yeah, he was just another one biting the dust!

Dora's attention was now drawn to the television crew who had arrived moments after the ambulances. Instantly she decided that she needed to be on the late news. Very quickly she turned to the mirror to check herself out. She either ignored or overlooked Chris who was standing in the entrance of the living room.

Chris was horrified as he realized that she was going outside in that red, revealing outfit she was wearing. As he watched, paralyzed, she took a final assessment of herself in the mirror and walked deliberately and quickly out of her door.

He stood there motionless as a few agents hurried past him. As Dora stormed out of the door, Dyanne instinctively spun with her pistol aimed at Dora! The agents, who had come through the house, stood behind Dora with their weapons also drawn. The two women stood glaring at each other for a moment.

Dora's expression turned to shear horror, but quickly turned to a scowl as the female holstered her weapon. She nodded to one of the male agents who immediately began to attempt interviewing the irrepressible Dora.

By this time, Dora had begun quickly walking towards the television crew. She stepped over Rommie's body with an air of detachment, as if he were some type of insignificant curiosity.

Many, who witnessed her display of total disrespect and disdain for the deceased, including Dyanne were visibly disgusted with her, while Sonia admired her. The now trailing agent lost a couple of steps as he walked around the body.

"Dat her man?", a disbelieving voice bellowed from the crowd.

"As long as he was giving her money!," laughed another.

The blinking lights from the emergency vehicles illuminated the scantily clad Dora giving her the appearance of a stripper and her walkway the ambience of a brothel.

There was a young man whose ghetto blaster provided the loud, rhythmic music that Dora used to strut her stuff. A woman in the crowd made the youngster cut the music off proclaiming "...I didn't much care for what he done around here, but everybody should respect the dead!

"Others in the crowd agreed that she should be respectful. An older woman proclaimed that if it were not for hussies like that Dora there would not be as many poor lost souls like Rommie. Others more or less echoed her sentiments, and none of what was being said escaped Dora's hearing.

Indignation, hate, and disgust for Dora seemed to be the prevailing sentiment of the crowd who were venting their all to real frustrations for the violence in their community and directing it at her.

Dora had unwittingly made herself the tangible symbol of all that they hated and despised in their community.

As she neared the television crew, a young man shouted, "Hey, Dora! You sure is looking good, baby! I got this five, if you wanna do a little something, something!"

Dora spun and uttered a barrage of obscenities directed at him and the rest of the crowd that was so vile that it angered just about everybody in hearing range!

A younger woman, Marlene, had to be restrained as she was so angry that she wanted to kick Dora "..in her whore ass!"

With every once of strength in her being, frantically she attempted to get her hands on Dora, who she never liked anyway, screaming, "You ain't going to disrespect my mother and children out here ! You ain't nothing but a disgrace out here in front of everybody dressed like that ! If you had any damned sense or self respect about you, you'd carry yourself in the house ! Nobody wants to see your naked ass!"

Marlene's mother, who too, lived in the same complex, grabbed her daughter and convinced her that Dora was not worth getting in trouble for hurting. She reasoned, "What about your children, child?"

"Yeah, I ain't got to do nothing to that fool! They got one of them body bags for her yellow ass, too!", Marlene responded and walked away with her five young children.

However, another woman in the crowd took up where she left off, "Why don't I just wax this bitch! I ain't got shit anyway and I don't like her any damned way! Ain't nobody as cute as that yellow bitch thinks she is!"

Dora, totally understanding that she was in clear and immediate danger, decided to go back into her house. Totally infuriated, she almost knocked Chris down as he was rushing towards her with a coat to cover her body. He was very hurt and embarrassed by the way his mother was dressed. Much to his surprise, she seemed to be glad that he had met her with it.

She put it over her shoulders and said to him softly, "Chris sometimes I don't even believe some of the shit I do myself."

She sounded so very remorseful that Chris felt that maybe now he would have a real mother for a change. He smiled to himself as they slowly walked into their home with her arm around his shoulder and with the crowd's blessings!

Once indoors, his hope and desire for a more caring mother seemingly bit the dust as she went straight to her room to get dressed announcing to no one in particular that she felt the need to go out and party.

"After all!", she assured herself, while pouring herself a drink, "It's Rommie's dumb ass that's out there dead, not me!"

Chris was totally stunned!

Jacque and Marcus had returned and learned of the demise of Rommie. Seeing the blanket covered body, they paused and prayed for Rommie's soul before going into their home.

Once inside, Jacque hugged Marcus and rushed to his room and looked out of the window at Rommie's body. He was so hurt that he was trembling as the tears flowed down his face.

While standing there he saw the irrepressible Dora, who was dressed to party, appear at her front door. He sadly watched her stop at the top of her steps and look down at Rommie's body.

Sadness filled his heart as he watched her laugh aloud and sashay up the now quieter walkway, those who remained, singing and swaying happily.

14. *"Here's a Quarter"*

Watching those crazy people laughing, joking, jeering, laying abuse, and grief on Dora had not been easy for Sonia.

"After all," she reasoned to herself silently, "the only reason that they're doing it is because they're jealous because Dora has the nerve to do just what she wants!"

Sonia wished that she could have said or did something to help, but she knew that there was nothing that she could do.

Even her next door neighbor, Miss Norma, approached her mumbling. " that . . . the 'ho should move the hell away from there! Maybe then, us decent people could walked around here without being scared of getting shot in the ass 'cause of Dora's thug-assed boyfriends!"

Sonia had merely responded to her with a wan smile. Now that all the excitement was over and the cute men were gone, Sonia decided to go in the house.

With all the excitement, cute men, and Dora, she had all but forgotten about Roy. But now she sure felt like being hugged and kissed, maybe do a little something before Virginia got home!

As she dialed his telephone number, she wondered how long it would take her to persuade him to return as she felt that he had to be crazy to leave her.

However, it didn't matter, because he didn't answer his

telephone. She was furious! Damn him! She was going to fix him! Maybe, never speak to him again! Who the hell did he think, he was leaving her? More important, where the hell could he be?

She turned off the lights and slowly walked up the stairs to her room, where she discussed the night's excitement with her dolls. Her dolls regretted that they had missed everything, especially the cute men!

Unanimously, they agreed that Roy was wrong for leaving, and that he was probably with some other girl somewhere kissing, hugging, making love someplace.

They agreed that another female could have been only reason for leaving her, and that he most certainly had to be taught a lesson.

While they were pondering Sonia's revenge, Sonia decided that she could call her mother to tell her about Rommie. Sonia really didn't care one way or another, but she didn't want Virginia to come home, see the broken window and blame her, asking a whole lot of stupid questions.

Also, she felt that it would be big fun to hear her mother freak out on the telephone as she was being told about Rommie getting himself killed and shit!

She took her favorite doll with her mother's room so that, the doll could hear Virginia making a fool out of herself because Rommie got himself killed.

Giggling, Sonia dialed the telephone, and it rang and rang and rang. Finally Sonia realized nobody was going to answer it, and Sonia became so very annoyed that Virginia nor anyone else answered that she slammed the receiver down.

Because Sonia's doll seemed amused by her reaction to the telephone not being answered, she threw it with enough intensity and force that its head flew off as it slammed against the wall!

"Serves you right!", Sonia screamed at it as it helplessly laid on the floor wondering why it had been treated so very badly. After all, the whole thing had been Sonia's idea! Sensing the doll's feelings, Sonia picked up its body and threw it into the hallway!

Too through, she snatched up the telephone and dialed Roy's number again, and again he didn't answer which confirmed to her that he was with some old bitch!

She was so furious that she screamed and, with tears in her eyes, she picked up the head of her doll and threw it into the hallway. Still crying she ran downstairs to the kitchen and poured herself a big drink so that, she could get herself together.

Meanwhile, down at the club excitement, and merriment filled the air, it was Eric's Amateur Night. Yes, the joint was really jumping as they were all being treated by a stellar performance by a very talented young lady and her four-piece band, which had the sound of a much larger group.

She opened her show with an upbeat version of *Midnight Train to Georgia* that caused feet to pat, voices to join in, and many including Eric and Virginia to dance with the joyous spontaneity of a feasible!

Then she captivated the audience with a real funky version of *Going to Chicago* which led many to believe that Eric had a real winner on his hands.

The jubilant chaos had prevented Virginia, Eric or anyone else from hearing the telephone as the entertainers had the complete attention, hearts, and souls of all who were there. Even the usually stoic Goldie was laughing, singing, and dancing with her girls.

She ended the performance by soulfully and skillfully

seducing the audience with a very emotional version of *Wildflower* which was so well arranged that many found tears freely flowing from their eyes.

As she finished the accolades from the small crowd was deafening, and only a promise from Eric that they would be returning after a brief break restored order to the emotionally charged crowd.

As they were leaving the band area, Dora made her entrance which was an event to many who thought she was "all that." Dora, if nothing else, had the type of personal presence that made it seem that she exploded into a room. She really knew how to make her presence felt!

As Virginia was going back behind the bar, she spotted Dora which made her instantly sick to the stomach.

Sensing Virginia's discomfort helped Dora feel great. That aside, Dora surveyed the club for a sponsor, and she saw Goldie. Slowly Dora walked toward Goldie gambling that she could replace the two that were with her or get some free drinks.

As she neared the table, the youngest of the girls, Lisa, became anxious as she knew that Goldie had a thing for Dora. The timid expression on her face was all that Dora needed to know that she could very easily get to Goldie who liked nothing more than for women to rival each other for her very special attention and gratification. She was especially attracted to women that were aggressive, and Dora knew it.

Loving the game, Dora snaked her way behind the anxious one and began to speak to Goldie very softly. Goldie was more than happy to see Dora come to her and was just loving the hurt puppy expression on Lisa's face.

Goldie savored the situation for a moment, than with lightning fast decisiveness ordered Lisa to give Dora her seat which was to Lisa liked being stabbed in the heart.

However, she relinquished her seat rapidly as she knew that the volatile Goldie was certainly not in the habit of repeating herself.

To add an insult to injury, Goldie ordered Lisa to go to the bar to get drinks for the party. As if an after thought, told her to get one for herself.

Lisa then felt that she had been reduced from a lover to a waitress. She also knew that some day, some way that she had to ". . . kick Dora's ass for doing that shit to her! Just wait bitch!", she thought to herself as she went to the bar.

Dora watched her and knew that somehow she would have to pay, but that would be then and all she was interested in was now. She felt rather comfortable as she watched Goldie mentally undressing her.

The other female was so high that it seemed that she didn't even notice what had happened.

"I got some bad news for you Goldie," Dora began slowly. Your brother, Rommie, done got his self killed tonight by 5-0 in front of my house."

Goldie took the cigarette out of the mouth of the other female and puffed on it a couple of times without taking her eyes off Dora.

Goldie picked up her drink and sipped it, again without taking her eyes off Dora. Dora's confidence took a dive as she now felt that she had made a very big mistake by telling Goldie about Rommie.

She didn't know what to do as her every instinct strongly suggested that she should get the hell away from there as fast as possible. But she stayed put.

Still gazing at Dora, Goldie slowly slid her hand in her pocket which seemed to confirm Dora's fear that she had made a fatal mistake.

"Damn!," she lamented silently, "this is one time that I really should have kept my big mouth shut. This crazy bitch might do any damn thing! Where the hell is that Lisa with my drink?"

Dora could see the shiny object in Goldie's hand as it swiftly shot out of her pocket. She just knew that it was either a small knife and maybe a gun. She gasped!

As Goldie now smiling said to her, "Here's a quarter, go call somebody that gives a damn! I sure as hell don't!"

As the thrown quarter handed on the floor, Dora jumped up running toward the rest room as she was sure that she was certainly going to wet her pants.

Goldie thought that Dora had run away, because she was grieving the death of Rommie. She sat there pondering her next move. She decided to go to the restroom to confront Dora, never even considering the possibility that she had scared Dora half to death.

Meanwhile, Sonia along with being lonely and angry had a few drinks felt that the whole world was against her and wanted desperately to hurt something.

She called the club, but this time the line was busy, busy. Damn! She had called Roy time and time again without Roy answering the telephone.

If there had been any doubt in her mind that he was with another female before, certainly the mere fact that he was not at home confirmed her every suspicion. Looking out of the window, she spotted the pathetic, solitary figure of Chris standing on his steps gazing into the sky.

Her first impulse was to open the door and scream something real mean to his sad looking butt, but before she opened the door she had a much better idea. With a diabolical smile on her face she dialed his phone number and chuckled loudly as she watched him run into the house to answer the telephone.

Anxiously Chris answered the telephone, "Hello, hello, who is this?" Remembering the events of earlier in the evening, he became frightened, "...uh, hello? Is anybody there? "

Finally, Sonia, controlling her laughter responded, began with a very soft babyish, "Hi, Chris, it's me. How are you doing, baby doll?"

Genuinely surprised, Chris answered softly, "Sonia?"

"Yes, it's your Sonia. I was sitting here thinking about you being home all alone after all the stuff that happened today. You are alone, I mean, you don't have some pretty girl over there keeping you company do you?"

Chris naively assured her that he was quite alone, and after being asked, assured her that he was not expecting anyone.

Turning on the charm, she told him that she was very lonely, too. She wanted some company like him. She laid in on thick by telling him that there was a bullet hole in her window which scared her, and she needed a strong man like him to be with her as she was still afraid. She pleaded to him to come over and hold her for a little while; so that, she would not be so afraid.

Feeling a surge of masculine ego, he agreed that she should not be alone if she were frightened, and that he would be happy to come over to comfort her, if he could.

15. *Joy and Pain*

Sonia greeted Chris with a big smile, led him to the couch and turned on the stereo. The station featured a late-night for lover's only format. She loved the way Chris sat watching her every move. She blew him a little kiss and asked him to wait for a moment so that, she could get them a little something to drink. Chris agreed as needed a little time to figure out his next move.

Seductively, she slowly ran her right hand around the front of her neck, then under the left strap of the nightie causing it to fall on her arm, exposing her left breast. Confident that move greatly affected Chris, she provocatively blew him another kiss as she went to the kitchen.

While she was gone the disc jockey, a really sexy sounding female, played a record by a guy proclaiming that he was going to make love all night long, and how good he was going to make the woman feel.

The female, calling it mood music, urged everyone "*to . . . hold somebody, to kiss somebody, and if you can't be with the one that you love, loves, love the one that you are with.*"

She added a few moans and groans to be sure that her audience got the message. Now Chris was burning with desire. The very idea of making love to Sonia was exactly what he had in mind. Although, he only had a vague idea of how to get started or exactly what to do, but he damned sure going to give it his very best shot!

Chris decided that when she got back he would just grab her and start kissing, hugging, and feeling! After all, she did invite him. By the way she was dressed, he'd be a punk or something if he didn't make love to her ' . . . all night long'!

He heard the click of the kitchen light being turned off, now. There were only soft shadows in the room. The reappearance of Sonia caused his very heart to flutter as both of her straps were now down totally exposing her upper body. Although it was fairly dark, he could see that the nightie was the only thing that she was wearing.

So overwhelmed with the sight of her hot body, he hardly noticed the two drinks that she had in her hands. He accepted the one offered to him and gulped it down. Well, he had intended on gulping it down, however, he didn't know that the drink was about two-thirds booze with ice and ". . . just enough soda to give it a little personality " as Virginia would say.

Being a thirteen-year-old nondrinker, his system was not quite ready for alcohol. Much to his chagrin, he spit the drink all over Sonia. Sonia looked at him with an expression that he could not comprehend, and he started to get up to find something to wipe the stuff off her and get the hell out of there.

Now he knew for sure that he was way over his head dealing with Sonia. All he wanted to do was to leave, and the sooner the better.

Much to his surprise, Sonia began laughing uncontrollably to the point of tears. He stood there dumbfounded, but soon he began to laugh as her laughter was so very infectious. Still laughing she pulled him back down of the couch and stopped long enough to kiss him.

This time he had caught on to tongue kissing which sent shock waves of ecstasy through his virgin body. Breathlessly she gently pushed him away and playfully informed him that he would have to lick the drink off her.

She firmly grabbed his head and directed it to her neck where he obediently began to gently lick the drink off her very smooth and desirable neck.

She pulled him on top of her, and started to demand that he suck her neck, harder and harder! The room was filled with sounds of animal lust as he continued to comply with her demands.

Just as he felt that he had this lovemaking thing all figured out, she started hitting, pushing and screaming at him angrily.

"Get the hell off me, fool! You better get of me before I kick your ass, Nigger!"

It took him a few moments to comprehend what she was doing and found himself on the floor looking up at her.

Seemingly calmer, she told him that he was a little too fast for her. She asked him to wait while she went upstairs to get some protection.

In total awe, he watched her run up the stairs. Anxiously he waited for her return. He began to believe that he was going to make love all night long.

Sonia went directly to the bathroom, turned on the light and looked in the mirror. There they were! On her neck she had three big passion marks.

"That will fix Mr. Roy's ass . . .", she said with a snarl. "Yeah, this will teach him to leave me all by myself."

Totally satisfied, she walked to her room, took of the nightie, and put on a pair of jeans, and her own pajama top. She watched herself button it up completely while gloating over being so smart. She calmly walked downstairs to where Chris was waiting for her.

Chris was surprised to see that she had changed her clothes. But before he could approach her, she walked to the door and opened it.

"Time for you to get your young ass outta here."

He could not believe his ears and tried to grab and kiss her to get that love making thing started again. She expertly ducked him for a couple of times, then she grabbed him and with all of the benevolence she could muster, kissed him on the cheek. Feeling that she really wanted him to stay, he grabbed and tried to get aggressive.

Without the slightest hesitation, she smacked him in the face and angrily told him "get the hell out!" Sheepishly, he apologized and asked her if he could leave by the back door. She responded that she really didn't give a damned if he flew out of the damned window.

As he backed his way toward the front door, she grabbed him by his shirt and told him that if he ever told anybody that he was there she was going to come over to his house, drag his young ass out of the house, and kick it all up and down the court! As he hurried out of the door, she slammed it almost catching one of his feet in it!

She went upstairs to shower and hide the nightie until she could wash it so that her mother would not know that she had worn it. Chris was so remorseful for trying to take advantage of Sonia that he was almost in tears.

When he finally got home and to bed, he cried himself to sleep, while Sonia was telling her dolls about the way she had handled the young rookie. They, too, thought that it was very funny.

Around 9:00 a.m., Virginia was awakened by the telephone,

the long evening's work, not to mention the considerable amount of liquor that she had drank, made the telephone sound like huge bells ringing.

Angrily, she yanked the plug off the telephone as she recalled almost everybody in the bar, especially Goldie and Dora celebrating Rommie's death. She knew that Rommie was nothing but a thug, but to actually celebrate his getting killed was just wrong.

She could still hear Dora leading the crowd in singing, "*Another One Bites the Dust, The Dust*" over and over and over again, until Eric made them quit. Virginia dozed off again, but when she was sleep, she could hear the telephone from downstairs ringing again.

She found the cord, plugged it in, and answered it. As she answered, she wondered why Sonia had not. Virginia didn't recognize the boy's voice, but he was so polite that she guessed that it must have been Roy.

She had never met him, because Sonia had never brought him around the house. Sonia had told her that he went to school with her, and she didn't like him enough to invite him over. Sonia knew that if Virginia had known that he was nineteen, she would have kicked both of their butts!

After a little small talk, Virginia called to and awakened Sonia, who was dreaming about being a rock star in her own hit video with hot men all over her. She knew that it had to be Roy on the telephone, and she just could not wait to fuss him out for being with that ugly female last night. She ran down to the kitchen and answered politely, waiting for her mother to hang up.

"Sonia, something truly wonderful happened to me last night after I left!"

"I bet it did", she responded sarcastically.

A little puzzled at her tone, he asked her what was wrong with her, and she mumbled that he knew. Roy chose to ignore her as he was really pumped up.

He began, "While I was talking to you last night and that thing with Rommie was happening, my uncles came pass with, of all people, the coach, the same coach that I met during the summer camp! He is a very close friend of my Uncle Ed! I had no idea! Isn't that wonderful?"

"Yeah, Roy, that's really wonderful", she responded, not even trying to hide her anger.

"Are you sure that you are all right?"

"Yeah, I told you that I was all right, didn't I?", she answered almost screaming.

"Anyway, Uncle Ed and Fred told me that they needed too . . . Did I tell you that I had uncles that were twins?"

By this time Sonia's patience was gone, and she shouted, "Did your twin uncles and coach bring you some of that North Carolina stuff, and you four stayed with them all night. Did your preacher father go with you to pray over the stinking 'hos?"

"Sonia, what in the world is wrong with you? "   "You know!"

"Know what?!"

Sonia would not say anything, mostly because she thought that she heard her mother stirring around upstairs.

Roy took a deep breath and began in a matter of fact voice, "Sonia when I got back home my uncles gave me some money to go to school with and over the objections of my parents, a new sport's car. I thought that I could pick you up in it this afternoon, maybe down by the basketball court. We could hang out all day and part of the night in a good motel."

"But it seems that for some reason you are too angry for

something like that. So, I guess that we can say our goodbyes right now, and maybe, I'll see you during the Thanksgiving holiday. You know that I have to leave tomorrow after church."

Sonia was stunned! Given a car? Money? Somehow that was beyond what she could conceive. As clever as she thought she was she could not think of anything to say. Her silence was interpreted by Roy as meaning that she was too angry, for some reason that he didn't understand, to spend the day with him, and he had just about had it with her moody behavior.

During the silence he recalled his father saying to him that every time a man made a move forward, he had to leave somebody behind. His father had preached many sermons about leaving folk behind when you are moving on. Maybe, just maybe, it was time for him to leave this child alone and move on.

He began slowly, "It is going to be hard to leave you like this, but I have to move on, Baby. Think about me sometime, and maybe, after a while when we are old enough to know what we want, we will meet and fall in love again and be together forever."

Sonia still could not manage to say anything. Roy softly said goodbye and hung up the telephone. Sonia cried.

She just sat there holding the dead telephone in her hand and crying. Finally, she hung up the telephone and melancholy made her way up the stairs. Her heart jumped as she heard the telephone ring. Her heart seemed to stop as she heard Virginia say that she was around somewhere.

Joy replaced the despair as her mother called to her to answer the telephone. She raced back to the kitchen, picked up the telephone saying "I just knew that you would call back, I love you, I love you, I love you!"

A surprised and stunned Chris answered,"What?"

Sonia called him a sneaky bastard and hung up.

Chris hung up the telephone and just gazed at it, totally bewildered. He didn't know what was going on and decided that whatever it was, and however much he liked Sonia, nothing was quite worth going through all this. He picked the telephone back up and called Marcus as he needed to talk to somebody and quick!

Marcus agreed to talk to him and asked him to meet him on the steps.

Roy's father happened into the kitchen where Roy was sitting at the table looking despondent. After a little probing, Roy told him about Sonia, having to leave her behind, and the fact that she was angry with him. He left out the fact that she was fourteen, and he definitely left out the motel plans.

His father advised him to call the young woman and try to at a minimum leave without hard feelings.

"Friends are rare, and sometimes people say and do things that may be negative, but in reality they're not. Maybe she just does not know how to say `I'll really miss you."

Roy hugged his father and ran to his room to call Sonia.

Sonia was upstairs talking to her dolls who agreed that Roy had no business upsetting her and they unanimously agreed and hoped that Roy would crash his raggedy car and kill himself.

16. *Little Al*

Sonia was annoyed when Virginia, who was in the bathroom, asked her to answer the telephone. "Sonia, Sonia, all I hear around here is Sonia!" She fussed all the way to the telephone. She answered the telephone in the type of monotone voice which reflected her mood.

"Hey, listen, Baby, there is absolutely no need in us behaving like ... uh, children. Maybe, we can have a ..."

"You forget one thing Roy. I am a child. You said so last night before you started doing me. Maybe, I should march right in the bathroom to my mother and tell her what you been doing to her little girl. She'll kick your ass and have you locked up, Mr. Roy! "

"What's wrong with you? I never heard you sound like that before. Did I do something? Tell me."

She suddenly realized that she really had no reason to be angry and decided that she did want to be with him. She apologized, even prophetically suggested that he should never have gotten himself mixed up with a crazy girl like her. Both agreed and laughed.

Sonia was interrupted by Virginia calling down the stairs asking her to hurry up and get dressed so that they could go shopping for her school clothes.

"Damned that!"

She was going with Roy. Hurriedly, she told him to meet her at the basketball court in about an hour. Sonia told him that they would have to do some shopping first, but the rest of the day and night would belong to them.

Roy was ecstatic and agreed to meet her. As he was already dressed, he went downstairs, hugged his father, and ran out of the door. He decided that he would spend a little time with the boys before he met Sonia, because he knew that there would be little chance of his seeing them before he would be leaving the next day.

Virginia was laying on the bed when Sonia entered the room. Sonia started a little small talk, then asked her mother if she could go shopping all by herself. After a little jockeying back and forth, Virginia agreed that she was old enough to go alone.

The two playfully wrestled until Virginia noticed the marks on the girl's neck. Not wanting to touch them as she somehow felt that touching them would confirm her fears, she pushed Sonia away pointing and asking, "What the hell is that on your neck girl? You look just like a tramp with that shit on your neck! I done told you that you had better slow your fast young ass down before you find yourself trapped in some hellhole like this one. I done told you!"

"So, get your little fast ass out of here before I kick it! I ain't even going to ask you how that shit got there, because I don't want to make you have to tell me a damned lie. She reached on the night table, grabbed some money and tossed it at Sonia. I hope the hell you slow down girl or you'll . . . just get out of here!"

Accepting the money quietly, Sonia backed out of the room, because she was a little afraid that Virginia would really get mad and go upside her head.

She closed the door behind her, but acknowledged her

mother's telling her to be sure to buy a couple of good bras. She hurried to the shower, wondering how she could cover up them damned marks that were, of course, Chris' fault.

Sonia searched all over her room and closets for a blouse, shirt, or something that she could wear which would hide her passion marks. Sonia finally chose a designer tee shirt with a pair of her tightest jeans.

Sonia really hated having to wear a top that was all closed because it messed up the way she liked to look. But after combing her hair, she looked in the mirror and really liked the way she looked except something was missing, maybe a little makeup.

While making up her face, she began having fantasies of being Roy's wife and liked the idea. She could get the hell away from the damned projects and live in North Carolina with him wherever in the world that was!

So, she hoped that she would get good and pregnant today. She reasoned that if she were pregnant he would want to marry her, especially if they had a boy.

Sonia wanted to get pregnant all along, but it had to be now. She certainly didn't him to meet somebody else while he was away from her.

Sonia yelled goodbye to Virginia, skipped down the stairs, out the door, and saw Chris and Marcus sitting on his steps talking. Being the gentle soul that she was, she taunted Chris with an erotic, "Hi, boyfriend! "

Chris returned her greeting with a very weak, "Hi Sonia."

Sonia and Marcus glared at each other for a moment, and she struck a pose, flipped her head with disdain, and walked away, strutting her stuff as she pranced away from them.

Chris watched her longingly, while Marcus watched her with disdain. Marcus thoughtfully examined the expression on his friend's face.

"Why do you like her so much?," Marcus began in his thick accent.

"You like her because she looks like a woman and acts like a...well? You want to be a man to her? You think she will have you rather than that basketball man, Roy?"

Chris answered with an expression of surprise on his face.

Marcus, sensing that he was surprised, continued, "You really didn't know that they were, uh, what's the word, close."

Chris lied, "She says that he is like a big bro . . . "

Marcus interrupted gently placed his arm on Chris' shoulder and began, "I don't know how to . . . Chris what could he want from that girl except sex? That is the reason that you want her too. She is a pretty young girl, but we need to have a little more respect for our young women."

Without much conviction, Chris countered by telling Marcus that she was not what he thought she might be. He mentioned that she was really a good person after you get to know her.

"She's, she's, I mean that we talk sometimes about sports, school, and other stuff. She is only fooling around about that sex stuff."

Marcus would not respond, and Chris immediately realized that Marcus knew that Chris didn't mean a word of what he was saying. On occasions like this, Chris almost hated Marcus, but he knew that Marcus was right.

Chris looked him in the eye, "Sometimes, well, you sound like my sister when I talk to her about Sonia. Maybe, I should leave her alone. I promise you that I will not marry her this week."

Both laughed and began horsing around. Sonia, by this time, had arrived at the basketball court, her body swaying as provocatively as she could manage. The boys and men on and around the court began to whistle, scream and carry on as if she were a celebrity! Boy, did she love it! She loved every word, sound, and gesture!

The females glared, stared, and dared her to make a move on their men which again made her feel great! As Dora would say, "When the other bitches hate you for out bitching them, that's when you know you got it!"

She would have gladly sold her soul to make that moment last. Out of the commotion, she somehow heard that familiar voice saying, "Hi, Sonia baby!".

There he was, all six feet nine inches of her lover, Roy, looking down on her with his whole body and soul seemingly smiling at her.

He lifted her up, spun her around, and kissed her. The crowd (well the males) went wild! The females were, for the most part, angered by this young girl having the prize, Roy. Sonia soaked all this in with total joy, and delighted to be the center of attention.

Although Roy was a little embarrassed by the type of attention they were receiving, the very nearness of Sonia made it all worthwhile. He stood there admiring her for a moment, and the couple joyously gazed into each other's eyes. The tall lanky youngster grabbed her by the hand began leading her away from the court to see his new car.

Suavely, he said, "Let's hurry up and do the shopping so we can start the stopping."

As they hurried away, the games continued, and the couple was all but forgotten. They all had to perfect their games; so that, they could make the big times, sign million dollar contracts, drive fancy cars, wear fine clothes, live in mansions, love fine women, and most important, have some basketball shoes named after them. So they play, play, play, and play! Nothing is more important than to play!

Roy had parked around the corner, because he didn't want to appear to be showing off. Roy had always been sensitive to the fact that he was blessed with things that his friends were not. He never intentionally tried to be a show off, except of course on the basketball court where he was "the man".

As they walked through the alley leading to the street where he had parked, he wondered whether he would ever see Sonia again as his girl.

Perhaps it would be best for them to be hundreds of miles apart so that she would have the chance to do whatever young girls are suppose to do. Sonia was considering various names for the boy child that she hoped that they would get started today.

When they reached the street Sonia, who had been holding hands with Roy, suddenly bolted away from him and toward three young men who were menacingly leaning against a black foreign sedan. As Sonia ran toward them one of the guys, a short, dark, muscular rascal stepped away from the car and spread his massive arms in anticipation of a hug from the oncoming Sonia.

This whole scenario made Roy a bit uneasy. His first impulse was to quickly retreat to the safety of the basketball court. He dismissed that thought as crazy and slowly walked toward them who were now hugging.

As he reached them, he heard her whining that she meant to come to see him and his responding that he knew that Virginia would not but he did expect her to come visit him.

As Roy stood there, waiting for an introduction or even better for Sonia to finish whatever business she had with these guys, he recognized the guy who was hugging her as the infamous Little Al.

Little Al, he knew, had the reputation as extremely dangerous although he was only about sixteen. His reputation was well deserved as he was personally responsible for many broken jaws, legs, arms, not to mention the other damage that he had caused to folks property and even animals.

It was even alleged, but never proven, that he had killed a former friend after a minor drug deal had gone bad. He also recognized taller and obviously the older of the guys (about Roy's age) still leaning against the car as Ricky, one of Snake's boys.

The other person was a really young looking little boy who was no older than about ten or eleven and seemed to be really dirty and neglected.

Roy found himself eye to eye with the volatile Little Al and knew that he was way out of his league if the situation were to break down into a fight. He knew that Little Al would need little or no incentive to bust him up.

The best that he could hope for was to get 'chumped down' by this maniac. Hopefully, he would be able to leave with or without Sonia who seemed to have some type of close friendship or something with him.

Without taking his eyes off Roy, Little Al gruffly asked Ricky, "Is this the one that Snake was talking about?"

Sounding bored to death, Ricky responded, "Yeah, that's the one. Is this going to take long? I got this thing that I got to do for Snake, and you."

"Just shut up!", Little Al screamed at Ricky, "All I want to know is if this the punk he told me about!"

Ricky nodded.

Without warning Little Al pushed Roy against the car asking,"You know who I am? "

"Yeah, I know you," Roy responded trying to sound unafraid.

"You know that this girl that you and your basketball playing bitch self been pumping is my little sis?"

Roy went completely limp with fear and horror. Of all things, this maniac's sister! What else could go wrong? He silently prayed that he would somehow get out of this and promised that he would never, ever come near her again.

Sonia started crying, pushing, kicking, and hitting her brother trying to protect Roy. This gave Roy a chance to run, and he knew that if he ran, Little Al would never could catch him.

However, as he was about to sprint away, he hesitated as he saw Little Al push Sonia to the ground. Sonia continued crying and screaming to her brother to leave them alone.

She told him that Roy was just a friend and she didn't care what Snake said, "Roy is just a friend, my friend! So leave us alone! "

Little Al looked at her for a moment and was satisfied that she was telling the truth. He even began to apologize to Roy. It seemed that things were going to work out. Now, it seems that the only problem that Roy would have was getting rid of Sonia and getting the hell out of town.

He decided that he would make up some story about wanting to beat the crowd on the highways and leave that afternoon. He knew that he had to distance himself from Sonia when possible.

Little Al picked Sonia up from the ground mumbling that he was going to kick Snake's ass. Sonia was so angry that she snatched away from him so hard that her tee shirt ripped exposing most of her torso, but more important the passion marks!

Little Al and Roy gazed at the marks angrily. Little Al was convinced that Roy had sucked her neck, and Roy was convinced that she had been out with somebody else as he knew that he had not been the one. Ricky's stare was totally lustful, and little Denny was amazed at the size of her breast!

"You dirty bastard! " Little Al screamed.

"The hell with you and that dirty bitch! I've been catching hell ever since I met your tramp sister, and I'm sick and tired of it! If you want a part of me, go ahead!

I didn't do that, don't know who did it, and now I don't even care! So, if you want to kick my ass go ahead, I deserve it!"

Sonia was completely stunned and began weeping uncontrollably as she felt that whatever happened there, she and Roy were through.

Seizing what he felt was an opportunity to get next to Sonia, Ricky suggested that he take Sonia away while Little Al who was now so angry that he was kicking the car.

Little Al ordered Sonia to get in the car and told Ricky to go buy her something to cover herself up. He also warned him not to even think about touching her.

Ricky protested that he was a trusted friend who would never do anything to his little sister (and he emphasized `little') for fear that Little Al would total him as he was sure he would total Roy.

Sonia obediently got in the car and they sped away leaving Roy, Little Al, and Denny. Roy stood there defiantly as Little Al was working himself up to a fever pitch of anger and rage.

Roy, too, was now angry enough to fight and started to pop Little Al to get the thing started and over with. But before he could hit him, he noticed that the guy was crying.

"Damn it all!" he sobbed, "all I ever wanted was for her to love me like I love her. She's, she's not like a sister to me but more like a woman. You know what I mean?"

Roy understood that his enemy was psychotic, with a thing for his own sister. Now he felt sorry for him, fully understanding that the guy was genuinely sick, but his major concern was getting away which didn't seem likely.

While Roy was trying to find out a way to get away from this maniac Little Al continued, "Down there at the school, her teacher kept on keeping her after school and taking her places until I found out and tried to kill the bastard!

I would have, too, if that damned principal had not jumped in the shit! I done already broke the punk-assed teacher's jaw when he got into the shit. I tried to kill his ass. Then when they locked me up, the judge say that I need time to think things over.

"Now, while I in that damned joint they keep telling me that some basketball playing bitch is out here pumping my sister. What am I suppose to do but kick your ass?"

Roy offered no suggestion.

"It don't matter." Little Al said, coldly.

"It don't matter." repeated the kid.

Little Al continued, "Damn! I don't want to but I got to do the thing to you. Ain't they got some women you age that you could be pumping except Sonia?"

Before Roy could answer, Little Al without any warning buried a tremendous left in Roy's stomach, followed by a thunderous left and right to the head. Roy tried to protect himself by swinging wildly at his opponent, but he was completely powerless to even slow him down.

The onslaught continued until Roy fell helplessly unto the pavement with a thud! His adversary then began to uncontrollably kick and stomp Roy into near unconsciousness.

With unbelievable brute strength, Roy was then picked up

and slammed against the wall. By now was so hurt that he was numb. The frenzied maniac started screaming at the boy to "give me the shit! Hurry up and give it to me!"

Denny reached in this pocket and handed him a couple of crack rocks. He ordered the helpless Roy to put it in his pocket. Helpless, bleeding, and hurt with a broken jaw, maybe nose and ribs, Roy struggled but somehow managed to comply hoping and praying that the maniac would stop, just stop!

A couple that just happened by as Little Al was smacking the helpless Roy in the face repeatedly. The male started toward them to help, but Little Al seeing him approaching, drew a pistol and began screaming at him, "Yeah! You want some of this! You want some, you old . . . "

The female grabbed her mate by the arm and they scampered away. He pointed the pistol at Roy who was now at best semiconscious and fired. The bullet struck Roy in the left leg. Roy screamed! With a diabolical grimace, Little Al fired again. This time in the groin, and again in the stomach.

He was fascinated by the agony, pain and suffering that Roy was enduring and grabbed him by the throat. Little Al emptied the three remaining bullets in Roy's head, wiped his hands on the wall and on his pants and turned to Denny.

Panting, he warned the boy that if he ever told anybody about ". . . this shit, well, I'll have to do it to you. I'll have to do it to you, because I ain't never going back in there. They ain't gonna do it to me again! I ain't never going back! They just going to have to kill my black ass!"

Denny was confused and certainly could not know about what had happened to Little Al while he was locked up. As bad as he was, he was no match for the thugs in the overcrowded detention center, and he could not protect himself from those predators who preyed on youngsters like himself.

Denny never seemed to fully understand what had happened. It was like something on television. They walked away from the scene to where they were suppose to meet Ricky and Sonia. They heard the sirens of the ambulance and the police cars.

Denny asked him what he was going to tell his sister about Roy. Little Al's only response was a blank stare as he had not even thought that far ahead.

While Little Al was pondering his predicament, Ricky pulled up with the now joyous Sonia who was now sporting a new tee shirt. As the pair climbed in the car, Sonia was singing along with the music on the radio and didn't notice the silent communication between Little Al and Ricky.

Ricky who had been having a good old time joking and playing with the effervescent Sonia looked in the rear view mirror and saw Little Al grimacing at him. He decided immediately to stop as he certainly didn't want to pay the price that he knew Roy had paid.

Everybody in the car, save Sonia, who was still singing, was silent. Suddenly Little Al ordered Ricky to cut off the damned radio and for Sonia to shut up! He leaned forward and asked Sonia to tell him the truth, "Did he put them on your neck?"

"No", she screamed, "I had some kid to do that to make him jealous. He was not paying attention to me." "Shit! So, he was telling the truth!", Little Al responded as he fell back on the seat.

Ricky wisely remained silent as Little Al sat motionlessly, trying to figure things out. Finally satisfied that he had discovered the truth, he asked Ricky, "So what you and Snake got to do with what my sister does?"

Ricky had no answer.

Now very calmly, he ordered Ricky to pull the car over to

the curb and made Sonia and Denny get out. Little Al reloaded his pistol and demanded that Ricky drive him to wherever Snake was.

Seeing the pistol, Sonia was now frightened for Roy. With genuine tears she pleaded to her brother to tell her where Roy was and what had happened to him.

He looked at her but didn't respond. He smacked Ricky in the face with the now loaded pistol and ordered him to find Snake so that, they could get "this shit straight!"

She watched the car speed away and turned to Denny with tearful inquiring eyes. Not knowing how to handle the situation, Denny ran away! Sonia sat on the curb crying profusely. Ricky lived only long enough to beg Little Al to believe that he really thought that Roy was pumping his sister because Snake told him.

The afternoon news featured the account of a local basketball prospect, Roy Govans, had been brutally murdered in what appeared to be a drug related incident.

The news person mentioned the many scholastic, athletic, community service awards that he had won. Then in an obviously impromptu editorial, she bitterly denounced those who dealt with drugs and the senseless violence that accompanied the execrable trade.

She went on to suggest that maybe we were putting to much pressure on our young men to succeed in a business that seemed to have too few winners, athletics.

She ended by asking the rhetorical question, "How many of you remember when sports were just fun and games, and drugs were something that you got from the corner drug store because somebody in your house was ill?"

Many found it quite easy to believe that Roy was somehow involved in drugs. Many in the community that had revered him were now very quick to judge and condemn him. Only those who heard the whispers of the streets knew the truth.

17. *Memories*

The sorrowful wailing and screaming of the nearby sirens accompanied by the squealing sounds of hard pressed brakes didn't draw too much attention from either Chris or Marcus.

After living in the projects, even for a short period of time, those sounds are as commonplace as the wind or the sun. Marcus was teasing Chris about being so short, and Chris countered by suggesting that he'd rather be short than some kind of tall, skinny, Zulu. They laughed.

Marcus asked Chris what he wanted to be when he grew up. Without hesitation, Chris replied that he'd love to be the first Black president of the United States. Marcus laughed and said that he would like to become the leader of his country one day, too.

"We share the same destiny of the lion!", Marcus laughed.

Just then, Virginia had come down to her kitchen smoking a cigarette and immediately reached for her bottle and poured herself a big drink. She was mildly surprised that the bottle was not fuller but dismissed it thinking that she had perhaps consumed more. She never considered Sonia was helping her.

Sipping her drink, she glared through her kitchen window at the fading chalk outline of where Rommie had fallen and died. She could not quite understand why she felt so much remorse for the man as he had been the worse thing that had ever happened to her. So why was she feeling so bad?

Before long she was distracted by the boys, who were seemingly having so much fun that she began to watch them wondering if Rommie had behaved like them as a boy.

"Hell! He was nothing but an old boy when I met him."

Virginia began daydreaming, remembering when she first met Rommie in the bar. She recalled that she had seen him around, but never up close until he entered the bar that day that now seemed so very long ago. So deep she was in her memories that she was not aware of the fact that tears were now flowing down her lovely but belabored face.

Gazing now into nothingness, she could clearly see Rommie walking into the bar with that slow swagger of his, nobody walked exactly as he did, wearing a very impressive light blue and gray sweat suit. She could almost hear him order that first drink with his raspy low voice and his boyish mischievous grin.

Virginia recalled being so nervous that she spilled the first drink she served him on his diamond ring decorated fingers. She had been so instantly attracted to him that she fantasying licking the drink off his fingers.

Virginia recalled the two of them being in constant eye to eye contact as he returned from making a telephone call. Virginia could still see that infectious boyish smile on his face as he approached her. She also knew that she wanted him without a doubt.

They talked too long that first time as there seemed to have been an instant soul connection. Virginia knew that she liked him and hoped that he was not just "running a line" on her.

She recalled being so engrossed with him that she ignored the rest of customers which not only annoyed them but totally irritated Eric. She recalled him looking at his diamond studded watch telling her that he had to go to "take care of some business."

He handed her a twenty, held her hand for a moment, and asked her if he could pick her up after work. She never, ever allowed customers to pick her up, because . . . well because even when they came off as okay, a woman could never be too careful.

But she heard herself accepting his offer and telling him that 6:30 would be fine. They smiled at each other momentarily before he turned to leave. She watched him with passionate eyes as he walked to the door.

Suddenly, she remembered his change and called out to him. He responded by asking her if she was allowed to accept tips, smiled, and continued out the door.

Immediately after Rommie left, she had been so very excited that she called her best friend Dora. Dora was not in the best of moods, because some man she had just met wanted to take her to some play. "I got some play for him all right. Girl, let me tell you what he said he wanted . . . "

Virginia knew Dora well enough to know that she would never be able to tell her about Rommie. She knew from experience that all Dora was going to do is complain about this guy. She wondered why she even considered sharing her good fortune with Dora.

She was so excited about going out with this guy that she just had to tell somebody. The only somebody to talk to was Eric. Talk about a bubble buster, Eric looked her straight in the eyes, sat her down on a stool and told her that the worse thing that she could do with her life was to start messing around with a fool like Rommie.

Although Virginia had been for the most part, a very levelheaded woman, the one area that she always seemed to mess up was her choice of men. She thanked Eric for his concern, but if being with Rommie was going to be a mistake, she was more than willing to make it. Virginia also knew that Eric liked, maybe even loved her, but she didn't like him that way.

Finally, 6:30 dragged in but no Rommie. Seven o'clock arrived, still no Rommie. As 8:15 rolled around in the door, wearing an all-white suit, white on white shirt, a white necktie with a huge, thick gold chain, and a big-brimmed white Panama Hat with a black headband, was Rommie.

There were quite a few people in the bar by this time, and they all seemed to stop to check the man out. Totally aware of the fact that everyone was checking him out and talking about him, Rommie walked to the bar and with his gold-tooth adorned smile, ordered a round of drinks for everybody in the bar which, of course, made him instantly extremely popular.

"These drinks," he announced, "are on this town's best and sexiest barmaid, Virginia!"

Virginia watched all this totally stunned! She was so astonished that she grabbed and hugged Eric. He sadly shook his head and walked away. She was totally and completely overwhelmed by the apparently charismatic Rommie and began to, at that point, consider him as her man.

She laughed at herself as she recalled giving curvaceous Vanessa, her relief and infamous tramp, the silent message that Rommie was all hers and back off!

In return, Vanessa with a smile silently expressed that she understood and walked down to the other end of the bar, but not before striking a pose and very provocatively asking Rommie if he wanted anything else.

Virginia was not amused worth a damn! As Rommie greedily checked out Vanessa's every curve, Virginia pretended not to notice.

After a couple more rounds of drinks, Rommie paid his check with a wink, a big tip and the two glided out of the door, arm in arm.

Once in Rommie's big, late-modeled automobile, they discussed hanging out for the evening. She convinced him that she had to go home to dress, check on and feed her child, Sonia.

Arriving at her home, Rommie became instantly interested in the effervescent, young, fresh Sonia. Again, at the time Virginia missed Rommie's lustfulness. However, while she was showering and dressing Rommie was scoring big points with her daughter.

Finally, they went out and began an affair which included all those things that they could find to do to enjoy each other. They went to clubs, bars, restaurants and quality hotels as she insisted that she never slept with a man in her home, because she had a young daughter.

The only thing that they didn't share was Rommie's appetite for cocaine which was Rommie's life and definitely his business. Virginia knew better but choose to overlook the fact that he was a thug, because she had instantly and completely fallen in love with him.

Now in the gloom of her lonely, lonely kitchen reality smacked her right in the face. She finally realized that she meant little or nothing to Rommie. Looking back on their brief affair, she realizes that he had never even told her that he liked her. He was never ever her man.

So, now Virginia did cry, but now for herself as she knew that she had again been a fool in love. As she slowly walked through the living room to the stairs, she wondered aloud when would she stop falling for losers and thugs.

She asked herself when and where could find herself a real

man to love her or was she just fooling herself. What decent man would have her? And more important, where in the hell would she meet such a guy? Certainly not at the bar, unless it was Eric.

But still, although she knew that he would be good to her and Sonia, she simply didn't like him that way. Maybe, she should start going to church. Whatever, she needed to make a move and quickly. By this time she was in her bedroom where she turned on the television.

While she was dealing with the reality of her relationship with Rommie, the boys were still just messing around. Marcus asked Chris if he had actually seen Rommie get shot, and Chris told him that he had not.

Marcus asked Chris what he thought about the whole thing. Chris answered that he was glad that Rommie was dead, because he didn't like Rommie. Marcus responded by saying that he hoped that Chris really didn't mean what he had said, ". . . because there, was good in everybody."

He went on to say ". . . everybody's life had a purpose and unless we understand that . . ."

"What damned purpose could he have had except keeping my mother away from me and selling dope?", Chris yelled at Marcus, now crying!

Jacque who had been in the living room heard the commotion and ran out to the boys to find out what was going on.

"What in the world is going on with you two? One minute you are good friends laughing and having fun. Then the next minute you are screaming at each other like crazy people. Believe me, nothing is as important as a good friend. Now calm down and tell me what is wrong?"

Both listened to him thoughtfully as Jacque usually spoke

much softer than his six-foot plus body would suggest and as usual he had a smile on his face. In turn, they told him that the discussion was about Rommie.

"Nobody was ever closer to Rommie as Mike and me when we were kids, I don't believe," he began slowly. "We were the craziest three kids in the world according to our parents, teachers, and Old Reverend Brown."

As Jacque began to talk, he sat on the steps and the boys joined him. They could tell from the expression on his face that what he was about to tell would be interesting as Jacque had a captivating way of talking.

"Yeah! We were like accidents waiting for a place to happen," he began with a big smile than a hearty laugh.

"Boys, you never know how things are going to turn out. A kindness here, a hateful or unkind word or act there can change a person's life for the better or worse.

Take us for instance, Rommie, Mike and me, we were like the three musketeers only without the swords. Nobody in their right minds would have allowed us to carry anything sharp!", Jacque laughed.

"We were not rich, but we all had parents who loved us and did their best to see that we had all that we needed. They saw to it that we went to school and took us to church every Sunday the Lord sent. They usually met us in church, because Rommie always made sure that we went to Sunday School.

You see, he was Old Reverend Brown's favorite and made sure that Mike and I got to Sunday School and on time. Most of the time we could have killed him, because Mike and I wanted to sleep Sunday mornings.

Then everybody thought that Rommie was going to be a preacher and Mike and I were going straight to hell!"

"Mr. Jacque!", Chris interrupted, "You can't be talking about the same Rommie that . . . "

"The very same one. You see there is good and bad in all of us. So, we must not allow ourselves the temptation of judging others. Chris, Rommie is, was and forever will be my friend, and I pray to God that his tormented soul finds rest.

"Sure what he was doing was wrong and there is no excuse for his actions, but it does nobody any good to hate him now as he is now in the hands of the good Lord who will judge him. Do you understand?"

"I think so", Chris responded meekly.

"Anyway, Rommie was the good one and we were, well, everybody thought we were on our way to hell! Rommie was a stubborn kind of guy. Once he decided to do something, it was done no matter what the odds were against him.

This was fine most of the time like the time that he decided that he was going to be on the honor roll. Well, while Mike and I fooled around all the time, very often he would be in the house, at school, or in the library studying.

We admired him, but we just did enough to get by. Well, by the end of the first semester he had the highest average in the whole school!

"Boy was everybody proud of him! Mike and I caught it, because our parents figured that if he could do it, we could. Man, that made him as popular as the plague with us!"

They laughed with Jacque!

"But that was all right because he was our friend and we were very proud of him, even if it did cause us some problems at home.

"Now, there was this dance one night down at the Y.M.C.A. I guess we were about fourteen or fifteen and we were . . . no, we were fourteen. Yeah fourteen. Anyway we all liked the same foxy lady, Juanita, uh, Juanita Stanton at the time. She was the prettiest, sexiest, stacked female in the whole school! Boy, that girl was something else! She was probably the sexiest young woman in the whole wide world! Man!"

"Well, the word was that she was coming to the party, and we decided that one of us was going to get her. We were so sure that one of us was going to walk away with her that we even made an agreement that the best man would win and that would be that.

We were so confident that we even practice what we were going to say to her. It was what we old timers used to call "rapping." The boys looked at him quizzically. Rapping then meant the things you said to a girl to get her or to win her.

So, we were ready to go Juanita hunting, and may the best man win and all that. But we each held a little surprise something back from each other, sort of a secret weapon."

"Like what, Grandpa!," Marcus interrupted.

"Each of us had a little secret something that we were going to use to win her. I was a very good dancer, so I learned this new dance I was going to teach her. Rommie had brought her a little ring, necklace or something. Mike had practiced this song by Bill 'Smokey' Robinson that he was going to sing to her.

He used to make us so mad, because he was always a quite handsome fellow and could sing! Lord, that boy could sing. Could sing them girls right out of their, uh, well, the girls really liked to have him sing to them.

"In all fairness to Juanita, she had no idea that we were planning on making fools out of ourselves that night. Looking back, I can honestly say that I wish that we had found something else to do with our time and energy. But we were young, dumb, and she was fine! 'Juanita, Juanita, oh there's no girl that's sweeta' we used to sing.

We were so excited that we got to the dance early, as clean as we wanted to be. 'Cleaner than the 'board of health' we used to say. Like I was saying, we . . . "

"Grandpa, what do you mean by clean?," Marcus interrupted.

"Well, it meant dressed, dressed to kill! We had on our brand new party khakis, all starched with creases so sharp that you could have cut through steel with them. We wore knit shirts with little animals right over the heart, and spit-shined shoes.

We wore shoes in those days when we were dressed. We felt that wearing tennis shoes when dressed was 'country', and a body would do anything to keep from being called 'country'. Oh! Don't let me forget the finger-tipped waves in our hair and the sunglasses, shades." By now the boys were hanging onto every word.

"We got there early so that we would be there when she arrived. Eight and nine o' clock rolled around and no Juanita. So, Mike and I started getting after the girls that were there.

There were pretty girls all over the place! They were not as fine as Juanita, but they were there. So, we sort of forgot Juanita except Rommie who kept pacing the floor and looking out the windows for her.

"Meanwhile, I was just teaching the pretty girls the new dance steps, and during the intermission Mike sang a few songs. The girls were grabbing and pulling on him so much that the people that gave the thing had to calm everybody down.

You see, some boys there didn't like their girl friends making such a fuss over Mike, but everything calmed down. Then, like a scene out of one of them movies somebody started yelling, 'Juanita is coming! Juanita is coming!'

Seems like everybody broke for the door! We three sort of cooled it and walked behind the crowd so that we would be cool, I guess.

"There she was our dream girl, the essence of femininity, sitting like the queen or something in the lo-o-ngest, blackest, shiniest Lincoln that we had ever seen. I still believe that car was about three, maybe four blocks long!"

The boys laughingly accused him of not telling the truth!

"Will you two behave so that I can finish? Anyway, behind the wheel of this magnificent machine was what we at first thought was a white boy, however, it turned out to be Theodore, the son of the biggest Negro funeral director in town.

His family was the richest people that we knew of. As far as we were concerned they had more money than God! Theodore was eighteen, nineteen, maybe even twenty and was known to be cold-blooded.

The guy never even smiled or at least, that was what they said about him. We sure didn't know for sure, because we didn't hang in the same circles. If you know what I mean?

"Mike and I knew that immediately that we were totally outclassed and so we got back to the other girls so that, we could find a couple that were willing.

Somehow the car, the fact that the dude was wearing a tailor-made white suit that complimented the white dress that Juanita was wearing didn't bother our stubborn friend Rommie. He just stayed far enough away not to be obvious, but within striking distance.

"Well, one of those really slow songs by the master beggar, James Brown, was played and Rommie somehow got to dance with her! By that time, Mike and I had found, let's say dates.

Everything was going fine as the very slow record, *Prisoner of Love* was filling the air. That song was always a good one to be dancing with someone that you wanted to get real close to.

"All of a sudden we heard Juanita screaming to the top of her voice that she didn't wear cheap shit! She didn't appreciate him offering it to her! She went completely off on him, calling him '...an ugly, black, young-assed Nigger'! She went on to even suggest that he may have gotten some black from his skin on her very dress!

"Rommie was hurt, stunned, and completely embarrassed. He stepped back from her without saying anything at first, but he had this wild look in his eyes. Finally, he called her a bunch of dirty names and smacked her!

Now we were shocked, because unlike us, Rommie never cursed or fussed too much, and he really believed in turning the other cheek. As I said before, he had this heavy friendship with Old Reverend Brown, and he did his level best to live by The Book. To my knowledge, he had never, ever hit anybody first and certainly not a female.

"The whole place was in an uproar, and everybody was looking through the chaos at Theodore to come to the girl's rescue and kick Rommie's butt for the lady's honor or something.

We were scared to death for him, because we had heard that he had learned some kind of foreign jungle killing stuff or something down there at that white school that he went to. But as scared as we were, we were prepared to go down with our friend. We wished that he had not smacked her, but he was our friend."

"But Theodore coolly finished his soft drink and gave it to somebody he was talking to and walked over to where Rommie and Juanita were standing sort of glaring at each other. He never even said anything to Rommie, but looked at him curiously like he was a monkey in the zoo or something.

The kids started clearing the floor for the fight, but

Theodore didn't seem to have any interest in fighting Rommie. Instead, he motioned for Juanita to come to him, and he examined her face like he was a doctor or something.

"He kissed her on the cheek, whispered something in her ear that caused her to laugh and they walked out the door without saying anything to anybody. But before they walked out the door, Theodore turned and looked straight at Rommie and gave him the coldest smile I've ever seen. I can still remember that look!

"After they had gone, we went over to Rommie who was still standing in the same spot where all the commotion had taken place. We were very excited, because he had chumped Theodore down. He just stood there with tears just flowing out of his eyes with that thing that he had bought for the girl in his hand. Suddenly he slammed it to the floor and stomped it over and over again.

Rommie looked me straight in the eyes and calmly said I got to go now. I'll see you later. We tried to stop him, but he insisted that he was fine and left. Mike had an older cousin who had a little apartment near where the Y was, and he was never home.

So, we took our dates around there for, uh, (Jacque looked a little embarrassed) some soft drinks. Well, the next morning when we got home our parents kicked our grown butts and promised to punish us for about two hundred years.

We saw each other in church that Sunday, but Rommie was not there. Well, he was not in school that Monday. Juanita was in our class and usually she sat up front flirting with the teacher because she was too everything for us.

Now that I think about it, I don't know whatever possessed us to mess with her in the first place as we were sure that she had a thing going with that dude, old Mr. Roberts. I usually sat in the back, because I didn't have too much to say in that class anyway, science.

"Anyway while he was writing some stuff on the board, she got up and walked over to me . . . Now, I was taken completely by surprise, because she never went out of her way for anybody, I mean, she very seldom had anything to do with any of the kids. She usually only talked to the teachers, male teachers.

Anyway, when she got to me she leaned over and in a whisper asked me if I'd seen my friend and laughed aloud. Mr. Roberts let me have it for disturbing the class and threatened to keep me after school if I didn't stop.

"Miss Sugar and Spice, much to his delight, claimed that she was just trying to sharpen her pencil and I started messing with her. If looks could kill, I'd been dead, he was not thrilled with me at all.

Later, while we were suppose to be reading about some worms or bugs or germs or something, she caught my attention and teasingly mouthed, "You want to dance?", with a big smile on her face.

You know, at that point I wondered what all the fuss was over her, because there was something quite evil and ugly about her. It took me a long, long time to even speak to her again.

"After school we went to his house to find out the reason he was not in school. His mother, who was always offering us milk and cookies and stuff, very coldly told us that he was not seeing anybody right now and closed the door in our faces.

She didn't slam it, but she closed it in our faces. All week we tried to get in touch with him. That Friday, Rommie was brought to school by his father. The vice principal came to our class and got Juanita, which angered Mr. Roberts.

After a very brief absence, she returned with a very smug look on her face. Soon, we were all saddened by the entrance of Rommie. He looked just terrible!

He had a bandage around what appeared to be a bald head, his right arm was in a sling, and he had very noticeable limp. The teacher, with all the compassion of a cobra, very coldly asked him to hurry up and find a seat. I was almost in tears.

"The teacher was diagraming something on the board and talking, while Juanita was blowing kisses at Rommie and laughing. That simple idiot, our teacher, thought that he had said something really smart and was really pleased with himself. I doubt that the class liked or respected him after that. I know that I certainly didn't.

"Rommie was never ever the same after all that had happened. Now, I believe, looking back, that the major problem was as terrible as it was for him to be mistreated as he was, the fact that he would not tell anybody what happened made it much worse.

He told nobody, not the police, not his parents, not us, and not even Reverend Brown which I believe had to break his heart. We always felt that Theodore and Juanita had something to do with it, but without Rommie telling exactly what happened everyone was powerless to do anything about it.

Well, time passed and things had definitely changed. Mr. Roberts was replaced by a new young female teacher who was just as cute as she could be. It was all of a sudden like, we left one Tuesday with a big home assignment from him and the next day the principal was there to introduce our new science teacher, Miss Conway. Wow! She was pretty and built like a brick...!

"Well anyway, Rommie got tired of the kids teasing him and hooked school until he got caught. Then he kept on running away from home, and he started getting into much trouble. He didn't have too much to do with us as he was running with a crowd that was a little too fast for us!

"When he did talk to us, he'd talk about all the money, fine cars, and women that he was going to have. He even started driving an old Caddy when he was about fifteen.

Anyway, he was not going to school, getting into trouble, and his family had to move to pay for his lawyers and many legal problems that he had. Finally, they locked him up for quite a bit.

"Looking back, I believe, I know that things didn't have to get completely out of hand as they did with him. If he had only talked things out with somebody, maybe he would not be where he is now.

So, boys, he pleaded, if you ever have a problem, no matter how serious it may be, please come to me if you feel that you need to talk. No matter how busy I may seem, I'll stop! God be my witness, I don't think that I could live with myself if I knew that I could prevent the same thing from happening to another human being and didn't do anything."

The three sat there silently. Chris broke the silence by sharply asking, "Whatever happened to that Theodore and Juanita?"

"Well, later Theodore met some guy and moved to New Orleans with him. As far as I know he is still there. Juanita messed around and around for quite a spell, then she found the Lord and married a guy who turned out to be the finest, young, and dynamic preachers that this town ever produced.

When she is not teaching school, she's working with young, troubled women. You know them as Reverend Doctor Michael and Mrs. Juanita Govans, and I know that you know their son, Roy."

Chris was dumb-founded. Marcus knew the Govans, but he had never been told the whole story. Jacque got up, grabbed, and hugged each boy before going into the house. The boys sat on the steps silently dealing with what Jacque had shared with them.

18. *The Terrible Truths*

Chris jumped up laughing, "These steps sure are hard on the butt!" Marcus smiled as Chris stood and walk around a bit. While he was standing facing Marcus, he noticed a sudden change in Marcus' expression.

Marcus' attention had been drawn by Dora and a companion who appeared so very strange, sinister, and potentially dangerous that he was noticeably shaken.

Seeing the look in his friend's eyes, Chris swiftly swirled around to see what had caused the look of urgency and concern on his friend's face.

His mother was walking a lot faster than she normally would walk as she always liked to give the world a good long look at her. But walking along side of her was a person that Chris didn't even know . . . it was difficult to tell if it were male or female.

Whatever it was about five feet eight inches, dressed in a black leather pants outfit with what may be gold studs, gold-studded boots, a no-brim leather hat which exposed it's short bright, golden colored hair.

Chris guessed that it was female as he could see the faint outline of the person's breast and the curvature of it's behind. However, he did share Marcus' concern as there was certainly something strange and sinister about this creature's appearance. She saw the boys gazing at her, and immediately returned their looks with a very sinister grimace.

Chris was also surprised by the new outfit that his mother was wearing. Instead of the outfit that he was sure that she had worn the night before, she was now wearing a tight-fitting red leather jumpsuit with a large gold zipper down the front, which was low enough (much to Chris' chagrin) to show much of her cleavage.

Her outfit was complemented by a pair a red leather boots and a white panama hat with a red hat band. The contrast between the two made the stranger look that much more ugly to the boys.

Chris opened his mouth to speak to Dora, but it seemed that she somehow didn't notice him or was for some reason ignoring him. Not wanting to be embarrassed in front of his friend he said nothing to the unpredictable Dora.

As the two entered the door, Dora looked over to where the boys stood and seemed to start to say something. However, a gentle push from her companion forced her inside before she could have spoken.

The stranger looked over at the boys with that awful grimace on her face and followed Dora indoors. After she had disappeared through the doorway, the boys had big fun laughing about how funny looking Dora's friend was.

After contorting their faces imitating the strange woman's grimace, a few jokes and laughs at the woman's expense, Marcus thoughtfully suggested that they really should be ashamed of themselves for laughing at the lady " . . . as she could not help being so ugly."

Chris tried to share Marcus' compassion, but she was about the funniest looking thing that he had ever seen and was not at all concerned about compassion. He just knew that she was about the ugliest female that he had ever seen.   It was nearing noon and both were getting hungry. Marcus invited Chris to join him and his grandfather for lunch. Chris refused saying that he really needed to go home in case he had forgotten to do something that Dora had asked him to do.

Actually Chris wanted to go home and get a closer look at Dora's friend. The boys slapped each other five, and Chris merrily walked toward his home with his curiosity peaking about the strange woman.

Arriving at his door steps, he noticed that both the screen and inner doors were closed, a fact that caused him to be concerned as he didn't have his key. As he opened the screen door, the inner door opened simultaneously.

What transpired after the door opened only took a few moments, but it seemed to Chris much longer; and everything seemed to happen in slow motion.

In the middle of the living room floor were the two with the stranger's back to the door. The woman was embarrassing, kissing Dora, on the neck, whose head was back and her eyes closed.

Dora's jump suit was open and precariously hanging from the hips. Neither heard Chris enter as the low, deep sounds of passion drowned out the little noise that Chris had made. Chris stood stunned and dazed. Involuntarily, Chris grunted! Dora lowered her head and screamed!

Goldie dove to the floor, rolled over, and from seemingly nowhere jumped up with a pistol! It was aimed at Chris who was so afraid that he could feel a warm stream of moisture jetting down his leg!

Dora screamed, "No! No! That's my boy! My boy!"

Goldie lowered the pistol grunting, "Well, he ought to know better than to sneak up on me that way! Damn it! I almost blew his . . ."

Before Goldie could finish, Dora had run over and grabbed Chris and held him as she would a much younger child. She begged Goldie to put the pistol away.

Chris felt as though he could spit up! Her warm, moist body felt like a large and hideous serpent trying to squeeze the life out of him. Then, he almost wished that the strange woman had blown his head off so that his nightmare could end right there. It would have been a favor to him.

He jerked away from Dora and ran to his room where he jumped on the bed and cried. Suddenly, he stopped crying. He got off the bed and defiantly walked to the bathroom.

As he snatched his wet pants off, he heard the two women involved in a high volume argument. As he was washing himself, he openly prayed the creature with his mother would blow her head off!

As he finished washing himself, he heard the front door open and close. He defiantly walked out of the bathroom with only his undershirt on his body, hoping for a confrontation with Dora so that, he could tell her precisely how he felt about her.

Walking slowly toward his room, the silence was deafening as there was virtually no sounds coming from any of the rooms. Just as he resigned himself to the idea that he was again all alone, Dora entered his room and began to talk to him.

She did her very best to explain to him that she needed somebody, anybody who was willing to spend money on her as she had no other way of getting the things that she needed for herself.

She went on to complain that there was no way that she could live off the little bit of chump change that them damn welfare people sent her. She rambled on about her new friend Goldie and asked him, " . . . to be good to her or him (snickering) or whatever the hell Goldie thinks she is."

Chris stared at his mother expressionless, thinking "this bitch is crazier than they think."

Goldie called out to Dora, and Dora asked her to come to Chris' room.

Soon standing in the doorway was this gruesome looking creature. If he were not so angry, he could have laughed right in her very face, she was uglier, if it were possible, when she smiled.

She had some clothing bags in her hand which she handed to Dora and told her to get dressed while she got acquainted with Chris.

"Man!", he thought to himself, now totally disgusted.

Dora greedily took the bags and hurried out of the room leaving Chris alone with "The Creature", which now his secret name for her.

"I know that you might not like me too much, I checked you out outside, but I would never hurt you. You see, you is family now that Dora is my woman. Do you understand that or is it too fast for you? "

Chris stared at her blankly.

"Most people don't like me because of what the hell I am, and I ain't dumb enough to think that you will. Your mother only likes me cause I got plenty of cash, more than my dumb-assed brother Rommie ever had."

"Rommie was your brother?"

"Yeah! But he dead as shit now and I am taking over ever'thing, including his woman, Dora. You under-stand?" Chris would have given anything to be anywhere, anywhere else.

One thing that she and her late brother had in common was the absolute willingness to talk about themselves. She talked on and on until finally dressed in a purple leather jump suit with color coordinated boots and hat, appeared Dora at the door.

Goldie's lustful eyes surveyed her lover, while Chris just shook his head in despair. Goldie turned to leave, but before leaving the room, she pulled out a huge roll of money pealing off fifty dollars. She gave it to Chris smiling, "Whether you like it or not we is family and I look out for my own. You understand?"

Before he could answer, Dora interrupted telling him that she and Goldie were going to Atlantic City and reminded him of what to do in case anyone asked about her whereabouts.

Sadly he nodded, indicating that he understood. Dora and "The Creature" left without saying another word to Chris. The feeling of total despair and loneliness overtook the boy as he heard the doors slam shut!

He wondered if he could feel any worse if they were closing a casket on him, but he decided not to cry. He decided that he would never cry again.

Virginia had all but finished her bottle and was laying across the bed still wondering why Rommie's death had caused her so much agony.

"Why in the hell am I torturing myself?", she pondered as she drank the last of the booze directly from the bottle.

Her attention was drawn to the news brief on the television as the news caster invited his audience to stay tuned for late breaking national scandal concerning a defense contract, a state of local school in the wake of the fast approaching new school year, and another senseless apparent drug-related death.

She sat there through the commercial, the other news items, waiting for what she anticipated would be a story about Rommie. However, the newscaster talked about a popular, young, scholarship winning, local basketball player who had been slain in what was apparently a drug-related incident.

He went on to name the youngster as Roy Govans, the son of a prominent local minister. As his picture was shown, somehow there was something all too familiar about the boy's face.

She was concerned as the newscaster mentioned that it had been the seventh drug related homicide in that area in as many days. Virginia was full of remorse as she realized that the boy could have been the son of Michael Govans, a fellow former schoolmate that she had flirted a little bit with in school.

He had never paid too much attention to her as he was a few years older. She smiled as she remembered how she and the rest of the girls would go crazy as he would sometimes sing in school programs.

"I pray to God that that's not his son."

By now the newscaster was editorializing about drugs, youngsters, and sports. His emotional, bitter attack concerning the lack of basic human values and the contempt for human life and decency showed by those who would sell, buy, or use illicit drugs moved Virginia almost to tears again.

However, she felt that Rommie, for one, had received the only justice that drug dealers should get, death!

After the commercial, there was an update on the Roy Govans homicide, the newscaster announced that there had been warrants issued for the arrest of four juveniles in the case and there would be an update on the evening edition or updates as warranted.

The newscaster was obviously emotionally involved as he could not continue and another commercial was quickly aired. Virginia thought aloud that whoever was responsible should burn in hell!

Virginia dragged her weary body out of the bed and went to the bathroom to take a long, hot bath. While the water was running, she decided to use some of Sonia's bubblebath and walked to her room to get it. She glanced around the room and was satisfied that it was reasonably neat and clean.

She very rarely went in her room as she felt that a young woman should have some privacy as she certainly didn't have any as a young girl. Seeing bubble bath on the dresser, she picked it up and left the room. She didn't notice the pictures of Sonia and Roy on the dresser.

Tired and emotionally spent, she finally settled down in the tub and began to feel refreshed. As she soaked in the tub thinking about the direction her life had taken, she thought that she heard some muted rumblings downstairs.

She listened carefully and hearing nothing dismissed it thinking that it was her imagination, the radio, or perhaps noise from next door.

Seemingly out of nowhere appeared three uniformed officers in the bathroom with her. The three had their weapons drawn, each barking out different orders. The lack of coordination almost caused her to laugh as they reminded her of the old Keystone Cops.

However, any chance for that type of relief was eliminated as one ordered her to " . . . stand with your hands up!" The other two officers looked at the younger officer who had ordered her out of the tub strangely but didn't say anything.

Virginia, in no certain terms, told them that she would not get out of the tub and what they could do with their guns.

Angrily, she demanded to know what they were doing in her damned bathroom in the first place, and that she had the mind to jump out of the tub and kick their white asses!

From behind the men a female voice began, "Ain't these

white boys a trip! I tell you, sometimes you would think that they couldn't cross the damn street by themselves."

Pushing her way through the three was a Black female wearing a white blouse, dark brown, long, pleated skirt matching vest with brown pumps and a large, brown, shoulder bag.

With a look of total disdain on her face, she asked them to leave the room and look around the house. "You did at least inform the lady that you had a search warrant, didn't you?"

The younger one nodded his head.

"Well, go do some investigating, and treat this place as if it were my house," she uttered.

Now turning to Virginia and choosing her words very carefully, "I don't know what Larry, Moe, and Curley said to you, but we have a very, uh, uncomfortable situation that we have to discuss. Do you mind if I sit here, pointing to the commode? I need to take this shoe off for a moment."

Virginia looked at her blankly.

"As crude as they may seem they're pretty good cops, but I can't tell them that, you know how that is? My name is Delois White, and I am a captain in the Homicide Division of our city's police department. She reached in her bag and showed Virginia her gold badge and simultaneously took out her pad and pen.

"Anyway, I am sure that you heard about the killing of Roy Govans. Well, we have eye witnesses that places your boy, Allen, at the scene of the homicide and he may be the one responsible for it.

Your daughter, Sonia, is somehow involved. We are not sure how or why she is involved, but one of our witnesses absolutely places her at the scene of the crime, also."

Virginia began to whimper softly.

"We have to ask for your cooperation in this matter so that we can get the truth, the terrible truth of this horrible crime. Now, can I depend on your coopera-tion or would you rather call somebody before we continue?"

Virginia protested slowly, " My son, Little Al, we call him is locked up, well, not really locked up but in a hospital. He couldn't have been the one who . . . "

"Well, according to our information, he was released three days ago. Can I assume from your response that you have not seen or heard from him in the last couple of days?"

"No, the last time I saw him was at the trial. I didn't know that he was even out. They didn't tell me, and Sonia left this morning to go shopping for school clothes. How or why should she be involved? I don't understand?"

"I'll tell you what. I'll go find the three wise men, and wait for you to get dressed and come downstairs."

She, then looked at Virginia sternly as she put her shoe back on, "Please don't do anything, um, unexpected. All we are interested in is the truth. You understand?"

She walked out of the room after Virginia said that she would cooperate. In the hallway she met an officer who handed her a few pictures of Roy and Sonia. Sadly, she took them with her downstairs and waited for Virginia.

As Virginia was dressing, she prayed that she could face the truth, regardless to what it was and promised that somehow, someway she would have the strength to change her life as she was sure that she was on a road directly headed for hell, here on earth and there after. She felt much calmer, at ease, and able after praying.

She walked downstairs where she found the detective using her compact to freshen up and pat her hair a little. She looked at Virginia and began rather casually, "You know I like my job, because I get to meet some very different and interesting people. Sometimes, I find people that I like and then there are the others."

With a puzzled expression on her face Virginia responded that she understood as she herself met many interesting people in the bar as she was a bar maid.

"Yes, I know," she responded finishing up her hair, "Eric's is the name of the bar, isn't? You like this hair do? I catch it trying to keep it in place, but you know a girl has to be sharp always. You never know when Mr. Right is going to show up?"

"That is a little off from where we are suppose to be. Tell me, uh, upstairs you were surprised that your son was out and that your daughter was involved. To your knowledge, did your daughter know the victim?"

"She may have seen him down at the basketball court. She liked to go down there to watch the boys play, but I think that he is, I mean was about nineteen or twenty. He would have been too old for my little girl."

"This is the part of my job that I don't even like. Your daughter may be young, but there is nothing little about her, handing her the pictures. Now you look at these pictures and tell me your daughter and the deceased were just casual friends.

I'm just an ole country girl, my papa and mama raised fourteen of us and let me tell you, even if any of us had been doing things like what I see in those pictures, some of which are quit explicit, there is no way that they would have been found in our house."

As Virginia viewed the pictures, some of which were framed, tears began running down her cheeks.

"Do you know where they were found? On your child's dresser! Now, tell me how in the world could your daughter be carrying on with pictures like that in your home and you not even know about it?

What else could she be doing and you not know? You're not under arrest, but you are going to my office and we are going to get some answers. I hope that you have more control over this child's life than it seems here."

Virginia was completely dumbfounded, scared, and visibly shaken.

Without the benefit of her siren or emergency lights, Deloris sped toward the police station, paying little or no attention to things like red lights and stop signs. Her driving was so reckless that Virginia temporarily forgot her problems as her only concern was getting to the station alive.

As they neared the station, Deloris was notified that the suspect had been apprehended.

19. *Uphill Climb to the Bottom*

The two women said very little as Deloris continued to race toward the station. Deloris was doing her best to remain objective, while Virginia could not stop blaming herself for all the pain and misery.

With a final defiance of the laws of speed and motion, Deloris whipped the car into the station parking lot to a space reserved for her. Yes, there it was on the wall in black letters "RESERVED CAPT. D. WHITE", which impressed Virginia.

Realizing that Virginia was glaring at the name on the wall, Deloris said with a big smile, "Girl, I had to work hard and take much stuff for this space, but I would trade it for a big, fat raise."

She gently nudged Virginia's arm, leading her inside the station which was a beehive of activity. Most spoke to Deloris, some handing her folders and whispering things to her.

A young man stopped her and began a rather long conversation with her which caused her to change her expression from a smile to one of deep concern. She asked a uniformed officer to take Virginia to her office and make her comfortable.

Left alone in the office, Virginia walked around looking at the various awards, certificates, citations along with Deloris' college degree and various other profession achievement certifications.

However, there was a painting on a wall by itself that took her completely by surprise. It was a beautiful painting of a Black Jesus Christ, with an inscription neatly painted in Gold on the bottom which read, "Forgive . . . for they know not what they do!"

This was the first time she had ever seen Jesus depicted as a Black man and the first time she had ever considered the possibility of Him being Black! The very idea that Christ and even God Himself could be Black completely boggled her imagination.

"Could this be really true?," she wondered aloud. "Look," she said to the picture, "I don't know if you are white or Black, or if you are really real. I may be standing here losing my mind, but if you are real and you be Black, you gotta understand what I've been going through. I'd feel like finding a gun and blowing my brains out 'cause I don't know what to do.

I don't know what to do about Little Al or Sonia, much less myself. If you be Black, you know that I been doing the best I can, and I cannot believe that any white man even a God would understand."

She paced the office with tears in her eyes, wondering if she had lost her mind. Virginia looked at the painting again. It seemed to be telling her that everything would be all right. She began to hum a hymn that she had not heard since she was a child in church.

She felt the need to pray again, but this time with much more conviction and hope. This time she prayed for not only forgiveness but for a way to make hers and her children's lives count for something. Virginia prayed that something would happen to make things much better.

Deloris walked into the office with two cups of coffee and

was pleased to see Virginia admiring the picture.

"The first person that I had to arrest painted and sent it to me. It was just the thing that I needed at the time and even more now. It helps me to keep things in order for me. Drink this. Maybe not the best coffee, but it will do in a rush.

Your son is here, and you can probably see him soon. We are waiting for a decision from the juvenile people before we, uh, interview a witness. We have sworn statements from a couple that saw some of what happened.

Your son is not very much help to anybody now, we will know more after the doctors have a chance to see him."

"Doctors?"

"Well, your son needs help. He is a very confused youngster, but we will know a lot more a little later. At this point and time, we do not have a lot of answers only questions. Just be patient and keep on praying, and we should soon know what direction we will be going."

Virginia told her that her boy had been emotionally ill since he was very young which was the reason he was in the hospital instead of in jail. She continued by briefly telling her about his troubles, the bizarre things that he had done.

Deloris listened patiently, looked at her watch, then said, "So, for the time being, please just take it easy. I have a few million things to attend to, and I'll be back as soon as possible."

"I need to use the telephone to call Eric to tell him that I will not in this evening."

"Sure, I'll close the door so that you can have some privacy. Okay?" Deloris left the room without any further comment.

Again the picture caught her attention as she dialed the telephone, "Yes, is Eric there? Sure, I'll wait . . . Okay, fine, and you?. . .Sure, thank you . . . sure.."

As she paced with her eyes still on the painting, the eyes of The Christ seemed to follow her which was beginning to unnerve her. Although she knew that it was impossible for the eyes of a painting, even of Jesus Christ to be following her around the room, or was it?, She was beginning to get really nervous.

"Thank God!," she answered to Eric. He assured her that he knew some of what had happened and expressed his heart felt concern for all that she must be going through, offering to help in any way that he could.

He also asked her not to be concerned about coming to work until she felt like dealing with it. Eric added that she would get paid for the time she could not work.

She thanked him and asked him why he was so very good to her. Although he did his best to sound as cheerful and as much in control as possible, she could detect a hint of sadness in his voice. Virginia knew that this whole thing was hurting him, if anyone in the world loved her, he loved her.

She knew it, he knew it, and the whole world seemed to know it, however she could not make herself like him that way. She wished that she did. It certainly would make life a lot easier for her, but somehow she always seemed to fall for losers like Rommie.

Overwhelmed with emotion, she thanked him, promised to call him and hung up before the tears flowed down her face.

Virginia slumped down in one on the chairs and looked at the painting which seemed now to be looking at her with love, tenderness, and understanding. She could feel a comforting warmth coming from it, and she wondered aloud whether she was losing her mind.

"Like I said, I do not know if you are real or not, but I hope you are. Like the old song, I feel like I am so low that it is an uphill climb to the bottom. Please if you are real show me, teach me how to be about something. Teach me how to make something out of myself and my children."

Through the door walked Deloris followed a man. "My God! It's Michael!" Her now panicked mind raced, "What do I do? What do I say?" She could not make herself look directly at Michael.

She focused her attention again to the painting. Now, the eyes looked so caring and so very compassionate that she was absolutely convinced that she had lost her mind.

Still not daring to look at the man, she could feel him approaching her. She froze as he leaned over her and gently wiped the tears from her eyes with his handkerchief.

"Virginia, believe me, I know that this whole thing must be very hard for you, but let me assure you that with the help of Jesus we will all get through it. Just believe in Him, and He will grant you peace.", Michael said softly and gently.

Deloris turned her back to them to hide the fact that she was, too, moved to tears.

"We must at this time hold on to our faith and believe in Him so that others can . . . " he continued, but he was interrupted by Virginia, who stood and tearfully responded, "I'm so sorry, please believe me, if there is anything that I could do to change what happened, I would. Please don't hate me and my children . . . I just don't know what to say . . . "

"My wife and I hold no grudge against anyone. My son is in His hands now and I know that we will miss him. He was a gift from the Almighty, and His wisdom cannot be second guessed by you, me, or anyone else. I hope and pray that we will act and behave according to His Divine Will."

Having said that, both hugged and Virginia glanced over Michael's shoulder at the painting and felt assured that everything would somehow work out.

The now composed Deloris walked around her desk and told Virginia that she could see her son, however she warned her that he was not responding to anything.

As Virginia was being led out of the door, she grabbed Michael by the hand pleading with him to go with her for support. He agreed and walked slowly beside her, hand in hand. Her grip was so firm that a pain shot up and down his arm, but he said not a mumbling word.

They reached a segregated area where there were padded cells. Through an observation window, they could see him laying on the floor in a fetal position. He was totally ambiguous to everything. Virginia wept. After a period of silence, Deloris assured Virginia that everything possible would be done to help her boy. The three prayed.

As they entered a small room, Deloris explained to them that they did have an eyewitness, but he was so young that they had to have someone from juvenile services with them to interview him.

They were joined by another detective, and Michael's wife who was as caring and concerned about Virginia as he had been.

Virginia wondered to herself whether she could have been as concerned for their feelings had the situation been reversed. She could not honestly say that she would, but she hoped that they understood how much she appreciated their concern.

They were all saddened by seeing the boy, Denny, who was obviously so very young through a one way mirror as he was being interviewed by a social worker and a policeman.

He appeared no older than about nine or ten. He looked too frail, and too dirty even for a boy his age. As the worker was cued, she asked Denny to tell her what had happened.

The boy in minute detail described everything that had occurred as if he were talking about a television show or a movie. Michael and Juanita supported each other as they heard the boy describe the details of their son's death, while Virginia softly sobbed.

"We are confident that he is telling the truth as this is the third time that I have heard the same account from him," Deloris added. "As you can see, he has no real sense that anything happened that was really that bad or wrong. It is just the way it is out there on the streets for many kids."

Juanita asked, "Well, what is going to happen to him?"

"It is very unlikely that he will be prosecuted in any way, however the juvenile services people are concerned as nobody seems to know where his mother happens to be or has been for some time.

Our information is that she is very often, let's say 'unavailable' very often. We suspect that he may be a neglected child. So . . . "

Back in Deloris' office, they sat there all emotionally, if not physically exhausted. Finally, Virginia broke the silence, "I know that you all think that I must be one of the craziest people that you have ever met because of all.."

Michael smiled, "Sure, you have made some mistakes, but you are far from being the craziest person..."

Virginia wept.

Michael added that none of them should or could judge her or anybody.

"Sure," Virginia replied almost sarcastically, "Anyway for the last few moments all that I have can think about are the words to an old song that I used to hear on the radio. I guess that you may know it too. The words are something like . . . `it's an uphill climb to the bottom' . . . and that's exactly how I have been feeling here.

So many things have been going crazy in my life that I feel like I've completely lost control, if I ever was in control. Do you know what I mean? It's like I'm in a deep, dark pit and can't find my way out."

Juanita walked over to her gently grabbing her hand while kneeling beside her, "What you are going through is the beginning of a wonderful change in your life. Sometimes something that we see as terrible and unfair has to happen to us in order for God to get our attention.

Just believe in Him to guide you through this, because He is able. Just believe and call on Him and He will make a way where there is no way."

Virginia could only manage to look at this woman. She wanted desperately to say something, but there were no words. She looked past this woman, at the painting which now was saying, "Go for it, my child."

20. *Shattered World*

The afternoon sun had come and gone. The tired sun had all but deserted the sky causing the cheap interior of the drab police station look grave and exhausted. Having worked much longer than her shift, Deloris was now very late leaving for an out of town family reunion.

The Govans had many arrangements and decisions to make. Virginia was dealing with the fact that her life was and had been a real mess which needed straightening out and soon.

The Govans insisted on taking her home. Deloris, looking very spent, "I'm going out of town, and I'm very late. I'm sure I'll be seeing you."

She reached for her bag with one hand, while writing with the other. She gave them the names and telephone numbers of the detectives who would be handling the investigation.

Deloris assured them that they would be available if there were any concerns and/or if there were some information that they should have. She looked at Virginia, "Girlfriend, get yourself a good lawyer so that your boy can get the help he needs. Take care of that young woman of yours. Sometime they grow up too fast and not it the direction we would wish. She needs a lot of structure! Whatever it takes, make sure she develops that brain . . . "

"Now, I know it is going to be hard, but I want you to go

home and wait for her. My people are looking for her and will find her or answer to me. If she comes home before they find her, please call this number to let them know she's home. We do not believe she will have any, uh, legal problems, but they do need to know if she's home."

Despite Virginia's objections, the Govans insisted that they would stay with her as long as possible. They walked to the parking lot together, well, behind Deloris who had put quite a bit of distance between them.

As they reached the door, Deloris was speeding off, tires squealing, nearly slamming into an oncoming police cruiser! Michael shook his head in disbelief. Virginia laughed, "I don't mean any harm, but it takes much nerve to ride with that woman. She made the drive over here an adventure, scared me to death!"

The drive to the projects began very quietly as each was reflecting on the circumstances that had brought them together. Driving was not easy for Michael as he often drifted into deep thought or prayer. He knew that he was going to miss his son and wondered how much his wife could take.

Knowing that she was relying on his faith and strength was frightening to him. He knew all the words but was not sure that he could be the rock needed now.

Juanita knew Michael well enough to know that his love for her and faith in God would oblige him to be comforting to her, and the many people who knew and loved their son.

She remembered one of the best sermons that he had preached. In it, he took the congregation back to the time and place where the Lord asked Abraham to sacrifice his son, Isaac.

After telling, reminding them that God was trying Abraham out and that he was stopped before he sacrificed his boy. Michael paused and smiled as only he could, "But glory to God

Almighty, He had found His man.

God made a covenant with Abraham. As you know, God always keeps His word! Our Jewish brothers and sisters believe they have a special relationship with the God of Abraham and his sons, Jacob and Isaac.

God Himself changed the name of Abraham's land to Israel for filling the covenant. This faith has sustained and nourished them even as they suffered and many were permanently severed from their home. Sometimes God's time is a long time to us mortals. But you look over there in Israel, and you'll see them, just where God told them they'd be.

"Now, we Christians see a much deeper significance with the relationship of Abraham and God. We often think of Abraham as the father of all who believe in God, whether belonging to Israel or not. And, and my brothers and sisters, I believe that the most significant part of this covenant was that fact that God would not let Isaac use his son as a sacrificial lamb.

"He would not allow Abraham to kill his son. But in His infinite wisdom, He had His mind on the ultimate sacrificial lamb, His own son, Jesus!"

Juanita's pulse began to race and although they were in air-conditioned comfort, she began to sweat. She recalled him stretching out his arms and spinning a couple of time in the pulpit as his voice sounded like a thousand trumpets, "Years later, when Israel was going through some stuff. The whole world was in an uproar over the social change caused by the Roman Empire, and God fixed it in His own way!

He sent the world a powerful little package. Without a whole lot of fanfare, without a special announcement or commercial on television He sent His only son, Jesus, to save us all.

"Not only our Jewish brothers and sisters, but for the whole world then and now. He sent His boy to save the hated

Romans, the Chinese, the Russians, the French, and you and me.

I can imagine the anguish that He must have gone through as He watched His son, the ultimate sacrificial lamb die up there on the cross for the world. I can also imagine the pride He must have had as the world didn't understand what had happened.

"Now, my brothers and sisters, tell me why are our sons dying in the streets? Whose covenant are they fulfilling? I ain't been on the job very long, but right here in God's house, I've been asked to pray for the souls of our fallen boys. Felled by the demons of greed, envy, and folks who'd rather turn their sanctified heads rather than face the truth.

Folks, too often their own parents, who profited by their son's ill-gotten gains, and those same parents got the nerve to come in here in God's house, saying they didn't know."

Juanita's thoughts were interrupted by the urgency in Virginia's tearful voice. "Maybe one day I will, but right now I don't understand you two! I don't mean no harm, but if the situation was reversed . . . I, I doubt that I could be around trying to comfort and ride around with the parent of somebody who done killed my boy.

I mean like, although Little Al ain't worth spitting on most of the time, but he is mine. If somebody were to hurt him for no-good reason, I'd be willing to go to hell 'cause somebody's gonna pay, big time! And my daughter, man, they'd have to lock me away to keep me from . . . what I really mean is that you two ain't real, and I love you for that. If you know what I mean?"

Juanita reached back squeezing Virginia's hand as tearful Michael pulled over to the curve. The women obeyed as he asked them to step out of the car for a moment with him.

The hot, humid breath of the evening caused the three to gasp for nonexistent cool air. Michael began to wave his arms vigorously as with his eyes surveying the empty lot.

The full moon made it easy for them to see all of the broken bottles, discarded cans, and the trash on the empty lot, which had been a residential block. He walked a short distance away, gently kicked a can and turned toward them.

"This, he stretched out his arms, is where the road that I now follow began. A few years ago, quite a few now (he smiled), I was seventeen. Like most of us geniuses at seventeen, I was wondering what all the fuss was about. I mean this life. I had it all figured out.

People, mostly the fairer sex, liked me a lot. I was, ladies please excuse my total lack of modesty, handsome, sharp, uh, Mr. It, a lover, a great singer, a song stylist, if you will."

Juanita laughed as Virginia looked.

"It would just be a matter of time before I'd be a great one. Nothing mattered except my music. I was destined to be one great recording artist. Other folks like my parents, sister, teachers, and friends could not see the big picture as well as I, but that was their problem.

My destiny was as clear as glass. Many had been discovered in joints like the ones that I was singing, and it would just be a matter of time before all the unbelievers would turn on the radio, and I'd be there singing my number one song. It would just a matter of time before they'd go to the record store to buy a copy of my already gold album. Anywhere there would be music, I'd be there.

"Living at home with my parents was pure hell sometimes, they insisted that I get an education. My sister, Loretta, was and is one of the most practical, independent females I know. She was wasting her time going to college and working as a nurse's aid to help pay her way, you see.

I kept telling her that I would take care of her when my career took off, but she'd just laugh saying that I could not take care of my self. I planned to take her on the road with me to watch my back. It is always beat to have family around you when you are rich and famous."

By this time Virginia wished that she had taken the bus.

"You should hear him around the house," Juanita began, "Sometime Roy and I . . . " She paused to compose herself. "Even better, sometimes during his sermons he will break down and lay one of those old-fashioned, down home hymns on you. You don't know whether to shout, cry, scream, or what? Sometimes I do it all!

Sometimes the kids in our youth gospel choir get a little angry with him. A sweet little sister said to him just last week, "When we are supposed to sing, you preach and let us sing." He promised to be more careful."

Michael chuckled, "Anyway, I was singing in local bars, clubs, and cabarets for folk who didn't want to put out the money for more experienced entertainment.

At first, my folks were opposed, often aggressively when I used to sneak out to do a gig. They had, thank God, no problem using a belt to make their point clear. Sometimes my sister would whack me a few times to save them the trouble. They all laughed.

"However, it was not long before they realized that the only way to keep from killing me was to let me have some of the freedom I craved. So, we decided that if I kept up with my schoolwork and reduced the number of gigs, they would support me. My sister volunteered to be my, uh, overseer.

Man, did she do her job! Well, looking back, I'm sure that they knew that I was setting myself up for disappointment, grief, and maybe mild disaster. I'd like to think that they felt that I'd have to find out what was real for my own hardheaded self."

Michael began to pace, "So, there I was, a legend in my own mind, singing my heart out in those little joints, seeing many things that a kid my age should not have seen.

Women my age became less and less attractive to me as those older women just wore my young butt out. But though all this I never even imagine that this was the beginning of what could have been a life shattering experience for me.

"By this time, I only had two teenaged friends Rommie and "Rommie?," Virginia shrieked as if being smacked in the face, "You can't possibly be talking about the one who got him . . ."

"Yes, and we are saddened by the way he choose to live, but who knows, maybe he had time to get it right with God! Ironically, it was Rommie who kept telling me that I was moving a little too fast. And there was Jacque, who lives near you."

"We don't talk too much, but he lives right across the court from us. I cannot get over you being friends with Rommie, because he was really bad news. I went out with him a few times and he was bad news, big time!"

"Well, he wasn't always like that. When we were youngsters, they thought that he certainly not I would be the preacher. He was our conscience then. He had quite a little crush on Juanita. We'll tell you about it some day."

"Rommie, I'll be damned, excuse my French. So what happened?"

"There were two types of people as far as I was concerned, entertainers and fools. Rommie had drifted away from us, and Jacque was the only person my age that I could even talk to, you see. Finally, I abused our friendship to the point that we even drifted apart.

With tears flowing from his eyes he continued, "One night a little club near here, my life shattering experience began. After I finished my first show, I met this guy named Slick or Smooth, something like that. That should have been a clue to stay away, but I was very full of myself.

Anyway, he talked to me smooth enough for me to believe that if he managed my career, I would certainly become a superstar. I was so green that he convinced me that he had big time connections in New York who were craving some young, talented singers like myself.

"He said that he had heard about me and was there to check me out. I was excited when he casually mentioned that I would be in a recording studio in a couple of days, if I were ready to go!

He talked about trust. He convinced me that I had to trust him even if others didn't. A funny thing, the barmaid saw me talking to him. She warned me to stay away from that snake."

Michael became so agitated that he was striding in little circles. The full moon was spotlighting his every movement, with the stars and the street lights keeping time as he paced while talking.

"Smooth was so slick that after my next show, we talked again. After telling me how good I was, and that I was a fine looking young man, I felt like I had known him forever.

I even told him about the money that I had tucked away at home that nobody knew about. He got truly excited about my career. My, uh, manager scribbled an address on a cocktail napkin and asked me to get my toothbrush, the money and meet him in the morning at nine."

Michael continued to reminisce, "Man! After I agreed to meet him, he sat there looking at me with this big smile on his face. He shook my hand, hugged me and told me several times that I would not be sorry.

It was time for my last set, but he said that he could not stay. But before he left he whispered to me that we were going to bust New York wide open! Sounded good to me."

When you feel good, it gets contagious. Slick told me to get used to being a star, and I believe just having somebody seemingly believing in me caused me to be great that night.

I let that joint out! Even the piece of band that played with me sounded fabulous! After I finished my last song even, they joined in the five minute standing ovations that I received. Nothing could stop me now!

"As I was about to leave the men tried to pat my back off, and the women just hugged and kissed me to death. Some offered me some money for a, uh, private performance. He blushed. Well, I just had to see Jacque before I left for New York.

It was almost three on a school morning when I got to his house. I threw a few pebbles against his window to wake him. He looked out at me smiling and came out to talk. After I finished telling him about my good fortune, he looked at me like I was a crazy person.

He pointed out all the things that were wrong with the arrangement, including the fact that I should not speak to a person named Slick or Smooth. I still cannot get his name right.

In my heart of hearts, I knew he was right, but nobody was going to take my dream away from me. So, I did the mature, adult thing. I called him fifty-two varieties of fool and said a few things about his mama.   "As I stormed away from his house filled with the self-indulgent omnipotence reserved for conceited idiots like myself, I truly felt sorry for Jacque as he could never share in the spoils.

Yes, my friends, he had in my mind turned his jealous back on me. Like I said, he'd never share in the spoils, the women, jewelry, women, cars, money, women, homes, women, vacations, and women! Did I mention women?"

Juanita and Virginia laughed as the air was filled with the omnipresent sounds of the streets. Their laughter was short-lived they noticed Michael was crying.

"This is the first time since then that I have been near this place. Uh, well, when I got home, I swaggered into the kitchen and noticed the basement light was on.

I skipped down the stairs and saw my sister sitting in the middle of the floor with about a million books, papers, and other stuff littered all around her. Asleep on the couch was her boyfriend Lester. He was still in his police uniform. Old Lester lived for two things, my sister and the law. He possesses one of the most astute legal minds imaginable. He laughed. I'm sure he knows every law since the time of Moses."

Virginia interrupted by asking them to join her at her place so that, Michael could finish telling them, and she had to go to the rest room. Soon they were in the car, but Juanita was now driving. Virginia turned to Michael, now sitting on the back seat, as he continued.

"Well, I think I stopped with my sister in the floor and Lester on the couch sleeping?"

"Full of arrogance, I said, "Guess who's going to New York to cut an album? My sister looked up at me responding, 'Guess who is going to get my foot in his butt if he does not go upstairs and leave me the hell alone.'

"I stood there with my little feelings hurt, absolutely stunned by her lack of interest in my apparent accomplishment.

"She jumped up, 'Album? What album? Tell me about it!'

"I felt like that was more like it! She was beaming as I began to tell her about my incredible show, and still smiling she said that she wished that she'd been there. Now strutting around, like a peacock, I told her about meeting the man who was now my manager.

Her expression was that of mild concern, but she was still happy. For some reason I still cannot recall the man's name. But when I told her his name was Smooth or Slick, looks of shear horror flashed across her face!

"Loretta was not a soul to be taken lightly. I'm sure that at that moment, she considered, I believe, he laughed, stomping me to death and being done with the whole thing.

She snatched the collar of my shirt dragging my dumb butt over to where Lester was sleeping and demanded that I repeat what I had told her.

"Being fellow men of the world, I expected Lester to see things my way. He was very groggy at first but became a captive audience as I repeated my story. Very calmly, he waited for me to finish. Lester began to question me like I was Jack the Ripper or somebody.

"What record company is this person affiliated? What is his full, legal name? Do you have a New York business address? Telephone number? Or even a business card?"

"All I had was a pathetic, wrinkled napkin with his name and address where I was to meet him in the morning. I never offered it to them. They took turns fussing me out.

He asked me if the clown had offered me drugs, taken any money, or propositioned me. I could not believe he was taking me there, and the question about being propositioned completely confused me, but I kept it to myself.

"My sister had heard quite enough! She demanded that I take

my dumb ass upstairs and go to bed. She added that she would stomp me into the very ground if she even thought that I was going to even speak to that, let's say person, again!

I decided that the safest thing for me to do was just what she said. So, I silently walked up the steps leaving my dreams on the basement floor and my sister crying."

Michael told them that he went to bed and finally drifted off to sleep. He told them about a very strange dream. It seemed that a bunch of excited people were around a palace anxiously waiting. Suddenly, they, many gorgeous women started screaming, yelling, some fainting, and chanting, "He's here! He's here!"

He remembered feeling confused as the crowd knocked him down trying to get to some guy, a singer. A large hand picked him up. It was Slick who with a diabolical laugh started yelling at him, "That should have been you! That should have been you! You! You!"

"The others began to laugh at looking like those faces you see at a horror show! I jumped out of bed wet as . . . I was shaking like a drunk with the DTs.

I sat on the bed and decided that Jacque, my sister, and Lester were dead wrong. I was going to New York and that was that!"

Michael paused to composed himself. "On that empty lot stood the house where I was suppose to meet him. Anyway, I wrote my parents telling them what I was about to do, and I would be back in a few weeks a superstar. I packed a few clothes, got my money, and eased out the house about 5:30. I was on my way to meet my destiny head on.

"Having time on my hands, I wandered around until my stomach started talking to me. I caught a bus to one of those all-night eateries and had a little something to eat. By then, it was about eight. So, I caught a bus back to where I was to meet my manager.

About six blocks or so from my destination the traffic got so congested that the bus was just stuck. I didn't have time to mess around as it was 8:35. I jumped off the bus and darted through the alleys.

Juanita pulled into the parking lot and parked the car. This action surprised Virginia as she didn't think Juanita even knew where those projects were and told her so.

Juanita laughed, "Girl, you don't know! I grew up not more than three blocks away from here. Now we live within shouting distance. So, as they song goes `we are neighbors'."

Virginia rushed to lead them to her home as she had to go to the restroom. Soon they were sitting in the living room drinking soft drinks and Virginia asked Michael to finish the story.

"Well, I was expecting the man to be outside waiting in his car to get going to New York. Before I turned that last corner, I even imagined him impatiently waiting in a limo. A strange thing, I then had my first doubts about him. I asked myself why he hadn't offered to pick me up, but I dismissed it.

"I had no problem finding the building, but again I had misgivings as the house was obviously divided into rooms or apartments. Having no apartment number, I sure didn't know what name to look for on the mail boxes.

You know as I stood there on the steps looking dumb, I believe I heard the sounds of sirens, but I cannot swear to it. But I can, and will never forget, this tremendous chill right down to my bones which startled me. Man! It was about eighty degrees, but for that brief moment it felt like, I do never remember feeling that cold before or even after that moment.

"Like a fool, I sat on the steps waiting. A lady dressed like what we called a domestic marched out the door. I asked her if she knew the guy that I was waiting for. She looked at me oddly and asked me to describe the man.

"She looked me up and down with her nose all turned up. Looking very bitter, mean, and angry with me, she asked me what I wanted with this man. Although I felt like she was trying the mind my business, I told her that the guy was my manager.

With pride, I told her that he was going to take me to New York to cut a record. She looked at me curiously, saying almost to herself, `Well Jesus, that's what they call it now "managing".

"That old soul certainly didn't bite her tongue . . . Why ain't you in school? You running away from home? Are you funny? We were taught to always respect our elders, even if we disagreed with them. The woman was getting to me to the point where I wanted to read her butt, but she talked so fast that I could not get in a word.

"Then she told me that his man that I was waiting for was about as much of a manager as she was a princess. He, she said, had many parties with young boys like myself. She told me that the one he had earlier this morning must not have liked what he was trying to do too much.

`They was up there cussing, fighting and breaking up the place so bad that we called the police. The police came in time to see the boy running down that hall screaming and all bloodied-up. The fool was dead on his heels with a straight-razor in one hand. In the other, he had a butcher's knife! The fool was butt-naked!

"She said that when he saw the police the fool went cold crazy! He charged them like he was one of them Indian's you see on television. Now, you know that the police ain't got no problem shooting a colored man these days.

They shoot the sh . . . out of him, but he wasn't shot bad enough to kill him. He just stood there like he didn't believe they done shot him. He was kind of dazed like.

"Somehow, he managed to get out here to the sidewalk, looking like he was going to quit acting like a fool. What with all the lead in him, we kinda of felt sorry for him. Then, he looked and a colored cop was talking to the boy. The fool went off again and charged that colored cop!

That was the last thing he ever did in this life. Them police really fired his ass up this time. They shot him so fast and so much that it sounded like the Forth of July out here! And I am happy that they kilt him, Jesus forgive me, but I don't like them kind of man the mess with boys like you."

"How did you feel?" Virginia asked.

"Like, I wished that the ground would open and swallow me. Well, she looked at me and told me that I should be in school somewhere. All I could do was to nod my stupid head as I was stunned, hurt, and disoriented.

She raised her pocketbook as if to whack me a couple of times and ordered me to go on to school and forget that manager business. I was not moving fast enough for her, so she did whack me on the head with her pocketbook.

As I retreated toward school, she yelled that she'd be watching me. If I messed up again, she would find me and kick my very butt! "I almost ran to school. In my mind I could hear her yelling at me, `I'll be watching you, boy!', repeatedly.

"Much later, when I had my first trial sermon the Good Lord arranged it so she was there. My nerves were shot, but I was comforted as I looked out at the audience and saw her face. Since then, every time I have a personal crisis, she is always there for me.

She (he smiled) is always around to keep me straight. I never knew how she found me, but I'm really sure that I have a genuine Godmother!

"It must have been about 10:30 when I finally got to school, it was time for my history class. I do not recall the teacher's name, but he was the most negative, insensitive, sarcastic, troubled soul I believe I have ever met. He was shorter than most of us, maybe . . . I hope he has found some happiness in life.

"Nullification dripped from his venomous mouth as I dared enter his classroom late. He continued by saying that none of us would amount to much as we were not scholarly historians like himself. As he continued to entertain himself with witticisms, I was summoned to the principal's office.

As I entered the office, I knew right away that something was wrong. The usually effervescent and flirtatious secretary, who was not very much older than us, didn't say anything to me. Instead of the suggestive sultry tones and gestures, she gestured toward the principal's inner office. She jumped up crying while running out of the office.

"It was only a few steps between where I was standing and his door. I didn't know what, but I knew that something was terribly wrong. The first person I saw was Lester dressed in his uniform which probably meant that he should have been working. He was holding my sister who looked very tired and drained.

I thought that it was all about me. To that end, I felt that their behavior was too drastic for what I had done. Then I wondered why these two were there. One of my parents should have . . . I began to cry as I knew that something had happened to one of them.

"Seeing me cry really broke my sister up. To add to the confusion, all three tried to talk to me at once. You know, there is no good way to tell somebody that a loved one has died suddenly. Their task was twice as difficult as they had the very sad duty to tell me that both of my parents had been fatally injured in an automobile accident about eight o'clock that morning.

"After my parents read my note, they started looking for me. An out of control tractor-trailer slammed into their car! I believe that was that reason my bus was stuck in traffic.

If I had used the streets instead of the alleys, I may have seen them. I heard the ambulances while . . . and the chill I felt was . . . could have been them trying to warn me or say goodbye . . . Well, then my whole world shattered."

Both Juanita and Virginia wanted to say something, but neither did. They were doing their best to remain composed.

"It was important for me, somehow, to go back to the classroom to get my stuff. The principal said that he would take care of it. But! I wanted my stuff! I was crying, irrational and felt maybe, if I could only go back there, somehow . . . someway, things would be different. If I didn't . . . After, I composed myself they let me go."

"When I entered the room, I was still an emotional mess. Mr. Mason, that's his name, Mason. Anyway, when he saw me, he really took off! He said that I was nothing, the whole bunch of us boys were worthless thugs, lacking discipline and home training.

He said that if our parents had done their jobs, his would be a lot easier. I stood there motionless, I just could not move. There were tears flying all over my face. The other kids didn't know why I was crying, but they were ready to get into his butt!

"Before any of us could do anything, Lester stormed into the door. Lester had followed me without my knowledge. Mr. Mason cut one them `I told you so' smiles, he knew that this big, bad, Black police officer was coming to arrest me.

But Lester went up to that man and just before he totaled the little man stopped himself. Mr. Mason was petrified as Lester called him a pathetic little bully. The whole class erupted in cheers, but it was short-lived as Lester's stare calmed them down. All was quiet as we left the room with Lester's massive arm around my shoulder."

Michael took a deep breath and a sip of his soda, while the ladies waited patiently for him to continue. Michael managed a smile, "Years later, when Lester was in a testifying mood, he told me that not long after that day, he hunted and found Mr. Mason and treated him to a free attitude adjustment session. The ladies laughed knowingly.

"I could not bring myself to view my parents until the funeral. Somehow, I felt that if I didn't they would still be alive. On the morning of the funeral, I just could not get myself together. They were very patient with me, but the guilt that I felt was killing me. I could not help but feel totally responsible. When we arrived at the packed church, I felt nothing. Many kids from school were there. Jacque and his family were there but no Rommie. His family was there but no Rommie.

"Most of the funeral I do not remember, but I do remember a couple of things that Reverend Brown said. One was . . . in every heartache, problem, or disaster lays the seeds of a greater victory. We do not know why things like this happen to good people, but we must have faith in Him.

The other was the greatest tribute to the departed is for all of us to live our lives in a way that would make God and them proud. I had no idea what I was going to do with my life, but from the time I promised my parents that they would be proud of the man that I would become. I hope to God I they are.

Michael asked for permission and used the telephone to call Jacque. He excused himself and walked over to Jacque's.

Virginia told Juanita that she was really blessed to have a man like Michael. Juanita laughed, "Blessed! Girl you don't know, I was speeding toward hell with gasoline clothes before we got really serious."

"You?" Virginia exclaimed as she had admired Juanita's moderate mannerisms and attire from the moment they met.

"From the time I was about thirteen, I discovered that boys liked having me around. I had a little looks and was really big for my age. Not by today's standards, but for then, I was big!"

Virginia laughed, "They must be born dogs!"

"It didn't take me long to find out that the boys my age were silly and broke. My first little boyfriend was fifteen. He made a little money working at the corner store, delivering groceries. Whenever I had to go outside, you'd best believe that I was dressed.

You know what I mean? I'd be sharp! So, whenever I would go to the store, he'd fall all over himself. I thought that it was and he was cute. There were always some unordered ice cream and cookies for me when he delivered our groceries.

"One day he got up the nerve to finally ask me to go to the movies with him. My mother almost had a heart attack when I asked for permission. It was just the two of us as my father rolled out to find himself when I was about two.

Took him a long time (she laughed), I've only seen him a couple three times since I was twelve. He always sent the money, but I think he is petrified by my mother.

"We had another long talk. She told me that I was a beautiful young woman, and all I had to watch out for was one thing, men! They laughed. She warned me that all they wanted to do was to have sex, sex, sex! With me and my fast acting self, I was not doing nothing, because my mother had spooked me so bad that the last thing I was going to do is have sex.

"Mother was something else, and she told me to always use the fact that they were lusting after me to my advantage. She told me that they would do anything for me as long as I kept my panties up and my head straight.

I was taught that as long as I remained a virgin, my options would be unlimited. So, by the time I was sixteen, I was a pro at dating and teasing older boys who had cars, money, and things. But I was not putting out for nobody, no time, and no how!

Virginia looked at her curiously.

"Almost, well, I wanted to a few times. Some of them were really cute and smooth as silk. Almost got myself raped, but I held onto my stuff!"

"Don't tell me until your wedding night?" Virginia teased.

"Real close, girl, real close! ... But let me finish what Michael didn't. The funeral was really hard on him as you can imagine. I was standing outside with the other curious souls as they were leaving the church.

I had never paid too much attention to him as, well, because he was my age which made him a young boy. But when he stepped out that door, my heart did a double flip!

I mean, he looked so sweet, so handsome, so, so, wow that I fell in love with him. I made my way through the crowd to get closer. As he passed me, I reached out and touched his hand. He looked at me and smiled a little. I melted. I knew right then that I was going to marry him or die trying.

"That was one strange day. First of all, I just happened past the church. But after touching his hand, I jumped into a car going to the cemetery with one of Lester's brothers and family. They were surprised but very nice. I don't know where I got the nerve, but I hopped right in there."

"By the way, before Lester and Loretta got married, Lester's brothers adopted him as their little brother. When Roy was born, they insisted that they were my son's uncles. Lester comes from a very large, loving family. You are going to love them as much as we do."

Virginia, realizing what Juanita was saying, began to cry.

"At the cemetery, everybody was astounded when three vans full of the most gorgeous floral arrangements imaginable arrived. I found out later that they were given anonymously. Years later, and quite by accident, we discovered that Rommie had sent them."

"So, Rommie did have a heart," Virginia said.

"Virginia, if nothing else, I have learned not to judge people. It is not wise. But I do know that there is sin in the best of us, and good in the worse of us. God is the only that can judge as we all have our challenges.

The two hugged as Virginia tears flowed.

Virginia ran upstairs to get some tissue.

21. *Virginia!*

As Virginia walked upstairs, she looked back at Juanita who was crying softly. She knew that Juanita was hurting, and only time would soften her anguish. Virginia wondered if she could have done anything to prevent the senseless murder of Roy. She knew that Sonia had too much freedom, but that was going to change big time!

In the solitude of her room, she prayed that she would have the strength to be the mother that she should be. As worried as she was about Sonia, she felt that the best thing for her to do was to wait as Deloris had told her.

Meanwhile, Michael had been standing on the steps trying to make sense of his son's death. Looking out at the broken sidewalks, broken glass and scattered debris, and the broken people milling around, he tried to resist the feeling that somehow he was still paying. Why was God still making him pay for being foolish when he was just a kid? Wasn't the death of his parents enough? When will enough be enough?"

He looked to the heavens for answers, but the full moon and the stars were busy exhibiting the plight of the projects. His thoughts were interrupted by a young voice, "Mister, you going to give me a quarter or what?"

Mechanically, he reached in his pocket handing the young boy most of his change. The happy youngster greedily grabbed the coins and jetted away. Michael realized, as the boy ran away, that he was the same neglected child he had seen at the police station. He wanted to talk to the child, but it was much too late as the child had disappeared.

He made his way over to Jacque's home and was greeted by a handshake and a hug. As always Michael was impressed by the way his friend kept his home. It really proved the expression, "I may live in the ghetto, but there ain't no ghetto in me."

"Man this has really been a week," Jacque began softly. "What with Rommie getting killed out there, and your son . . . man, I'm so sorry. He was such a good kid and really didn't deserve that. God! I'm sorry."

"Thank you, man. It's hard, very hard. But I've got to hold in together or Juanita may . . . God knows what? She wanted us to move away from here a long time ago, but I said that we needed to be close to the people we were ministering to. She always asked me to think about Roy, but I always said that all we had to do was bring him up right and keep an eye on him. Juanita hasn't yet, but I'm sure that one day she's is going to say that our son would still be alive, if we had moved.

"What am I going to say?"

Jacque looked at him sternly, "You don't sound like yourself. You sound like somebody who never listened to your own sermons."

Michael yelled back at him, "My sermons? My sermons? Maybe I'm in the wrong business. Maybe I should just hang it up and . . . "

Jacque laughed, "And do what? Sell insurance, or maybe you should sell used cars. If you never believed all the stuff you said from your pulpit, selling worthless used cars should be a breeze to you! Gonna give it up! Yeah, do that! Let everybody know that you have been bullshitting them for years!

"Let's go down to the corner and get ourselves a bottle and drink our troubles away. Even better, let's find a pusher and really get down. If you want to quit, I'm your friend and will quit with you!"

Michael managed a slight smile, "Do I sound that bad?"

"Worse. I love you like a brother, you know that, but shouldn't you be with Juanita?"

"She's across the court with Virginia."

Shocked, Jacque responded, "Where? You know that her son..."

"Yes, I know but we got to keep on looking out for each other. Even through tragedy, we must look out for each other. We've been trying to keep her occupied until the police find her daughter. I'd better get back! Come go with me."

Jacque hesitated.

"What's wrong? Don't you ever visit with her? When is that last time you were over there?"

"Counting today?"

"Yes, counting today."

"Never, she reminds me too much of Claudette. They looked enough alike that they could have been... Man, she looks so good to me that I could . . . "

Michael interrupted, "Yes she does. I've been looking at that woman. She looked so familiar, yes, Claudette. How long has it been?"

"Almost ten years, now."

"I am not trying to be a matchmaker, but you need somebody, and she certainly needs somebody. I'm not saying that she can replace Claudette, but man! Ten years of not having a close female friend is a bit much, brother. Now go over there with me. We may need you."

Without further hesitation Jacque went along.

Virginia was surprised to see Jacque at her door. He had always been cordial but distant. Their greeting was friendly but cautious. Juanita was delighted to see him. She ran over to and hugged him. They shared a much needed laugh.

Jacque's laughter was so infectious that everybody began to laugh. Soon they were talking like old friends, which was a pleasant surprise to Jacque and Virginia. Virginia teased Jacque, "Thought the only words you knew were good morning and good evening. But now, after all those years I find out, you are, well, all right."

"I don't want to be a drag, but Michael will you please finish telling me? I sure Jacque will not mind."

Jacque fully agreed after being told briefly what they had been talking about.

"Well," Michael began, "at least now I have an impartial witness to confirm what I've been saying."

"Amen!", Jacque laughed.

"Now, where was I?"

Virginia eagerly exclaimed, "At the funeral. Juanita told me about the flowers."

"That was really something", Jacque added, "Old Rommie was really a person filled with contradictions." Michael began, "I became an instant introvert. I stopped singing and devoted myself to school and studying. The next year, I was a straight A student in everything except music. I just could not get into it. I received the lowest possible passing grade as the teacher was really annoyed with me as I would not participate.

He walked over to the still standing Jacque, "This guy was the only person with whom I could talk . . . And I didn't talk to him too much. However, I did manage to develop a close relationship with Reverend Brown.

He was really patient and loved me through those most difficult periods of my life. He also planted the seeds of my understanding of unconditional love and responsibility.

"Sometimes I feel like I did learn my lessons well enough, but thank God I've always been surrounded by people who keep me from getting too lost. People like my good friend, Jacque."

Jacque smiled and nodded.

"Close relationships . . . Well, I began my close relationship with God. I prayed so much that God, Jesus and I got real close. My sister and I, well, those first few months, I must have worried a few grey hairs in her head. She and Lester got married that following summer.

Man! was that a big wedding. Lester's parents had thirteen children and they were a very loving bunch. Yes, they had thirteen children all girls except the twelve boys, and . . . "

Virginia interrupted laughing, "Maybe I'm stupid or something. But how many children were there thirteen or twenty-five, male, female, or what?"

"You'd have to live with him to understand him sometimes." Juanita interjected. "I believe he talks like that to see if folk are paying attention. There were twelve boys and Nancy. Nancy is the anchor of a big television station in New York. She is something else. Wait until you meet her."

As Michael began, Virginia was again touched by Juanita's obvious intention to have a real friendship with her.

"They adopted me as their little brother and took turns taking me to places. Sometimes I had to hide from them because I couldn't keep up with them. That's how Roy, he paused, had so many uncles, and one very wild aunt! I was really happy when Roy was born. It took some pressure off me.

"Lester was like a father to me with his love, patience, and understanding. I had the support and stability that I needed. I think I may have been the world's oldest teenager. Everybody that I hung out with was much older, including Reverend Brown.

Old Jacque over there had a part-time job and a full-time romance with one of the most attractive and intelligent young ladies this town has ever produced. Those love birds got married and had a beautiful daughter. Both have gone on to Glory!

"Maybe I'll lose a lifelong friend by saying this. He looked at Jacque. You may have noticed that at times I could not keep me eyes off you, I . . . "

Virginia blushed, "I didn't notice, but thank you!"

"Well, you reminded me of somebody, Claudette, Jacque's late wife. You are as attractive as she was . . . and sharp, too. I understand you work down at Eric's. There is nothing wrong with you making an honest living, but I feel that the Lord is going to move you in another direction. Maybe working with youngsters."

"I always wanted to work with kids. Maybe, I'll . . . "

"I think you should. Juanita can help."

Juanita echoed Michael while a slightly embarrassed Jacque mockingly thanked Michael for telling Virginia that she was attractive to him. She laughed as Virginia blushed again. Jacque moved quickly toward the door, saying that he was going to treat them to some juice. Virginia didn't want him to leave for fear he would not return. Michael assured her that Jacque would return.

"I sure hope so, he's kind of handsome."

Smiling Michael continued, "Well, my sister would not move, which was a suggestion that I made a couple times a day.

Sometimes, when I came home I expected to be greeted by my mother and father.

During that first summer, I spent much of my time sitting on the steps watching life go by. One evening, while sitting there, Juanita dressed in a pink shorts set sat on the steps beside me. She didn't say a word, just sat there."

Juanita blushed and this time, Virginia laughed.

"After sitting there for about five minutes, she took my hand telling me that it was time for us to go to the movies. I told her that I was not going anywhere! And I meant it! She sure had nerve! I'll tell you about Jacque, Rommie, and me trying to, uh, date her another time.

"Anyway, I made the mistake of looking at her infectious smile and her dreamy, big, bright, brown eyes. The next thing I knew we were leaving the movies, holding hands and laughing. It felt good to laugh! It felt real good to be with this wonderful woman!"

Virginia teased Juanita who was hopelessly blushing. She asked if Michael was always that sweet. She answered that he was all the man any woman could ever want.

Virginia said, "I heard that."

Michael continued, "I don't know about all that, but we became instantly close. My sister and Lester were tickled as I stopped moping around the house like a zombie, making a drag out of myself.

As our friendship developed, our families started doing things together. We had Sunday dinners and picnics. Sometimes Reverend Brown would be with us. We started going to church together. Juanita's mother even married a deacon! That's how much she liked the church! It was a real mess!

"It was not always easy for me. As much as I talk now,

sometimes it was hard for me to express my love for Juanita. One Sunday morning, I remembered that I had written a love song. From what I remembered, it described what I felt about her.

As I searched for it, I found a picture of my parents and me at an amusement park. I developed a major case of the blues and wanted to be alone in my misery.

When it was time to go to church, I told my sister that I was not going. Don't get me wrong, she's really a sweet person, but she has always had very low tolerance for nonsense.

She looked at me and very calmly told me that either I was going to hear the day's sermon preached to me or the rest of the world would hear him pray over me! That narrowed down my choices, she (he laughed) hits like a mule. She should have been a prize fighter!"

Jacque, who had returned with the juice, nodded his head and laughed. He asked Michael to tell them about the time she beat up a gang.

"Loretta and I were walking down the street, minding our own business. She was wearing a pair of them shorts. As we passed these guys, they began to comment about how fine she was and what they wanted to do to her.

When she would not say anything to her, they started calling her a bunch of b's. One of them eased up behind her, patting her on the butt!

"She spun around and punched him in the face a few times! Blood and a tooth went flying everywhere! She snatched another and slammed him into the wall and punched in the eye!

The others backed away apologizing their hearts out. The one that she hit first was laying on the ground trying his best to die. She lifted her foot to stomp him, but I stopped her at great personal risk!

"If you knew Rommie, you know him. They call him Snake. That gold tooth is no cap thanks to my sister. Even now, when they happen to cross paths, he always retreats and politely calls her Miss Loretta."

Everybody laughed as Virginia rushed in the kitchen to get ice and glasses. As she was filling the glasses with ice, she realized that she thought about how rare it was to be filling glasses with ice without alcohol. She liked the change. Virginia returned with a big, beautiful smile that didn't go unnoticed by Jacque.

"So, I sat there in church with a major case of the blues. I would have left except Loretta had that eye on me. Reverend Brown's sermon changed my life and from then on I knew exactly who I was.

He said that when your world gets all busted up, shattered into pieces, if you are like I was, you want to go somewhere and just die. You feel hopeless and helpless.

"That's because you are suffering from an identity crisis. You don't know who you are! You feel forsaken and lost, because you are suffering from an identity crisis! I came here today to tell you who you are. You are, my brothers, and sisters, sons and daughters of the King of Kings."

"So what are you all worried to death about? It matters not if you have lost your job, get another one! If you have lost your money, go out and get some more! When it is all said and done none of that material junk means too much! The most important thing in your life is your relationship with God!

"Let me tell you, even when friends and kinfolk mess around and disappoint you, don't worry about it because you have God! When death overtakes those that we love, don't even get yourself upset. Our Lord and Savior done kicked death's butt a long, long time ago! Yes!"

Virginia felt a surge of power and began to cry tears of joy.

The man told us that we should be ashamed of ourselves. While the Negroes here in America were suffering from the bondage, dehumanization, degrading pain, and suffering of forced servitude, they had faith in God.

Every chance they would get, they would sneak down to their private place to have church. They were not as concerned with themselves as they were for their children and their children's children. They celebrated in advance, the day that all Black folk would be free.

"Slavery could not last forever, and Pharaoh would have to let his people go. Even as they were whipped and beaten, shot and lynched, they knew that God would deliver us in His own time! Many freed them, proudly proclaiming, before I'll be a slave, I'll be buried in my grave . . . and go to my God and be free!"

Michael wiped the perspiration from his face, "I sure wish somebody right here would help me sing, *All is Well With My Soul!*"

Before they made a conscious decision, they were all singing with him. Virginia surprised herself by remembering the lyrics, *When peace, like a river, attendeth my way. When sorrows like sea billows roll . . .*

After they finished singing, they in turn hugged each other. A very joyous Michael continued, "I was just like you, Virginia. Sometimes the Spirit just sneaks up and grabs you as It did you tonight. Now, I know that I talk too much. Virginia protested him even saying that. And I know that I bored people sometimes. Jacque disagreed. But let me tell you what happened to me that glorious morning.

"Reverend Brown led us in singing *Jesus Is the Best Thing to*

Ever Happen to Me! I heard an old familiar voice singing with strength and conviction. I discovered that just like the tears of joy in my soul and eyes, the voice was mine!

It seemed like the sun was shining brighter through the stained glass windows. It seemed like the Spirit was walking and talking about the church!

Michael calmed his voice, "Let us not fall prey to the temptation of feeling helpless in these days and years that we shall have to deal. Even as our world seems to crumble and shatter, all is not lost. I believe that if we look at the ninth chapter of the book of Nehemiah, we will find the clues to the answer. We need to be right when the time comes when every knee shall bow. We may as well commit ourselves right now to . . . seek ye first the Kingdom of Heaven and all these things will be added unto you.

They realized that they had church right there in the living room. They all felt much better, even joyous. Virginia shared the fact that she had been brought up in church, but was ashamed of the fact that she had strayed far, far way.

She said that she could remember how much she had loved Jesus as a child, but the world had helped her to forget. God does not care how long you have been away. It's time to come home. Jesus is always waiting, waiting for you and for me.

22. *The Beasts*

Since early evening Kingsley had been impatiently pacing from his porch to his kitchen where he drank himself a shot of whiskey and just enough beer to take the bite off.

He would check his watch as the sarcastic red evening sun abandoned the projects, and the night slowly engulfed it with its hot, humid, unrelenting breath, providing an aura of suspense and forbearance. The full, bright moon seemed to be a hole to forever with a pleasant but not too optimistic expression for those below.

Kingsley was hoping and praying that his son would be there soon as he didn't like to be even on his porch at night. He feared that one of them dope fiends might sneak up on him and steal him, even though he had his shotgun near the door.

He was a frightened, lonely, old man especially at night. However uneasy, he waited for his son who had promised to be there when he could that evening.

He rehearsed several times how he was going to tell his son about Chris, but it never sounded quite right. It had to be done because he knew that growing up with that woman would ruin the boy as she was a real beast.

Again he glared at his watch waiting for his son who lived at least an hour away. Kingsley had begged his son to come over as he had something very important to talk to him about.

Jerry, his son, eagerly agreed as he hoped that his father had finally tired enough of the projects to come live with him. His wife and two young daughters loved the old buzzard, and their home was most certainly large enough.

He had done well, married well to a successful real estate agent who now enjoyed a six-figure income. The son had been worried for the last few years as the projects had become more dangerous.

Kingsley was becoming extremely anxious as the projects had become clustered with people. The sights and sounds of the restless folk with very little to do but exist in the night heat.

A sleek, dark blue sports car maneuvered its way through the glass and debris on the parking lot, and out jumped a man in his mid-forties, wearing the uniform of an officer of the United States Air Force.

Smiling Captain Jerry Clark walked briskly toward his father's home. He didn't go unnoticed by the folks who were around. The younger women who were hanging around the parking lot with men with their beer, wine, and smoke were impressed enough for a couple of them to speak to him seductively.

An older, more aware gentlemen in the crowd thought that Jerry was a bus driver and made a derogatory comment about bus drivers.

Jerry completely ignored the guy but was flattered by the attention of the women. One was gorgeous! Looks, build, pretty enticing smile, however, he knew better! He had been that way before. Poison he thought to himself smiling. The green hand of jealousy and envy grabbed the hero who thought Jerry was a bus driver.

Kingsley was about to give up and go inside, when he heard

that all too familiar voice call out to him playfully, "You going to drink all that rot gut by yourself or can a man get a drink around here?"

"Hell no!", Kingsley beamed, "I don't serve officers here!"

By this time Jerry had leaped onto the porch and hugged his father laughing, "Well, I guess that I'll have to settle for a big hug!"

Their reunion was interrupted by the hero from the parking lot who had nothing to do but follow him. He felt he had been disrespected and insulted. He was followed by the crowd from the parking lot.

Bored with nothing to do, they hoped to see a good fight. With a their encouragement, the man had worked himself up to a fever pitch.

"You the bus driver that put me and my woman off your bus. You had 50 at your back then, but now you by yourself. I think I'll beat your ass like you stole something from my Mama!"

Kingsley, immediately reached around the door, grabbing his shotgun, while inviting the thug and his following to a one way trip to hell.

Jerry snatched the shotgun from his father and began to unload it.

"You bus driving faggot, I'm gonna kick yo ass out here!", shouted the hero. "Or is you man enough to come down here and . . . ?"

Kingsley had heard enough and retreated into the house to get other pieces of artillery! Knowing his father, Jerry ran in the house after him.

Misinterpreting Jerry's move as a retreat, the man charged in the house after him. Before his companions could follow, the hero staggered backwards out on the porch and fell backwards on the walkway, holding his now bloody face.

The crowd, which, by now had increased by number and volume, was silenced by the obvious defeat of their self proclaimed companion.

Jerry had followed his opponent to the walkway and was wiping the guy's blood from his hand. Out of the crowd emerged Dora and Goldie who had happened along.

Jerry and Dora stood with fixed looks at each other for a moment as Goldie watched briefly.

"Still kicking ass, ain't you?" Goldie said to him with childlike enthusiasm. Uncharacteristically, she appeared very happy to see him.

Jerry and Dora were still frozen in that moment, continuing to look at each other with that "I knew you when" smile.

Kingsley was now standing in the door with two very lethal looking guns in his hands demanded that the crowd go. Jerry and Dora paid little attention to him.

Goldie leaned over the now whimpering hero and told to him that he was very lucky that Jerry had not gotten really mad. She punched him in the ribs, chest, mouth, and ordered him not to show his ugly face in the neighborhood.

She yelled at the retreating soul that if he lived in the neighborhood that he'd better move! Many blood thirsty spectators went wild, slapping each other five and coercing Goldie to finish the dude off.

Caught up in the frenzied mood of the crowd, she considered blasting the chump! But she decided against it. The guy got up silently and retreated to wherever heroes go.

Meanwhile, Jerry had managed to say to Dora that it had been a long, long time since he had seen her. She agreed and added that it had been twelve maybe thirteen years.

As the crowd had gone, the four sat on the porch and talked

about days gone. Goldie who knew that Jerry and Dora had a thing for each other years ago was a bit uneasy.

Answering Dora's questions, Jerry talked about his career, his wife, and daughters. Goldie managed to interject that she and Dora were now lovers which mildly surprised Jerry.

After catching up on all the 411, they discussed the death of Rommie. Kingsley had very little to say and was quite agitated.

After Dora and Goldie had departed, Jerry commented to his father that Dora still looked good. However, he was glad, very glad that she had run away from him years ago. Back in the day, he thought that he had loved her enough not to go into the Air Force.

Looking up at the moon, "Man! There was a time that I would have gladly gone to hell to stay with Dora. She had a way of making me feel like doing anything to make her happy.

I thought I was going to die when she told me that she was tired of my broke ass and started dealing with Pickles."

Kingsley retorted gruffly, "Well, boy I was really worried about your ass for a time there, but I should have known that I didn't raise no fool for a son."

Gazing at the moonlight that he and Dora had shared many years ago, he said to himself more than to his father, "You know, Kingsley, she double-crossed both of us and ran away with that musician.

There is no telling where I'd be now, if she had stayed with me. So, I guess that in a way I owe her, because if I . . . The hell with it! Now! What did you have to tell me that was so darn urgent?"

Kingsley looked at him wondering to himself if it would be best to let sleeping dogs lay.

"I know that after driving over here after working all day, almost breaking my hand on that fool's face, seeing Dora, and hearing about Rommie, you are going to tell me something!"

"Look, don't talk to me like one of them boys on the base. Now, I done told you that we had to talk and we will. Let me pour us another drink, and then we talk."

"I can tell that this is going to be a long one, so let me go get some things out of the car, come back and call Pat, then we can talk all night if you want. Okay?"

Kingsley nodded, and Jerry walked toward his car shaking his head.

On the parking lot he was again greeted by some youngsters who had been there when he first arrived. The pretty woman wanted a ride. Laughing as he thought of Dora, he politely responded, "Maybe another time."

Being totally transparent, she answered, "Anytime, I mean it, anytime."

As he walked away, he heard a familiar voice shout, "Attention!". He immediately turned toward his good friend, Jacque smiling, "How you was, Cuz?"

They rapidly approached, shook hands and hugged each other.

"Jacque, how long has it been since I've seen your ugly face?"

Jacque playfully looked up at the sky as if attempting to remember, "Oh! I would say about two weeks."

Both laughed heartily. Jacque greeted the youngsters that were there, and Jerry excused himself as the two headed toward Kingsley's home.

The pretty woman's desire for Jerry was noticed by Jacque, who shook his head. They exchanged small talk as they approached the porch. They laughed as they saw the two pistols that Kingsley still had tucked in his belt.

Jerry shook his head and told Jacque that he would take the gunslinger in the house to put away his guns and call his wife.

He also suggested that the three of them go somewhere and drink some coffee. Kingsley could sure use some.

Jacque agreed but insisted that he go check on his grandson first. They agreed to meet back there in about fifteen minutes.

Michael was telling Virginia that all parents, especially he and his wife (he smiled), didn't always make great decisions while raising their children. He added that however bleak things may be at the time that she did indeed have a chance to make changes.

He asked her to help her children be the type that they and most importantly God would be proud of. While they were talking, Juanita was walking around the room looking at the pictures.

She interrupted, "Is this a picture of your daughter, Sonia?"

Looking at the picture Virginia replied, "Yes, I believe that it was taken about a month ago."

"And she is how old?"

"Almost fifteen."

"That child is gorgeous! Michael look at this picture!", she said in very excited and disbelieving tones.

"No wonder Roy liked her!"

Michael looked at the picture and was also astonished, "Well, at least I know who this mysterious girl was that Roy would not talk to me about. You see, I was in his room talking to him and saw a similar picture and asked him who the woman was.

He sort of blushed and said she was just a girl that he had met. I looked at the picture then looked at him and wondered to myself if he was old enough to be dealing with a woman that old. As God be my witness, I thought that she was older than my boy and was really concerned about him. Fourteen? My God!"

Juanita added, "She's so, so . . . "

"Big?", Virginia offered.

"Yes, and so attractive, pretty! I really don't mean any harm and maybe shouldn't even say this. I, uh, I am really glad that she, I mean that I didn't have to compete with her when I was her age. She would have given me a sense of low self esteem that you would not believe! Boy, would she have!"

Virginia totally understanding what she meant, shook her head and with an uneasy smile replied, "You should try living with her."

They looked at each other knowingly and laughed. Michael just shook his head. Michael was about to speak but was interrupted by the ringing of the telephone.

Virginia ran to the kitchen and answered it anxiously. "Hello? ...Yes, it is? ....you have? (Now crying) . . . Yes, I understand . . . I . . . well, no . . . you will? ....yes . . . no . . . Thank you very much . . . I'll be here. Thank you! Thank you, very much!"

She walked back into the room, still crying. Juanita immediately jumped up and hugged her and led her to a chair.

"That was the police. They found my baby and are going to bring her here. They say that they're satisfied that she had nothing to do with . . . (now lowering her head) you know."

After a moment of complete silence, the Govans asked Virginia whether she wanted them to stay. After pondering it for a moment, Virginia told them that maybe she needed to talk to her daughter alone at first.

Michael smiled, saying that he understood, and reminded her to bring the girl to church in the morning. He added that she should pray with her child.

Michael reaffirmed that everything would turn out for the best. After a brief prayer and hugs, the Govans departed.

She watched them walk hand in hand toward their car. Before they disappeared around the corner, they turned and waved at Virginia. She returned their waves with tears again in her eyes, again wondering if she could have been as kind, gentle, and understanding as they had been.

She wondered exactly what she was going to say to Sonia. Pondering it, she turned and walked into her home. Just as she entered her kitchen, Jacque walked out of his door on his way to Kingsley's home.

Chris was in his room trying to make sense out of all that had happened the last couple of days. He heard his mother and Goldie laughing and talking. Although, he desperately wanted to talk to somebody, he knew talking to Dora was definitely not an option.

A sudden coldness began to engulf him, and he promised himself right there and then not to care nothing about nobody. He felt a thrill out of hoping that one day Dora would be as sad and unhappy as he felt.

Ironically, a sense of motherly concern somehow grabbed Dora then as she heard him in his room. She looked at then walked to his door to say something to him while Goldie poured a drink for herself and Dora, but she decided against it.

She had no idea what she would say to him. Dora paused at his door, shrugged her shoulders and simply walked back to the living room where the two drank to their future together.

Goldie was telling her about all of the things that they would be doing together, while Dora paid very little attention to her as she gazed in the direction of Chris' door.

Michael and Juanita said very little on their way home. Both were deep in thought. Finally, she asked him what he thought about Virginia, and he replied that he felt that she was certainly a good person who had got lost somehow.

He hoped that she would be in church in the morning as he felt that it would help. She asked him how in the world he planned on fulfilling his promise to always be there for her if they were going to be thousands of miles away.

He answered by saying that he was not sure that he should go, he may not be fulfilling God's will but his own. He told her that he was leaning in the direction of staying. He looked at his wife and repeated something that he had heard or maybe read in a book, . . . "Only a fool will go to put out a fire in someone else's house when his own home is burning."

Juanita said nothing but snuggled up against him. He kissed her on the forehead and said, "We should hurry home and meet the crowd that I know is there by now."

Before the police car could come to a complete stop, Sonia jumped out of it and bolted toward her home. The two Black, male detectives watched her helplessly as she ran. The older one grabbed the bags that she had left in the car and followed her as the other stepped outside the car and began smoking a cigarette while surveying the area.

Sonia was so shaken that she could not manage to do anything but scream and bang on the unlocked door that would not open for her.

Virginia ran to the door and immediately began to kiss and hug Sonia who was crying, screaming, and speaking incoherently. The detective stood by the steps, waiting for an opportunity for them to pause from the apparent grief and sorrow before he would say or do anything.

Virginia did what she could to calm Sonia down, but Sonia was nearly hysterical. She kept crying, and screaming much of it incomprehensible. But she finally started making sense, "Why? Why did he have to do that to him? Mama why?"

As Virginia held her, the sound and the feeling of her

daughter calling her Mama resounded through her ears to her very soul. For the first time in a long time she thought of Sonia as the young daughter that she was instead of the young rival that she had often thought of her.

Tonight she was just a little, well- a young, frightened, fourteen-year-old girl. The officer excused himself, offered Sonia's bags, said that he was very sorry that it all had happened, and slowly walked away. He started to turn to tell them that they would be contacted and the rest of the usual stuff that they usually tell suspects, but he felt that the only thing to do was to leave them alone.

His partner, who was now leaning against the car, greeted him by saying, "Look at them. They're just like animals down here. I hate like hell to come down here with these people. They make me sick with their . . . "

"Now, boy! You have finally shown that you have lost your damn mind. Do you really mean what you are saying or does your brain know what your mouth is doing?"

Not waiting for an answer, he continued, "Don't you know that you are less than a heartbeat from being right down here with them? You see them as beasts. Look at your skin, fool!

"Don't you know that all that you have can be taken away in a moment? What the hell would you be right now without your badge, gun, and most important, your paycheck? You are one, maybe, two paychecks away from being right down here! Mr. Can't Stand These People!"

His partner lowered his head and silently got into the car, while still agitated he taunted him by asking him if he felt that he could handle driving "down here." They drove away.

About the time that they were leaving, Virginia and Sonia had settled down in the living room. A very remorseful Sonia told her mother very candidly everything that she had experienced and witnessed since she left home that morning.

Virginia was relieved that Sonia had not witnessed the slaying of Roy, but she could not within herself help feeling her personal responsibility in the tragedy.

Perhaps had she been a better mother, this whole thing would not, could not have happened and for that, she could blame no one but herself. She thought about that picture of Jesus that was in Deloris' office.

She thought about what the Govans had said, and more importantly what they had done for her. She hoped upon hope that this Jesus Christ that she knew very little about would truly forgive her.

The tears flowed from her eyes as she told Sonia that Roy's parents had spent much of the evening with her. Sonia responded by beginning to cry again, "They must think that I am terrible. Bet they never, ever want to see me."

Virginia put aside her own anguish and told Sonia how wonderful they had been. Virginia shared some things that they had shared with her. She told Sonia that they were invited and were going to the Govan's church in the morning.

Sonia considered the prospect of going there for a moment and much to the surprise of Virginia decided that she wanted to go. They hugged, and Virginia described Roy's parents to the curious Sonia.

As the mood lightened a bit, Virginia told her that they thought that she was pretty. Sonia seemed pleased but not as impressed by the compliment as she normally would have. There was no air of conceit in her voice or expression.

Finally, Virginia told her that they should go to bed as they would have to get up early in the morning to go to church. For the first time in a long time Virginia tucked Sonia in, but only after to the two prayed.

Virginia kissed her on the cheek, said good night and quietly walked out of the room. Before the now drowsy Sonia drifted off to sleep, she glanced at her dolls who were silent.

Kingsley had been, for the most part, quiet in the car however, after they were seated, he became a real pain. He made fun of and insulted the waitress, the table was not clean enough for him, the coffee was too weak and tasteless, and he liked nothing on the menu.

Try as they may, neither Jerry nor Jacque could calm him down. So, tired of apologizing for him, they attempted to ignore him, and Jacque began telling Jerry about the death of Roy.

Jerry was visibly upset and angry as he, too, was a friend of Michael. He had also been friendly with, even taken Roy to the base with him to play ball. Once, he had taken Roy up in a trainer jet. He remembered aloud how brave, thrilled, impressed, and thankful the boy had been about flying.

The three men shared some experiences that each had with Roy, and agreed that his death was a shame and a waste. They held hands and prayed for Roy's soul and his family and friends.

The waitress cautiously served them their food. She certainly didn't want Kingsley to get on her case again. Jerry began, "Don't get me wrong, I love my two little daughters, I would not trade them for anything in the world, but very often I wish to God that I had at least one boy. "

Kingsley almost choked when he heard Jerry say that he wanted a boy. After wiping his mouth, "You really mean that?"

"I would like nothing better, but Pat says that she would not go through all the pain again for love nor money."

Looking like the cat that swallowed the canary Kingsley announced, "She ain't got to do nothing, because you already got you a boy. That's why I asked you to come here. I wanted to tell you about your boy."

A very confused, speechless, and shocked Jerry looked to Jacque for some help in understanding what Kingsley was talking about. Since he was as surprised as Jerry, all he could do was to answer his pleading eyes by shrugging his shoulders.

"Kingsley, that does it. You are losing your mind living alone. I'm going to take you to live with us as soon as possible and that's that.That's sick, you ought to be ash..."

"Boy, ain't nobody crazy! I sure ain't a fool! But I'll tell you what, the day that you take that boy of yours home with you, I'll go. And that's that!

"You two calm just down," Jacque interjected.

"Mind your business, 'cause you know what I'm saying is true," Kingsley yelled.

"What!?", Jacque exclaimed, "I really don't know what you are talking about."

"Chris! Chris, damn it all! Chris, your grandson's friend is Dora and Jerry's boy!"

Jacque considered the possibility silently, then leaned his head back on the seat. Almost immediately he knew that what Kingsley said could very well be true.

Jerry was absolutely stunned and exasperated! He looked at Jacque and asked him about this Chris. Jacque told him all that he knew. After he finished, Jerry asked him if the boy looked a little like him. The response was ". . . Just like you spit him out."

Kingsley pleaded, "Once you see the boy, my grandson, you will know that it is true. A man always knows, Jerry. Please meet this boy and take him away from that crazy-assed Dora.

We all know that she is like a beast, and we can't do a thing about her attitude. But you got to save that boy, because if you live with a beast you gotta become a beast. Will you at least see the boy?"

"I bet that I'll never forget this night!," Jerry began. "Okay, but how do I get to see the boy? Even if what you say is true there are some things that have to be considered."

"Like what?", Kingsley retorted.

"Like about a million things. Like what or how do I tell Pat? Like what, I mean what will the boy think? How in, what will Dora do or say? I don't know."

Jacque volunteered that Chris was going to church with him and his son the next morning and he could be at least seen there. Kingsley promptly agreed that he should go and that he would go with him. Jerry begged the two for a moment or two to think it over. After a short while, Jerry looked at his watch and agreed that he would go to church to see the boy and to offer his condolences to Michael and his wife.

He asked the two to ride with him home so that he could get something to wear to church. As the two men headed down the highway, Jacque began to laugh. When Jerry asked him what he was laughing about, he replied, "You know, I had always heard that a man should be careful about what he asked for, but you take the cake! You asked for a son and five seconds later, you got one."

Jerry joined him in laughter, but his was nervous.

23. *Victory*

As the lazy, hazy early morning sun was beginning to paint the projects in soft gold, the party folks were heading on in after a long Saturday night of joyous bedlam and mayhem.

The more gentle folk were easing in their last moments of sleep. The sun was setting the tone for the day by rapidly pushing the darkness aside and brightly illuminating all below in its glory. It was announcing that this day would be something extra special!

Kingsley was impatiently standing in his son's driveway, watching the sunrise and feeling good considering the probability of his being Chris' grandfather. He could hardly wait to get back home so Jerry could meet Chris.

He never wanted anything as much as he wanted to live with his son and family which he hoped would now include Chris. The girls were all right, but they were girls. He and Jerry needed a boy.

After spending the night partying, Dora and Goldie were stretched out in bed, totally exhausted. Goldie had plenty of money, and Dora sure damned had the time.

Jerry was lying in his bed beside his wife with his eyes wide open. They had decided to stay there and get started early in the morning. Jacque had been anxious about leaving Marcus home alone but was convince that it was best, safer as neither he nor Jerry could keep their eyes open.

Jerry pondered the possibility of being the father of Dora's boy. He knew that if it were true his life would be changed forever, big time. There were so many unknowns such as, how would his wife react?

He was fairly sure that she would be amiable, but one could never tell. How would the girls feel? Would they be happy to have a brother or would they resent him?

What would Dora do, and more important than anything, how would the boy feel? Whatever the consequences, he committed himself to finding the truth and would begin on this day.

Chris was restlessly waiting, sitting up in his bed waiting for the very slow clock to signal time to get up, wash, dress up and go over to Marcus' home for the big breakfast that Jacque had promised them. After which, the three of them were going to church.

He had never been to church there and hoped that it would be much like church that he had attended with his grandmother. A gentle tear slid down his cheeks as he remembered his grandmother and all the folks down in Georgia.

Marcus was surprised to hear his grandfather enter as his grandfather had always been there when he woke up. Jacque called out to Marcus, who had finished a book that prior evening, telling him that breakfast would be ready soon, flipped on the radio, and sang his way through the shower.

Marcus was happy to hear that breakfast would be ready soon as his stomach was on 'E'!

Virginia was on her third cup of coffee as she wondered how her son was doing over there in jail. She was also concerned about the now sleeping Sonia who had whined and whimpered a lot in her sleep.

Virginia had spent much of the night sitting in Sonia's room, watching but not awakening her troubled daughter.

Little Al was on the floor of his cell in the fetal position blankly gazing at the wall not aware of who or what he was.

"Chris, you sure look like a young minister or young executive this morning! Maybe you're too sharp to be traveling with us poor folk this morning. Maybe we should order a limousine. Just come in, breakfast will be ready in a few minutes."

Chris thanked him for the compliment and in advance for his breakfast. It sure felt good to be in a home full of love and genuinely caring, instead of the caustic place, in which he lived. He hoped and prayed that somehow, someway, he could live in a home with love and affection, too.

They had so much fun laughing, talking, and listening to Marcus sharing portions of the book that he had read that they were running late. They hurried to the bus stop in time to catch a glimpse of who might have been Virginia and Sonia boarding the bus that pulled off before they could get there.

By the time they arrived at church the service had already started, and the choir was singing *Peace Be Still*, led by a female with one of the strongest voices Chris had ever heard.

The whole church was jammed and packed as usual, however, there was an air of anticipation, thick enough to cut it with a knife! Most knew what had happened to Roy and were really curious to see how Michael was going to react.

In the pulpit, dressed in a bright red robe trimmed in gold and white was Reverend Michael Govans. He held up his arms with a big smile on his face signaling the church to be quiet.

"Let all who love the Lord say, Amen!"

Most responded. Michael shook his head and said, "Now!

This time, say it like you mean it! "

The response was much louder!

"This time, my beloved, stand tall and shout it to the very Heavens, "Amen!", which was followed by a brief upbeat interlude by the organist which created an aura of intense excitement! Some clapped rhythmically, while some others danced.

"Sure feels good in here," Michael proclaimed loudly, with a broad smile on his face, "Shake somebody's hand, hug a loved one and tell them that you love our Lord, Jesus Christ."

Michael hugged everybody in the pulpit, left the pulpit shaking hands as he made his way to his wife. He hugged her, kissed her on the cheek and said loudly, "I love this woman!"

As he made his way back to the pulpit, the joyous interfacing began to subside, and the church for the most part had settled down to a mild roar.

Michael began softly, "I don't know why but (he began to sing), . . . *If anyone should ever write my life's story (the choir joined in) for whatever reason there might be, He'll be there! He'll be there! He'll be there!* ' *Cause Jesus is the best thing that ever happened to me! ... Oh! There were times when times were hard . . .*'(one could clearly see the tears freely flowing from his eyes.)

By this time the whole church was singing, swaying, and crying tears of joy along with Michael. At the conclusion of the hymn, most hummed as Michael began to speak, "You know, my beloved, sometimes we think that we are in charge, in charge of all we survey.

We make, what we think are, flawless plans for ourselves, our families, our friends, and in my case when and where I will serve my Lord, Jesus Christ. As you, many of you know, today was to be my last sermon here for quite a while. My wife and I were eagerly anticipating going to West Africa to do some missionary work.

To help our brothers and sisters to, uh, be nearer to our Lord and Savior, Jesus Christ. We, no I, felt that we could do His work, and see the magnificence and splendor of the Mother Country. I had it all planned.

"As I said, we have been planning this day for a long, long time, but we are not going to follow that, our, or rather my program this morning! We are going to follow His!

Save the program that you have in your hands that was so carefully and lovingly put together by the church's staff. We just may do that another time, but now, now, we, well, we are going to let go and let God!" The church responded with a tremendous ovation!

Next an assistant ministers offered an exhilarating prayer of thanksgiving. Very softly, a young lady in the young choir began to sing, *He Will Remember Me*. While singing along, Chris looked all around, there was not a vacant nook or cranny in the church.

However, as more folk entered, the ushers were making places out of no place. He spotted the old man, Kingsley, standing next to a man with a white military uniform. Somehow, the man appeared familiar to him.

He was really surprised to see Virginia and Sonia. Sonia! He could not believe his eyes, but she looked different somehow. Chris was so distracted by the sight of Sonia that he didn't notice that the hymn was virtually finished, and everybody else had sat and was now humming. Marcus gently tugged at his sleeve. Chris sat.

Michael stood in the pulpit silently surveying the congregation. He softly cleared his voice and began slowly, "This week, the week that just passed us seemed to have been a particularly busy one for Satan on our streets. Many who were among us are no longer walking, talking, singing, and doing all those things that we all take for granted that we will be doing forever.

We all are seduced into a feeling of immortality. Although, intellectually we know that our days are few, we act like tomorrow is promised to us. Some have gone on to be with our Lord. I was tempted to say death or the thing that we call death is untimely, but we all on His time.

"To some of us it may very well seem that Satan has taken over and run amuck in our homes, our schools, our streets, even in our churches. The senseless violence in our lives tempts us to throw up our hands and say what's the use. But Somebody told me to tell you this morning! He said to fear not! Be ye of good faith, because even in our darkest hours, God is in charge and He is able!"

"Last week we were reminded of our fragile existence here on earth, and the reason that we must pray and honor God every moment of every day. None of us knows if we are going to see another day here on earth, which is the reason that we need to keep our only real insurance policy in force, which is a working, praying, loving relationship with our Savior and Lord, Jesus Christ.

Among those who have gone on was a life-long friend of mine and a person known to many of you. Mr. Jerome David Johnson, known to most of us as Rommie, is no longer with us.

"Now I'm not going to, to stand here and pretend that he lived the type of life that made us proud of him, but those of us who knew him in this life knew that he was often capable of great kindness, tenderness, and generosity.

I do not know what was on his mind or in his heart at that

critical moment, but I do hope and pray that his very soul found peace.

"My boy, Roy, will never be with us again on this earth doing those things that made us proud, those things that disappointed us sometimes, those things that youth and seemingly boundless energy that he possessed.

Never again will he come home hungry, tired, and with that infectious smile of his tell me and his mother about his victories and frustrations of the day. We have been blessed to have been the recipients of the gift of a fine son. But whatever his mission in life was, it is now over.

"To tell you the truth, it has been hard, a hard thing to know that the boy that you have raised the best you could will no longer be with you. However, this Morning, My Lord let me know that Roy is fine and with Him! So, many of you will understand me when I say I in many ways envy my son because he is with Him!"

The church was absolutely still and quiet. The only sounds were the occasional clearing of throats. Michael led the church in silent prayer, before which, he reminded them that death had no reason to be proud as the Lord and Savior, Jesus Christ has already paid the price for each and everyone.

As he and the church prayed, a solitary bell resounded, 'Bong . . . Bong . . . Bong'! The sounds of amen, and open sobbing, rejoicing filled the church. Chris prayed and looked around the church. He saw the old man weeping while a man in uniform was lovingly hugging about the shoulders. Somehow, Chris felt a kinship to them.

He could plainly see the tears flowing from the Sonia's eyes as she snuggled against her mother. He could see the trembling lips of Jacque silently praying with his head lowered. Marcus also had his head lowered in prayer.

Chris drifted into deep thought as the service reminded him of Georgia, his grandparents, other relatives, and friends. He slipped in a little prayer, asking that he could, again, live with somebody that truly loved and sometimes even fussed over him.

His thoughts and prayers were interrupted by a thunderous ovation from the congregation. He looked up as Michael was continuing, . . . " Yes, my wife and I were prepared to go Africa to, uh, help spread the word to those who we believe do not know as much about Him as we do. We were all packed, been packed, to take on this noble cause.

"Yeah! We were feeling real good about being messengers and such, But! But! ....He turned to his friend and mentor, the now Bishop Brown, . . . but, I believe, well, among the many of you the are here this morning were at our home last night, helping my wife and I deal with the sudden death of our son.

Some of you said that you'd keep on fighting the fight and remember us in your prayers. And then it hit me like a bolt of lightening . . . I, I still believe that we will help save or gain some souls for the Almighty which is good.

"However, my beloved, the best way I can explain what I feel is God's plan for me, and my wife is by using an old African expression which translated means only a fool will grab a bucket to put out a fire in another man's shanty when his is on fire!"

The congregation became more excited as Michael continued, "My beloved, our streets, our schools, our homes, playgrounds, even our churches are on fire! The flames are being fueled by Satan!

His intention is to create even more havoc and damnation for God's children. His fuels are greed, lust, drugs, guns, despair, and hopelessness. He has us so confused that often we don't know good from bad, sin from righteousness.

Parents, teachers, preachers, and politicians point out that the decay in morality in our very own children is the major cause of our plight. We take no, absolutely no responsibility for the fact that many of our youth, our babies are lost. But we will not accept the blame!

Instead, we blame the victims, our children, our babies. We reason that they should know better, but there is no one to teach them. Folk say, well we told them. But, let me tell you, a big ingredient in the fraud that Satan uses is us. Sure, we tell them. We tell the babies, sometimes, how to act, but we do the exact opposite. Forget, we do, that they hear what we do must louder than what we say.

"I cannot remember the name of the movie, but there is a line in it which we need to remember. `You only covet what you see.' As long as our babies see us drinking, smoking, gambling, fussing, fighting, and seemingly happily living in sin, that's what they're going to do. They say that our kids cannot learn, but they have learned. They have learned from us in our greed and selfishness to love things and use people.

"While Satan is burning holes in our souls, we must keep in mind that we are only a decision away from His righteousness! Like I said, Satan has decided to use the fires of negativism to cause God's children to burn for eternity. But the everlasting fire of Jesus' blood will defeat old slew foot if we only believe.

We, here in God's house do accept Satan's challenge in the name of Our Lord and Savior, Jesus Christ. Let's commit ourselves right here, and right now to kick his butt! A committed congregation can kick his butt out of our homes, our schools, our streets, and everywhere we find him and his fiends.

Yes! Let it be known that this church, on this day, is serving notice to the Prince of Darkness that we have had enough and are taking over in the name of God Almighty!

We will be with you fighting the fight until that day when in the words of Martin Luther King, Jr., we can say, 'Free at last, free at last, thank God Almighty, we are free at last'!"

The congregation erupted!

"Now, be careful, I'm not talking about passively wishing these influences out of our community. Like Malcolm X, I say that we need to take back our community by any means necessary!"

Most shouted their approval!

"Now, before we get out of hand here, (he smiled) please do not think I'm advocating violence. Brothers and sisters this is not a call to arms, except, the full armor of our Lord!

"Like you, I have had it with the present system of slavery. As you know, the present system is supported and carefully guarded by those who would profit from drugs, gambling, prostitution, and liberalism.

Yeah, like you, I am tired of going to jails, prisons, and the morgue with our overburdened mothers to see our young, Black, confused, hopeless, frightened males who feel alone and helpless.

"Like you, I'm tired of seeing lawyers, bail bonds-men, and oh yes, the judges, politicians, and the like get fame and fortune off the backs of our youth. The criminal justice system, known as just us, is one of the nation's biggest growth industries. They make the big bucks while we toil in factories, restaurants, and yes, scrub the floors, raise their children.

"But being on the bottom of the social-economic ladder is not enough to satisfy the beast. Even as all our resources are being sucked up by these vultures, more is required. They're won't be satisfied until we have the grim tasks of viewing the lost generation alone and cold in their caskets.

"Like you, I am sick and tired of being sick and tired. So, whenever there is a child who is hungry, we'll be there. Whenever, a child gets lost, needing to find his way, we'll be there! Yeah, whenever or wherever, the waters get rough, we'll be there! And when it seems that there is no way, even to the River Jordan, we'll be there!

Only then do they feel safe as our babies, cut down in the their youth, long before they can know the real joys of life and can never compete for the abundant blessings of this life.

"We will be there . . . full of the real deal of life which is, regardless to what they say on television, He is in charge! He is able! Victory! Yes, brothers and sisters, victory is here! Ain't no C.O.D., no charge, no easy payment plan! For He has paid in advance, in full by our Lord and Savior, Jesus! ..."

Chris looked around the church. He saw Sonia being hugged by Virginia which made him feel good. It reminded him of the way his grandmother had held him in her loving arms.

He looked over at Jacque and Marcus holding hands while absorbing the sermon. Only then did he notice that he and Jacque were holding hands which made him feel that he belonged.

He and the old man, Kingsley, made eye contact. Kingsley's nod and big smile made him feel warm inside. Kingsley whispered to the man next to him in the bright, white uniform. The man turned looked at Chris quizzically for a second then he, too, smiled at Chris.

Chris was distracted by Michael's conclusion ". . . and so believers, as we have faced what many of you have faced, we will hold our heads high! My wife and I agreed this morning that we will not yield to the temptation of questioning God. What we call death, even premature death is but God's way.

And as we are tempted to feel it is an injustice . . . a mistake . . . from He who cannot make a mistake, we must praise Him, anyhow . . . Love Him anyhow! ....Trust Him, anyhow! ..."

Michael looked over the packed church and smiled, "Let us leave this place singing praises to Him! Please join me in singing a hymn that my son loves. Let's sing it the way our gospel youth choir sings, *Hallelujah Anyhow!*"

Although Michael started the hymn, the youth choir took over with a young lady who had been a close friend of Roy's leading. Her melodious voice was so strong that the church and the heavenly choir seemed to join the soul stirring rendition.

In perfect harmony, Michael led the congregation to the front door. Tirelessly, he thanked them for attending while challenging them to seize the victory.

Meanwhile Dora's sleep was interrupted by the repeated rings of the telephone. A very hung-over and annoyed Dora finally answered it. She screamed at the non-responsive caller, until she became angry enough to cuss and hang up!

Tearfully, Christee held the dead telephone in her trembling hand.

ISBN 155395852-7